In Dependence

Sarah Ladipo Manyika

Legend Press
Independent Book Publisher

Legend Press Ltd
Unit 11, 63 Clerkenwell Road, London EC1M 5NP
info@legendpress.co.uk
www.legendpress.co.uk

British Library Cataloguing in Publication Data available.

ISBN 978-1-9065580-4-8

Set in Times
Printed by J. H. Haynes and Co. Ltd., Sparkford.

Cover designed by Gudrun Jobst
www.yellowoftheegg.co.uk

Legend ▌▌ Press

Independent Book Publisher

For James

I

In the beginning

Chapter 1

September 1963

One could begin with the dust, the heat and the purple bougainvillea. One might even begin with the smell of rotting mangos tossed by the side of the road where flies hummed and green-bellied lizards bobbed their orange heads while loitering in the sun. But why start there when Tayo walked in silence, oblivious to his surroundings. With a smile on his face he thought of the night before when he had dared to run a hand beneath the folds of Modupe's wrapper. Miraculously, without him even asking, Modupe had loosened the cloth around her waist. Of course they had kissed many times before, usually in the Lebanese cinema when all was dark, but that was nothing compared to Friday night. And while Tayo was lost in his thoughts, his father, who walked alongside, noticed his son's smile and read it as excitement for the forthcoming trip.

They had set off early that morning to visit relatives, as was the tradition when someone was about to embark on a long journey. They began with Uncle Bola in the hope of finding him sober because by midday he would almost certainly be drinking *ogogoro* and this was not a day to meet Uncle Bola under the influence.

"An old man should be contemplating his mortality rather than dreaming of women," Tayo's father said, alluding to his brother's raunchy tales, which Tayo knew his father secretly enjoyed.

And although his father made it sound as though Uncle Bola was old, Uncle B. liked to joke about his age and boast that he was young enough to still make babies and thank the Lord God Almighty. And he did make babies – dozens of them. As for thanking God, well, that was simply a manner of speaking. Uncle Bola believed only in beautiful women – not Allah, Christ, or Ogun. In turn, women loved him, in spite of what he lacked by way of height, teeth and schooling. Tayo had long since concluded that Uncle Bola held the secret to a woman's heart, which was why he looked forward to this visit. But on this particular morning Uncle Bola did not seem himself. Upon seeing them, he became quite weepy, so weepy in fact that he forgot about his atheism and offered prayers to Allah, Ogun and Jesus on behalf of his favourite nephew. With tears still in his eyes, Uncle Bola gave Tayo his best *aso ebi* as a going-away present, and then insisted that they stay longer to take *amala* and stew with him.

"Here is some money for the ladies when you arrive," Uncle Bola whispered, stuffing the newly minted Naira notes into Tayo's shirt pocket before waving a final goodbye.

Tayo had hoped to stay even longer, enjoying the company of his sentimental uncle, but there were many more relatives to be visited and several more lunches to eat. Everyone insisted on feeding them and then, just when Tayo thought it was all over, they returned home to find more relatives gathered to wish him well. Several of Father's friends were sprawled across the courtyard drinking beer and palm wine while the children chased each other in the dirt path by the side of the house. The women sat in one corner, roasting corn on an open fire, with sleeping babies on their backs.

"Tayo! Tayo!" the older children chanted as he made his way through the throng, stopping to pick up the youngest. Tayo expected his father to usher people away, but after the day's copious consumption of palm wine, he had apparently forgotten time, preferring instead to continue boasting about his eldest son.

"*Na special scholarship dey don make for de boy?*" somebody asked.

"Oh yes," Tayo's father beamed.

In actual fact, the scholarship was not created just for Tayo, but because he was the first Nigerian to win this scholarship (such things being reserved, in the past, for whites), Tayo's father decided that he might as well claim it just for his son. Tayo closed his eyes while his father boasted, and thought ahead to Sunday, imagining how he would move swiftly through the crowds at Lagos Port to the ship and over the seas to England. "And then to Balliol College, Oxford," Tayo whispered, thinking how grand it sounded.

At dawn the following day, the entire Ajayi family said prayers before gathering around Father's silver Morris Minor, washed and polished by brothers Remi and Tunde so that it glistened like a fresh river fish. Everybody was dressed in his or her Sunday best, ready for the photographs and only when the cameraman ran out of film did they clamber into the car. Father parped the horn and all the doors slammed shut. The key turned and turned again, but the motor wouldn't start, so everyone stumbled out again to push. Even Father pushed, with one foot pumping the pedals and the other pressed firmly against the ground. They rolled it down the path, out of the compound and onto the road, until the engine lurched into action and hurriedly they all piled back in. The children followed the car down the dirt road, running and waving, not caring about the dust being blown into their faces, but jogging along until they couldn't keep up. Sister Bisi ran the fastest, thumping decisively on the car boot before they sped away, out of Ibadan and onto the high road that would take them to Uncle Kayode's place in Lagos. There were five of them in the car: Mama and Baba seated in front, and Tayo and his two aunts in the back. Father forbade talking in the car, claiming that it distracted him, and for once Tayo was happy with this edict knowing that his aunts would be eager to lecture him on how to behave in England. It didn't matter that his aunts had never travelled outside of Nigeria; it was their right and duty to instruct. Tayo closed his eyes and thought again about his sweetheart and their final goodbye. He remembered the poem he had composed for the occasion and the lines that did not quite rhyme, but thankfully in the end there had been no need for sonnets.

By the time they arrived at Uncle Kayode's house, the car was caked in dust and its weary passengers covered in sweat and grime, but all would soon be forgotten in the luxury of Uncle's home. Uncle Kayode was a big man in Lagos, recently returned from abroad as a senior army officer. Maids cooked for him, and large fans hung from the ceilings, whirling at high speed to keep the house cool. Tayo had never seen anything like it before.

"When you arrive in England, my son," Uncle Kayode was saying, "you must make sure to contact the British Council and don't forget to write to cousin Tunde and cousin Jumoke."

Tayo listened carefully, hoping not to forget any valuable advice, but by the time he went to bed he couldn't remember half of what he had been told. Annoyed with himself, he tossed restlessly on his mattress. For weeks he had been looking forward to travelling away from home – to having his freedom – but now he thought only of what he would miss and how frightening it would be to travel alone. He took Modupe's photograph from his bag, quietly, so as not to wake his uncle, and kissed it. Reassured by her smile and remembering the events of Friday night, he rolled over and eventually fell asleep.

The next day, Tayo stood at the ports, holding tightly to his bag. He dared not ask his uncle another question (he had asked so many already), but he still wasn't clear about what to do when he disembarked. What if the arrival halls in England were just as chaotic as the confusion he was seeing now with everyone shouting and gesticulating, willing people to move forward? Nobody bothered to queue. Exasperated by the late-afternoon heat, men took off their cloth caps and flicked away beads of perspiration. Then, as the folds of their agbadas kept slipping off their shoulders, they hitched them back, raising their arms like swimmers. Meanwhile, women herded children, straightening little dresses, trousers, and shirts, while hastily tightening their own wrappers and head ties, continually unravelled by heat and bustle. Tayo, like everyone else, had been standing in this crowd for hours. He smiled, but not as broadly as the day before. His parents, uncle, aunties, and several Lagos-based relatives were with him as well as Headmaster Faircliff and some teachers from school: Mrs Burton (Latin), Mr Clark (Maths), and Mr Blackburn (British Empire History), but none of his brothers or sisters had come and he missed them, especially his sister, Bisi.

Tayo shook his head wistfully, staring at the *Aureol*, which towered high above them like a vast steel giant with hundreds of porthole eyes. You will be missed, he told himself, recalling the rumour started by friends that a particular Lagos girls' school – the one that occasionally visited their school – was supposedly in mourning over his departure. He glanced around for these girls, but all he saw were family, easy to recognise in the matching clothes worn specially for his send-off. The men's agbadas were the same eggplant purple as the women's short-sleeve bubas and ankle-length wrappers. Tayo's mother had chosen the material, fine Dutch waxed cotton, embroidered in gold thread at the neck and sleeves. Tayo had wanted to wear his agbada like the rest of the family, but Father insisted on Western attire, claiming it more appropriate for an Oxford-bound man. So instead of loose flowing robes, Tayo wore grey flannel trousers, white shirt, school tie, and a bottle green blazer that stuck to his skin like boiled okra. His agbada was neatly packed away in the trunk with extra clothes, the Koran, the Bible, half-a-dozen records, and several large tins of cooked meat with dried okra, egusi seed and elubo.

"*Jeun daada o, omo mi. F'oju si iwe re o, de ma jeki awon obinrin ko si e lori.*" Eat well, my son. Pay attention to your studies, and don't be distracted by women, Mama whispered, tugging at his shirtsleeve.

"Yes, Ma," he nodded, turning to face her as she adjusted his collar, which needed no tweaking but that was her way. He hugged her tightly so that her head tie brushed against his chin, and the weight of stone and coral necklaces clinked against his blazer buttons. It took him back to his childhood days when he feared thunder and lightning and would rush to his mother's arms to bury himself in the reassuring scent of her rose perfume tinged with the smell of firewood and starched cotton. He squeezed her again before his father called him away.

"So long, my son," Baba spoke in English, which was his custom when in the presence of expatriates.

Tayo held out his hand and was surprised when his father pulled him into the voluminous folds of his agbada and held him there for some time. Baba then started sniffling and fiddling with his handkerchief behind Tayo's neck, which compelled Tayo to cough and break Father's hold so that they stood for some moments, disentangled but silent, each searching for something to say.

"Now, Tayo," Headmaster Faircliff interrupted. "You're off to be a Balliol man."

"Yes sir," Tayo nodded.

"You ought to be jolly proud of yourself, Tayo, and soon you'll return to lead your country and make our school proud." He grasped Tayo's hand and threw a friendly slap across his shoulder.

Tayo nodded again, feeling strangely irritated by the man

whom he normally admired and felt indebted to for the scholarship.

"Right then, off you go," Mr Faircliff ordered, releasing Tayo, and pointing to the gangway.

Tayo turned to leave, holding tightly to the large canvas bag that hung from his shoulder. Mama had assured him that in it was all that he needed for the voyage – a few changes of clothes, a bar of Palmolive soap, a tin of kola nuts, some dried meats, a map of England, chewing sticks, and Uncle Kayode's old winter coat.

"Write to me as soon as you arrive," Father called.

"Yes sir." Tayo glanced back at his father before making his way slowly up the steps. He waited for his father to shout one last instruction, but it never came.

Chapter 2

Dear Baba,

Greetings from England and dry land! And what a journey it was, Baba, with that mighty sea constantly slapping against the ship and spraying the deck with salty water. There were many days when we saw no land at all and no other ships, just dolphins and flying fish, and once a group of sharks attacked our dolphin friends, turning the water red. Occasionally we passed another ship and our captain would blare his horn loudly, saluting the vessel while we waved, but usually it was just us and that endless, frightening sea. The waters were particularly rough when we entered the Gulf of Guinea, and the notorious Guinea current. They were also rough in the run up to the Bay of Biscay, but the worst was entering the Mersey Estuary from the Irish Sea. From a distance, the Irish Sea was cloaked in fog so that we could not see the rough, heaping waves that are legendary among mariners. Mind you, this was the only time when I succumbed to seasickness (and everyone suffered from motion sickness that day!).

On board the ship, I made friends with two students – Mr Lekan Olajide from Ogbomosho and Mr Ibrahim Mohammed from Kaduna. The three of us were well received by the Captain, and even invited to the first-class cabin where the British Broadcasting Corporation was making a film about Nigeria. Perhaps we are already famous! Sadly, Mr Olajide and Mr Mohammed were not Oxford-bound, but we have exchanged addresses, and in this way we remain in touch. The boat made several stops along the way at Takoradi, Monrovia, Freetown, and the lovely Las Palmas. Once in Liverpool, they tugged us into harbour and I travelled to London, and then up to Oxford where I am now in my college rooms.

My first two weeks at Oxford have been busy and filled with invitations of all sorts. Yesterday I had tea with my moral tutor and sherry with the Master. Today it was a new members' drinks party at the West African Society, and chapel was followed by sherry in the Old Senior Common Room. I have also been introduced to a British Army Colonel, a Brigadier, and a Lord who dined in college. King Olav's son (from Norway) is a student here at Balliol too. As you can see, there are many important persons at Oxford, which is part of what makes it such an impressive institution.

In other ways though, Oxford is not as I had expected. The sun sets by 5pm and I am told that it sets even earlier in months to come. This, and the fact that darkness descends so slowly, are so strange for me. The people can be a little strange too and on the whole not terribly friendly. I have come to the conclusion that because the English are a minority in Nigeria, they are obliged to be cordial in our country whereas their true temperament is somewhat cold – much like their weather. You will also be surprised to discover that in this country, people do not greet each other in passing, not even Balliol men. In fact many Balliol men do not look very distinguished at all. Some sport long hair, and bathing is not a daily occurrence on account of the cold. The tutors look more distinguished, but many are surprisingly ignorant about Africa. I am grateful to Headmaster Faircliff for his letter of introduction to Professor Edward Barker and his wife, Isabella, who have invited me to lunch next week.

I am also excited to report that I have met three other Nigerians at the university. Mr Ike Nwandi, who is reading History, Mr Bolaji Oladipo reading Law at Magdalen, and

Christine Arinze who reads Modern Languages at St. Hilda's. We live and study in the colleges and each has its own library and tutors. I am also friendly with Percy, my scout. He is the man who cleans my room every day, and has been most helpful in explaining the origin and meaning of certain English customs. Can you believe that he addresses me as 'Sir'? Life is different here, but a great adventure. I intend to join the college football and table tennis teams, and also the West African Students Society. I will, however, devote most of my hours to reading, starting with Kant and de Tocqueville, as well as many other notable scholars for my tutorials.

I wait anxiously for news from home, and for some letters. My greetings to everyone, and please tell Mama that her food has served me well (I have made several friends by sharing it with chaps on my staircase). English food, with the exception of custard (like ogi) is not too appetising. Please greet Auntie Amina, Uncle Tunde, Auntie Titiola, Auntie Mary, Uncle Kayode, Uncle Joseph, brother Remi, brother Tope, sister Bisi, sister Kemi, sister Fatima, and all the family.

Yours truly,
Omotayo.

PS – As my colleagues find it difficult to pronounce my name, I am now known as 'Ty' for short.

Dear Son,

We received your letter dated 27th October, two weeks hence. We are delighted to know that you arrived safely and in good health. Praise God! It was most interesting to hear of your experiences in Oxford and I have informed colleagues at work about your meeting with King Olav, the Lords, and the army generals. They are duly impressed. In your next letter, you will please apprise me of the <u>precise names</u> of these gentlemen so that I can provide complete statistics to colleagues and Uncle Kayode.

We are all well here. Thanks be to God. Bisi received highest honours for Geography, and Biyi made school prefect. So you see, the Ajayi family continues to excel in their studies. Marvellous. We are looking to you now to make us even more proud. Meanwhile, things in Nigeria are running splendidly. The independence celebrations (three years of independence now!) were quite fantastic. In short, there were many fireworks, dancing, eating, and general gaiety. We were proud and now the government is working for increased Nigerian leadership. Indigenous responsibility is what we call it. Rumour has it that a Nigerian will soon replace our Chief of Police, and we hope so. God willing. And yet some white men here are still thinking they own our land, not acknowledging that it is a new Nigeria. In short, to keep you informed I send you forthwith these articles from The New Nigerian *and* The Daily Times *newspapers. I have underlined, for your benefit, the important points.*

Your mother is preparing her trip to Mecca. She informs me that she will offer special prayers for you when she arrives, and that upon her return, she will dispatch hence-with to you some additional provisions. In short, she would like to know how much to send your esteemed colleagues. It is most encouraging to hear your news. Write again immediately upon receipt of this letter. Read your books, and always remember that you are an Ajayi

man. *Don't forget the Ajayi motto* – <u>*In all things moderation,*</u>
<u>*with exception of study.*</u>

God bless you.
Your father
Inspector (Mr) Adeniyi Ajayi

Chapter 3

All that Tayo knew about Mr and Mrs Barker, prior to their first meeting, was that Mr Barker and Headmaster Faircliff had attended Oxford together in the 1940s and that Mr Barker was a History don at St. Johns. Tayo presumed on this basis that the two men would be similar – that Mr Barker, like Faircliff, would be highly intelligent, pompous and patronising. Tayo was surprised therefore to discover that the man was not at all as he expected, and even more surprised to hear Mr Barker freely joking about his old friend as an old colonial 'type' and a remnant of a dying era. Mr Barker was nothing like Faircliff; he was soft-spoken and married to a much younger (and very attractive) Italian woman who preferred to be called Isabella rather than Mrs Barker. The Barkers had no children of their own, but seemed to have adopted a number of foreign students at Oxford. Isabella cooked wonderful meals in a way that reminded Tayo of his own mother while Mr Barker talked politics like his father. Mr Barker had visited Nigeria on several occasions, which was what made Tayo feel so at home from the beginning.

Today the Barkers were having a drinks party for foreign students at their house on St. Giles. Isabella welcomed Tayo with the usual hug and kiss before whisking him through the kitchen and into the garden where everyone else was gathered. Tayo felt disappointed that they had to mingle outside rather than inside where it was warmer, but it seemed to Tayo that this was the British way. People spent all day talking about the weather, complaining about how cold, damp and miserable it was until the sun poked its head around the clouds and then everyone cheered up and started talking about lovely weather. But 'lovely' to Tayo could only be warm weather not this cold, pale orange sun sitting high up there in the sky. Tayo was thinking of an excuse to return indoors when he spotted his friend, Bolaji, and the woman standing next to him. He had only ever heard of one Nigerian woman at Oxford so he guessed it must be her – the famously beautiful third year, Christine.

They were talking literature when Tayo joined Bolaji's small circle of friends who stood by the back door, which was at least warmer than standing under the apple trees where everyone else had congregated. Bolaji was in the process of arguing that Shakespeare was the greatest author of all time while others argued for Tolstoy and Homer. As Tayo listened, it became obvious that the group knew much more about literature than he did. Even Bolaji was able to reference an impressive number of literary theorists in support of his position.

"What does Christine think?" Tayo asked, curious to hear her thoughts for he knew that she read Modern Languages.

"Poets are the greatest writers," she answered.

"And why?" he asked, knowing that the safest way to avoid being questioned himself was to do the asking.

He noticed, as Christine talked, that she appeared quite serious, never smiling despite the fact that the conversation had taken a jocular tone. Tayo had heard men say that Christine was arrogant on account of her beauty. Others thought it was the result of having lived in England for such a long time. It was rumoured that both her parents had schooled in England and she had been sent to boarding schools as a child. Whatever the reason for Christine's apparent seriousness, Tayo was determined to make a good impression on this beautiful woman. She spoke eloquently like an actress, poised and confident so that Tayo quickly lost track of what everyone else was saying until he heard someone call his name.

"What do you think, Tayo?"

"Me?" he replied, stalling for time. "I think if I had to choose it would also be Shakespeare – his sonnets," he said, with the sinking feeling that someone would now ask him to say more, to explain or, God forbid, name a favourite sonnet. To avoid further questions, he mentioned in passing that one of his old teachers had been a poet.

"Christopher Okigbo was your teacher!" Christine exclaimed.

Later that evening Bolaji marvelled at Tayo's good luck.

"Did you see how she lit up when you spoke of Okigbo? She even smiled!"

Tayo laughed, pretending not to have noticed, but of course he had; everybody had noticed.

Tayo did not see Christine again for several days until they bumped into each other the following Monday as she was dashing out of the Covered Market, heading toward Schools Examination. He invited her to have coffee with him at the Cadena the next day, which to his surprise she accepted, and it was all he could do to stop himself from grinning while saying goodbye.

The next day he was struck by how made up Christine looked. She was the sort of woman who would always look beautiful, but it seemed to Tayo that she had put extra effort into styling her hair and adding rouge to her cheeks. He didn't care for the rouge, finding it artificial, but the fact that she had gone out of her way to look good for him was all that mattered. Perhaps she really did like him, he thought while she talked again about Okigbo and some of the other new Nigerian authors. He asked her why she was so interested in these writers. Wouldn't it be more interesting to talk about other writers that she must know from all over the world? No, she replied, insisting that her knowledge of Nigeria and Nigerian writers was not good enough. It seemed to matter a great deal to her what other Nigerians thought of her. If only she knew how in awe they all were of her! Tayo was beginning to think that she was sharing things with him that she might not have shared with others, when she changed the subject and asked him how many girlfriends he had.

"So far I've counted five," she said, referring to the number of women who had passed by their table to say hello to him.

Tayo tried to laugh it off, but Christine wasn't laughing.

It took some days to convince Christine that he wasn't the playboy she took him to be. She kept commenting on the number of women that liked him, but at the same time she was seeing him more often so that he grew bold again and asked if she would like to come to his rooms for coffee. On Friday night she came, and this time, when she made yet another dig about his so-called girlfriends, Tayo decided to play along with her story. Rather than be defensive, he told her all about his teenage fantasies for Indian women and how he used to go to the Lebanese theatre in Ibadan to watch Indian films which was the only cinema available. Unable to understand Hindi, what else was he supposed to do but look at the ladies? Christine laughed a lot this time, which gave him the courage to turn serious and tell her how beautiful she was. He still half-expected to be pushed away or for her to say something about how silly and young he was, but she didn't, so he grew bolder and took her hand. And then, because she didn't resist, he drew her close for a kiss.

For the rest of the term they spent as much time as they could together. Often they took walks by the river and now it wasn't only him telling her about his background but she also shared hers with him, telling him more about her family. There were moments when Tayo felt guilty about Modupe, but he reasoned with himself that he and Modupe had been too young to make promises to each other. Three years was a long time to be apart at their age and now, when he re-read Modupe's letters, they struck him as childish. Modupe was just a girl next to Christine and with Christine he had gained confidence, so much so that he no longer felt the need to talk about long-term commitments as he had done with Modupe. He was, after all, only nineteen, and now that he had won the chase with Christine he still hoped to meet other women and further expand his horizons.

Chapter 4

Vanessa cursed herself as she and her friends left the pub. A wet October night was not the time to have worn, of all silly things, a strapless dress with summer sandals. And what on earth was she doing splashing through rain and stubbing her toes on paving stones as she ran towards Balliol? Who was this person that everyone was talking about as though he were a god? Supposedly good-looking, from an aristocratic family, captain of boats at Balliol, and a million other marvellous things, none of which meant much to her. Certainly not the aristocratic bit, but she had to keep going because it was late and too dark to walk back to college alone, even though she still felt tempted to try.

When Vanessa and her friends arrived at the party, someone was thoughtful enough to lend her a towel. She dried herself off, realising only then that the men who stared were looking not *at* her dress, but *through* it! Oh well, she sighed, feeling tired already, let them look.

"Care for a drink?" someone asked.

"Would love one,"

She took the glass and drank it quickly.

"I'm Charlie," he smiled, "and you?"

"Tired."

"Well tired is no good," he laughed, "let me get you something."

He took her empty glass and returned with another and a jumper.

"Not a bad match," she said, and smiled at his choice of clothing.

"Oh, look who's here!" Charlie grabbed her hand and pulled her along. "Mehul meet…"

"Vanessa," she offered, shaking free of Charlie to greet the newcomer whose handshake was firm but a little too lingering. What was wrong with these Oxford men? Still, she liked the deep tenor of the man's voice and watched him as he wandered off, stepping gingerly over empty wine glasses, toppled bottles, and a body sprawled drunkenly across the floor. It was rare that a man's looks made her stare, but he was Indian, or possibly Arabic, with dark, shoulder-length hair and eyes that reminded her of Omar Sharif. Everyone seemed to recognise Mehul, or at least pretended to know him as they slapped him on the back in inebriated greeting. Apparently he was a well-known artist.

"He's terribly good-looking, isn't he?"

"He is." Vanessa nodded, trying to remember the woman's name, but by now she was finding it difficult to think straight. The woman was in the same college as her, that much she remembered.

"They say he's a prince."

"Really?"

So a prince *and* an artist she thought, until seeing that it was someone else the woman was referring to. And God he was good-looking too. Tall and dark, with beautiful hands that gestured as he talked. *Oh no-no-no*, Vanessa thought to herself, when he looked her way. She was a little drunk, but still sober enough to care about looking bedraggled in front of a man like him.

The next morning Vanessa woke up shivering and with a throbbing headache. Every time she moved her head the pain got worse so she lay still, trying to recall where she had been the night before and what she had done. She couldn't remember how she had managed to get back to college and swore to herself that she would never drink that much again. She hadn't intended to get so drunk but part of the problem, she realised as she got a whiff of burnt toast from somewhere down the hall, was that she hadn't eaten very much. Food was so dreadful in college that she had taken to skipping meals. She lay still for a few more minutes, hoping for some sun to brighten the room, but it never came so she tugged at the covers, pulling so hard that the blankets slipped to the floor. She scooped them up, startled a little by the static as she tucked them back in the hope of more sleep, but now the relentless toll of Oxford bells had begun. She tried folding the ends of the pillow over her ears to block out the noise, but that didn't help, so she gazed at the fireplace wishing it could light itself when she spotted the lump on the floor. *Shit*, she whispered grabbing fistfuls of blanket. Thinking it might be a rat, she cautiously craned her neck and squinted for a better view. "Thank God," she muttered. It was only last night's garments lying in a crumpled heap – her red dress and Charlie's jumper that she had forgotten to return. She pushed back the blankets, and swung both legs out of bed and searched around for slippers. Next she found her dressing gown and padded across the wooden floor to the desk. She took her notebook and hurried back to the warmth of her bed, plumping her pillows so she could lean comfortably against the wall. But then she remembered something else. Music. She had to have music and what could be more appropriate than Dylan's *Times They Are a-Changing*.

The Trouble with Oxford men, she began, scribbling on her notepad. Or better still: *The trouble with ~~Oxford~~ men*. Either way, there would be no confusing which article she was referring to given that *The Problem with Women at Oxford* had been published in the same student paper for which she now wrote. She jotted down a list of ideas and then changed her mind.

Dearest Jane,

I've just spent a frustrating hour trying to write something on the status of women in Oxford. If only you were here then we could talk about it, but by the time you receive this I will either have written the article or abandoned it. Perhaps part of the problem is that I'm trying to write this piece in response to a silly article arguing that Oxford women are to blame for distracting the men (as though men have nothing to do with their own distractions!). In any case, I think I've now decided not to bother writing a response. I'll write a totally separate piece on the ways in which we're treated like second-class citizens and how it must change (can you tell that I'm listening to Dylan!).

And now, after all of that, how are you? I miss you so much and can't wait to see you in London next week. You haven't told me what your rooms are like. Do you like them? I love my room with its view of the college gardens. The birds love it too and each morning I'm greeted by a choir of finches and robins who perch on my windowsill and serenade me in warble and chirp, which is far more pleasant than the clanging of college bells. Do please tell me that you are not cursed with the same at Cambridge! Everyone says that after a while one stops hearing them, but I can't see (hear!) how that's possible.

Have thus far made two friends in college. Gita (from Kenya), who reads English, and Pat, who is a Physicist like you. Pat's father is a Balliol scout, which must make it terribly uncomfortable for her among the more snooty girls here in college, such as the Roedean girl who speaks incessantly of family connections and refers to Churchill as 'Uncle Winston.' Silly girl!

Vanessa readjusted her pillow and took another biscuit, reflecting for a moment on her own family. It was far more posh than she cared to admit. She had a grandfather in the House of Lords and a father who talked endlessly of his time in the colonial service. At least there was Uncle Tony and Mother who didn't believe in taking themselves too seriously.

I've signed up for the Labour Club, JACARI (Joint Action Committee Against Racial Inequality), and the college music society. Maybe more if there's time. And you? Do tell me whom you are meeting and all the things you are getting up to at Cambridge. I'll be dreadfully unhappy if you tell me that all you're doing is work.
Write to me soon!!
Lots of love
Nessaxx

Vanessa folded the letter and glanced at the clock. Twelve noon. Lunchtime, but college food was dreadful – overcooked and flavourless. "Dreadful, dreadful," she muttered, looking down at the empty biscuit tin and feeling sick. Time for a cigarette, which was at least one small consolation for being away from home – but not as good as Mother's Sunday roast beef with horseradish, or lamb with mint jelly and rosemary-flavoured potatoes, peas, carrots, Yorkshire pudding, treacle tart, apple pie… "Oh stop it!" Vanessa berated her growling stomach.

Chapter 5

Tayo hummed to himself the tune of Count Basie's *One O'Clock Jump,* clicking his fingers to keep pace as he stepped out of Hall into the cold. He lifted his shoulders and drew the tips of his coat collar tightly beneath his chin. All around was the lazy English drizzle which floated aimlessly in the air, like harmattan dust – only worse. Nigerian rain always fell with purpose, in serious torrents, watering the earth and then stopping; in England it lingered for days.

Tayo tugged again at his collar and kept walking. As he crossed the quad, he nodded to some young men on their way to dinner who looked surprised that he would acknowledge them. They each wore their gowns as was mandatory for Hall and tutorials, the lengths of which varied according to a student's performance on entrance exams. Tayo felt thankful not to be a fresher again with first-year anxieties only exacerbated by these visible markers of alleged intelligence. He still worried about work, but not at all about his social life, except for today as he thought of seeing Christine after the long summer break.

They had had an argument just before the summer holidays and a few weeks later Christine sent him a letter telling him that their relationship was over. She had taken offence at being called clingy and had accused Tayo of looking for an excuse to court other women. In Tayo's mind he had only been trying to tell her that he wasn't ready for a long-term commitment. He didn't want to make the same mistake he'd made with Modupe, but nor did he want the relationship with Christine to end. He kept hoping that Christine would change her mind but as the weeks went by with no word from her, and as he began to meet new people, he decided that perhaps the break had been a good thing.

The room booked for the first West Africa Society meeting of term was in the basement. It wasn't the best of rooms – cold and damp – but it would do. Someone had set up the film projector so that all Tayo had to do was rearrange the furniture. He rubbed his hands wondering how it was that English people never seemed to feel the cold. He concluded that it must be genetics, as he pulled out the chairs and pushed the tables against the wall for food and drink. College rules limited refreshments at these meetings to *hors d'oeuvres*, but nobody ever took this seriously and Tayo had started to dream of spicy jollof rice with fried chicken when Christine arrived with Ike and Bolaji carrying the food he was dreaming of. They exchanged animated greetings in Pidgin, which was their language of fun – a verbal jazz of broken English interspersed with Yoruba and Igbo, and a good dose of gesticulations.

"*Wetin you cook?*" Tayo asked, circling his hands above the food that Christine had brought. "*Na jollof and dodo I dey smell so?*"

"*Comot!*" Christine slapped his wrist.

"*Eh en. Na so e be? Okay-o!*" Tayo surrendered, laughing as he walked back to the film projector. It was a good sign that she was joking with him.

"Don't worry," she called after him, "I've made special jollof with dodo and moin-moin."

"Special for who?" Ike asked.

"For you, my darling," she said, without looking at anyone in particular.

"For me?" Ike purred, draping an arm across Christine's shoulder.

Tayo stared in shock for a moment before lifting the reels from the steel containers and attaching them to the projector, willing himself to be calm. A few seconds later, casting another glance their way, Tayo saw that Ike's arm was gone, and Christine had started laying out the food – her back turned to him. She wore a grey woollen dress, long-sleeved and tight across the hips. He thought of the times when he had placed his hands around that tiny waist and spread his fingers over the curve of her hips. How dare Ike! Why had Ike not consulted with him first? Tayo continued to stare, watching Christine balance on her high stiletto heels as though they were a natural extension of her legs.

She turned and he looked away, knowing she had sensed him watching even though the room had filled with people. After a few more moments of tinkering with the projector (pretending to Christine that this was what he had been doing all along), Tayo stopped to mingle and welcome new guests. As usual, several pretty women smiled at him, but he wasn't in the mood. Let Bolaji entertain the women while he talked to the men. He greeted a Nigerian, some West Indians, and several English students before the meeting began. At least the turnout was good, which served as a temporary distraction from thoughts of Christine. The President made the initial introductions, and then Tayo played the film on Nigeria.

Tayo had not had time to review the reels beforehand, and so it was a relief to find that the film played smoothly. It started with a brief history of Nigeria's colonial rule, which served as the backdrop to a much longer treatment of Nigeria's recent independence. There were shots of Nigeria's artisans and village life, as well as modern scenes depicting technological advancements, including aerial shots of Kainji dam and the new Niger Bridge soon to link the commercial town of Onitsha with the ports. Tayo felt satisfied with the film, which ended on a positive note for Nigeria's future. As the credits rolled and lights were turned back on, it was Ike, as usual, who spoke first.

"That film is a disgrace. Where were the Nigerians?"

Tayo raised his eyebrows, somewhat taken aback but not entirely, as he knew where Ike was likely to go with this. Ike had lived in England longer than most Nigerians at Oxford and now had a tendency to interpret British pronouncements on Africa as racist, or at best patronising. In his first year, Tayo found Ike's reactions extreme but he was used to it by now and the longer Tayo remained in England the more he saw Ike's point-of-view. Were it not for Ike's behaviour with Christine, he might have nodded in agreement.

"And I don't mean showing photographs of Nigerians, as in some anthropological study of Africans in their natural habitat," Ike continued. "I mean, why aren't Nigerians directing these films? Or, at the very least, why aren't we narrating them? And why must filmmakers always start with the colonial period as if that's where Nigeria's history begins? Why not the 10th century with the Benin and Hausa kingdoms or, if one must start with whites, how about the slave trade?"

"Okay, Ike, we all know our history." Francis interrupted.

"But we don't!" Ike retorted. "I'm willing to bet that you know English history better than your own Ghanaian history. You spout English law, but what can you tell me about the Akan and their legal system? And if colonialism is finished, why do British people still speak for us as though we are children?"

Tayo glanced at Christine, wondering what she thought of Ike's tirade.

"What do you propose?" Francis challenged Ike. "You want Nigerians to seize control, just because they're Nigerians. You can't just take Africans with no experience of Westminster-style democracy, and expect them to step in overnight. If you ask me, independence came far too early."

"Well, the question surrounding the timing of independence is certainly a topic for future meetings," Simon interjected.

'Oh Simon!' Tayo thought to himself. When Simon spoke like this, it made Tayo think that Ike had been right to object to

Simon's nomination as President on account of him being British. At the time, Tayo had supported Simon as a friend and also as a matter of principle. But Simon was naïve and increasingly out of touch with what Africans were thinking about their continent. No sane African would waste their time revisiting the timing of independence.

"We could invite Margery Perham back for a debate with Sir Hugh Trevor-Roper?" Simon continued.

"No, I don't think so," Tayo answered, remembering his first and only encounter with Trevor-Roper. Ike had warned him not to bother with the man, but Tayo had been new to Oxford at that time and naively thought he could win the man over by the power of his argument.

"What you're suggesting, Simon, is precisely what I'm talking about," Ike snapped. "Why must we always invite *British* people to talk about *Africa's* future? Don't we have enough brilliant people of our own? And as for brilliance, this certainly does not pertain to Mr Roper. Anyone stating that Africa makes no contribution to history or culture is not only racist, but also stupid. And by the way, Perham's not much better with her patronising nonsense."

"That's not a fair assessment," Simon protested, reddening around the collar, because although he did not say so, Ike and others knew that he was related to the woman. "Perham may be conservative in her politics," he added, "but surely not patronising?"

The question dangled in the air for a few uneasy moments.

"Any other ideas for speakers?" someone asked.

Names were proposed and the discussion moved on, but as soon as someone suggested the topic of negritude, Ike was back.

"And this is the other problem. Negritude is an ideology of the elite completely devoid of meaning for the masses. No, you must listen," he insisted, responding to grumblings from the floor. "Negritude is an ideology suggesting that Africans are blessed with a soul and not reason. They would have us believe that Africans can sing, dance, and feel, but not think. To merely emphasise the supposed African capacity to hear rhythm only supports the racist views of people like Trevor-Roper and Gobineau."

"Hence an excellent topic for discussion."

Everyone's eyes turned to the speaker with the long brown hair swept over one shoulder. She had not said a word until now, but Tayo had noticed her earlier and had the feeling that he had met her somewhere before.

"I think it could be argued," she was saying, "that proponents of negritude, such as Cesaire and Senghor, do not see African culture as Africa's *only* offering to Western civilisation, but rather one of many contributions. Moreover, isn't it Senghor who speaks of the importance of cross-cultural breeding?"

Tayo smiled to himself at the look of shock on Ike's face and wracked his brain for where and when he had seen this woman previously. A pretty woman so she had to be from St. Hilda's, but what did she read? A Historian perhaps, or a Classicist? He would have to find out once Simon drew the meeting to a close.

"I don't believe we've met." Tayo extended a hand.

"Vanessa Richardson. Pleased to meet you."

She stood a few inches shorter than he, fixing her gaze on him so that he found it impossible to let his eyes wander down the rest of her body. He had to content himself with her face and eyes, which were blue and clear like a child's, and the colour of her hair he now noticed was more golden than brown.

"My name is Tayo. Tayo Ajayi. Ty if you like."

"Yes. Tayo Ajayi."

"You pronounce it well." He smiled, liking the fact that she opted for his full name. "And thank you for your contribution to the discussion. We need people like you to take on our radicals."

"But I didn't add much. Besides I thought the other speaker

made some valid points. What do you think?" She slipped her hands into her pockets.

He admired her dark brown cashmere coat with its large chestnut buttons and thought how stylish it was.

"I thought I should give others a chance to expound," he said, "although I was going to take you up on your point about cross-cultural breeding."

"Oh were you?"

"Yes." He laughed, remembering now where he'd seen her. It was at Charlie's place. She was the woman in the little red dress, but too engrossed with the Indian man for him to have paid much attention to her because he, unlike others, would never dream of taking someone else's girl. Not that Ike had really taken his girl, given that he and Christine had broken up, but he still felt annoyed.

"Come and eat." Tayo pointed to the table at the back and winked at Christine. "My friend here cooks the best Nigerian food. I'm sure you'll like it. We have moin-moin made from beans, and what else?" he paused, realising he had no clue what else went into the preparation of such things. "We also have plantains, which we call dodo. They're tasty and sweet like banana. I'm sure you'll like them. Try some," he urged, handing Vanessa a plate, and catching the pleasant fragrance of her hair. He liked the way she helped herself to good-sized portions, not the cautious amounts that English people usually took.

"So did you come with a friend?" he asked, as they moved from the table.

"Is that a requirement?"

"No, not at all," he said, bemused by her wit.

"I came on my own." She smiled.

"Really?"

"You sound surprised."

"I am. How can such a beautiful young lady be without an escort?"

It was meant to make her blush, but it didn't.

"And why is that strange?" She held his gaze. "Don't tell me you're one of those men who believes women need protecting."

"Oh no, it's the men, Vanessa, who need protecting from fighting over you."

He smiled but then decided he had gone too far with the fighting bit and adopted a serious tone to ask about her interest in Senghor.

"It's the combination of poet and politician that appeals to me," she replied, resting her fork on the plate. "He's different, and I like that. I suppose that whether being in touch with one's feelings is African or not, I'm all in favour of it, be it Senghor or novelists like Forster or Woolf."

"Ahh, the Bloomsbury group. So you must also be an admirer of Maynard Keynes?"

"Absolutely. And you?"

"I admire his economics, but not…" he paused, distracted by the noise coming from the other end of the room.

"I'm sorry," she said, "I seem to be keeping you."

"Oh no. They're just being too loud, and I don't fancy seeing the Dean, but now I've forgotten what I was saying?"

"It was your hesitation concerning Keynes."

"Oh yes, I think I was going to say that I questioned his lifestyle, perhaps his morals."

"But that has nothing to do with his economics."

"True, and no doubt you will tell me that Keynes was a man in touch with his feelings."

Tayo found himself staring at the fullness of her lips. God had definitely blessed this English woman with some other country's lips. A shame though, that the rest of her was all covered up. This was the other problem with England being so cold – women always bundled themselves up. Just as he was about to say something to that effect, she started coughing.

"Here," Tayo reached for a glass of water. "I'm sorry, our food is spicy, isn't it?"

But before she could respond, another uproar of excited voices burst upon the room.

"Oh goodness! Here's the Dean. Will you excuse me for a moment, Vanessa?"

Tayo put down his plate and gently touched her arm, telling her he would be back.

Once the Dean had left, Tayo berated his friends.

"Cool down Tayo! Noise never hurt anyone," Ike replied, dismissively.

Tayo shook his head, mildly irritated. He looked for Vanessa and found her buttoning her coat.

"You're not leaving already, are you? I was just beginning to enjoy our conversation."

"Just beginning?" She smiled.

"Well yes." He laughed. "I was clinging to your every word, even as you coughed, so you must at least allow me to walk you back to your college. As a believer in feelings, I'm sure you wouldn't want to hurt mine, would you?"

"No," she smiled, "but I've got my bicycle so I don't think feelings come into this."

"Then I'll take you to the porter's lodge. This is a dangerous college full of crazy Marxists, including our Master." He was keen to make a good impression, but seemed incapable at that moment of anything but a silly grin as he extended his arm and guided her out of the door.

They stepped out into the still damp and foggy evening, and crossed the main quad, passing in front of the dimly lit Junior Common Room where a student band was playing dreadful music to a drunken audience of freshers.

"Well at least that should keep the Marxists out." Vanessa laughed.

"Terrible," Tayo winced.

They walked from the old building, past the porter's lodge

and onto Broad Street, where Vanessa had left her bicycle.

"It was lovely to meet you, Vanessa, and I hope you come back." He steadied her bicycle as she got on and waved goodbye, watching for a moment as she pedalled away.

"Tayo! Tayo! Tayo!" Ike grinned when Tayo returned. "Quite a stunning girl you found there."

"*You dey craze!*" Tayo tapped Ike on the side of his head.

"And a white woman, too," Christine added.

"And what's wrong with that?" Tayo asked, detecting the sarcasm in her voice.

"Yes, so what's wrong with white women?" Bolaji asked. "I want to know too."

Everyone else had gone and the four of them were tidying up.

"I didn't say anything was wrong," Christine replied.

"But you implied it," Bolaji added.

"Well," Ike laughed, "I certainly think something's wrong with black men always going for the so-called English honey."

"Look, I was just doing my job by talking to the new members," Tayo replied. "*Don't vex me now, abeg.*"

"So you're feeling guilty as charged?"

"Don't mind him." Bolaji dismissed Ike with a flick of the hand. "But Christine, I think you need to explain what's wrong with English women."

They had finished straightening the furniture and were sitting around the film projector, where Tayo was putting away the reels.

"I never said anything was wrong with English women, I just don't understand why you men always fall for them, that's all. When do you ever see white men coming for black women?"

"So you want a white man?" Tayo asked.

"No," she snapped, glaring at him. "Not everyone's like you, Tayo."

"Ohhhhh!" Bolaji whistled.

"And what's that supposed to mean?" Tayo persisted, ignoring the laughter from the others.

"Well, you obviously noticed her."

"Meaning what? That you never notice other men?"

"Look," Ike insisted, placing a hand on Christine's shoulder. "Let's carry these plates outside. We don't want to get locked out of college."

Tayo kept quiet as he fiddled with the films that he had already finished packing.

"Tayo," Christine called, lingering after Bolaji and Ike had left. "Why don't you come to my place for some coffee and we can talk."

"That sounds nice. A happy threesome – you, me, and Ike?"

"Are we jealous?"

"What's there to be jealous of?"

"Your choice," she shrugged. "And for your information, Ike won't be there. So maybe I'll see you later."

Whenever he stepped into Christine's flat, Tayo thought of home, never quite knowing why. Perhaps it was the smell of Christine's cooking that reminded him of Mama, or the fact that she frequently played Highlife and Juju music. Perhaps it was now simply nostalgia for what used to be. Whatever it was, he had missed it, and by the time he arrived, Christine had put the kettle on, and the flat felt invitingly warm after the cold and damp of outside. They exchanged news of their summers and while Christine got the mugs and the milk, he stared aimlessly round the room.

"You can sit if you'd like." Christine waved at the table.

He sat and picked up one of her books.

"I think you might enjoy that one," she said, watching as he flipped through it.

"And I suppose that this *Lonely Londoners* will tell me why I shouldn't look at English girls?"

"Oh don't be silly." She laughed, handing him a mug and sitting down at the other end of the table.

"So why am I here, Christine? Why me and not Ike?"

"I wanted to talk to you, Tayo."

"Why can't you talk to Ike?"

"Why do you keep bringing up Ike?"

"Well, it looks like you and he are…"

"Are what?"

"Are some sort of couple."

"And if we were?"

"Well are you?"

"What do you think?"

"I really don't care."

"Then why do you keep asking?"

"Why do you keep avoiding an answer?"

"Because Ike has nothing to do with this. I just thought I could talk to you as a friend."

Tayo waited for her to finish speaking, watching as she stared blankly across the room.

"I feel scared," she said. "I'm scared about my next tutorial, I'm scared about exams, I'm scared about what my parents will think if I don't do well."

He stood up and went to sit in the chair next to hers.

"Christine, you're going to do fine. You'll do fine in all of those things, and you've always done well."

"But that's the point, Tayo." She glanced at him for a moment. "I've always done well, which means that everyone now expects me to continue doing well, but what if I don't?"

"You will."

"But I won't," she said, shaking her head. "It's just luck, Tayo, and everyone else is so much brighter than I am. It's only because I study so hard that I think…"

"Please don't cry, Christine." He moved his chair back so he could reach and hold her arms. "And just look at these tears of yours – they're soaking up my shirt!" he said, trying to make light of it. She lifted her head and because he didn't know what else to say, he started wiping the tears awkwardly with his thumbs. She smiled a little as he pulled her face to his and, without intending to, he started to kiss her. It seemed the only thing, the best thing, to do under the circumstances.

Chapter 6

It was a perfect day for walking. The paths were a rustling carpet of golden leaves, and the air hung heavy with the smell of dry brush and bonfires. She and Tayo were, as far as she could tell, not walking to any particular destination, just walking in the direction of the meadows and talking. They spoke at length about Malcolm X's visit to Oxford, she being eager to hear the story of how a member of the West Africa Society had been instrumental in organising his visit, and he wanting to know what most English people (not just those at the university) thought of someone like Malcolm X. She found his questions challenging and felt torn between reality and her own idealism.

"I wish that England was less racialist than America," she said, "but then, when you have politicians like Enoch Powell saying the things he does, it doesn't really inspire hope."

"It is discouraging," Tayo acknowledged, "but people do change, especially the younger generations, and I have hope in the British."

Vanessa raised her eyebrows, wondering if he was just being polite, but he seemed not to have noticed her scepticism. Instead, he had begun to talk about some of the encouraging interactions he had experienced with school children and church groups, and she began to think that he was in fact being sincere.

"Besides," he added, "in Yoruba the meaning of my name is someone who brings joy, so I have no choice but to be optimistic!"

She smiled, thinking that the name suited him.

As they continued their walk, Vanessa noticed that Tayo had a habit of picking up twigs that he would play with for some minutes before sending them twirling away into the bushes. She liked the way he carried himself – so at ease in his body. It was obvious that he was clever and highly-accomplished and yet in his manner he was humble, never once flaunting his knowledge in the way that she had grown to dislike in men like Charlie and Mehul. Tayo also seemed to be more serious and less flirtatious than she remembered from the first meeting, which prompted her to share something that had been bothering her. Oxford was a small place and she preferred that Tayo should find out about her family from her.

"I have a small confession for you, Tayo. A small confession." She laughed, tapping him playfully on the shoulder when he stopped dead in his tracks. "I just wanted to say… well, do you remember when you asked me about my interest in Africa? I felt a bit embarrassed, in the light of the debate that evening, to admit that I actually do have connections to Africa."

"But why so embarrassed?" he asked.

"Because my father and grandfather were in the colonial service."

They had stopped on a bridge and were leaning against a wooden railing, peering at the water flowing gently downstream. Two ducks paddled cautiously, close to the riverbank, leaving room for a punter to glide silently past. And there, as they stood side-by-side, she told him about her father's colonial tours in West Africa. She chose her words carefully, not wanting him to form a bad impression of her family and as a result found herself saying more positive things than intended.

It was not true that her father had been won over to the idea of African independence, so when Tayo told her she ought to be more proud of him she felt guilty. He mentioned that his father had also worked in the British Administration as a way, she thought, of making her feel further at ease. His father had been a court messenger in the 1950s and an interpreter in the Native Administration before becoming a policeman. According to Tayo, his father had made many British friends including some District Officers, so he wondered whether their fathers might have met.

"Maybe," Vanessa replied, knowing this was doubtful. Her father did not fall into the category of colonial officers who were loved by locals, and now she regretted having misled Tayo into thinking so. Hopefully he would never have occasion to see the less attractive side of her father. At least she could count on her father to put on a good act.

They walked in silence, in single file, for a few moments along the narrowing path. She wanted to ask him more about his family but didn't want to seem rude, so they talked instead about college and the people that they knew in common. She had not realised how far they had come until she saw they were nearly at The Trout, where she had been several times before but always by car, never on foot. Her feet hurt from her new boots and she was weary, but Tayo didn't look tired at all, no doubt because of all the sports he played.

"Do you play any?" he asked, when she commented on the fact.

"No, not at all."

"None?"

"None," she confirmed. "Why, is that bad?"

"Terrible! So come on, let's run. I'll chase you to The Trout."

"Oh no – I can't run!"

"Yes, you can." He tugged at her arm. "Last one buys the drinks!"

"Then I'm buying." She laughed watching him crouch like a sprinter, waiting for her to start.

She was breathing heavily by the time they got to the pub, and could only nod when Tayo offered to relieve her of her coat. He laughed, showing no sign of being short of breath.

"My goodness, you are fit, aren't you," she muttered, noting the slim waist and broad shoulders.

"I'm sorry, what did you say?"

"You heard me, and I'm not repeating it!" she laughed.

"What can I get you, love?" the bartender asked, interrupting.

She ordered a beer, and Tayo took a pineapple juice. They were looking around for a place to sit when two men passed in front of them and bumped into Tayo.

"Do you mind?" Vanessa said crossly when no one apologised.

"Maybe the bloody wog ought to look where he's going."

"Maybe you two fucking idiots should learn some manners."

"Just leave them," Tayo whispered, placing a hand gently on Vanessa's wrist.

She started to protest, but he was restraining her so she just stood, staring in shock.

"It's fine," Tayo insisted, quietly brushing pineapple juice off his cardigan. "Here, let me fetch you another." He reached for the empty glasses.

"No. But thank you." She looked nervously at the bar. "Could we go outside?"

"Come then."

They stood up, and passed close to the bar where the men now sat, beers in hand. Tayo stopped and looked one of them straight in the eye. Alarmed, Vanessa tugged quickly at his sleeve, but he stood still, staring at the men until they were forced to look away.

Outside, a smoky haze had fallen across the meadow and squirrels darted excitedly across the paths and into the bushes. It was mid-afternoon, but the sun had already begun its descent and a cold wind was lifting pocketfuls of leaves and tossing them recklessly into the air.

"Were you afraid?" Tayo asked, softly.

"No," she lied. "I felt like punching them."

"Ohhh – not such a gentle butterfly after all! I tell you what," he said, smiling at her. "How about I give *you* a new name."

"A what? Why?"

"Something to capture your fighting spirit. How about Moremi?"

"What's that?"

"It means as tough as a nut. A little Miss Cassius Clay. Legend has it that Moremi saved the Yoruba kingdom."

"Well I'm not sure that Mora–"

"Moremi,"

"Moremi. I'm not sure that's me. But Omotayo is certainly you."

"Omotayo Oluwakayode," he added. "Oluwakoyde is another of my joyful middle names."

She looked up and found him smiling.

"Do your names *really* mean what you say they do?" She started laughing. "Or is this how you like to charm the girls?"

"Now why would I possibly wish to lie to you, Miss Moremi? I'm sincere – really sincere."

"Okay," she laughed, "so what is Mr Sincere doing over the Christmas holidays?"

"Nothing that can't be changed," he said.

"In that case then, come to my grandparents' Christmas party."

Chapter 7

The next day, Vanessa took the train back to London for the holidays. She slept through the journey but woke as the train drew into Paddington and passengers with luggage began bumping their way down the aisles. She waited for others to get off before retrieving her cases – dragging them down the steps and over the gap onto the platform where her parents were waiting.

Her parents looked older and shorter than Vanessa remembered, each wearing tan raincoats, which was the first time Vanessa had known them to wear matching clothing. Father's was open at the front, Mother's buttoned to the chin. Mother's hands were clasped around her handbag as though grasping a horse's reins – fingers curled tightly around leather, hands drawn back, close to the waist – while Father kept his arms folded over his chest in order to keep glancing at his watch, eager to get home.

"It's lovely to be back," Vanessa said, pretending, for Father's sake, not to have noticed Mother's nervous chatter or the rancid smell of whisky on her breath.

She knelt to remove the day's letters from the entrance so that Mother wouldn't trip, remembering as she did this having crouched by front doors as a child in eager anticipation of Father's letters. Usually he wrote on flimsy blue aerogrammes, but occasionally he remembered to send a white envelope with a row of colourful West African stamps that she saved for her stamp collection.

Juma and Saratu sauntered in, greeting Vanessa as though she had been gone for just a few hours. They stepped nonchalantly between her feet, tickling her calves with the tips of their tails, and arching their backs to better rub against her ankles. Soon, the gentle patter of Mother's slippered feet summoned them down the stairs to the kitchen, and Vanessa followed down the carpeted steps, where the feline two waited in expectation of milk or a tin of something fishy.

"I've made your favourite chicken pie," Mother said, standing by the oven, hands clasped in front of her tweed skirt.

"Vanessa," Father called from the lounge upstairs. "I'll take your suitcase to your room, darling."

It was just the three of them in the large, three-storey Georgian house, but already it felt crowded to Vanessa – crowded and strangely cold. She glanced at her mother standing by the oven, twirling her wedding band round and round, like an anxious schoolgirl. Above the thick gold band sat a slimmer band pulled up to the knuckle to give room for the latter's rotation. This was her engagement ring: a large opal encircled by sapphires. Vanessa remembered touching the stones as a child, turning the ring this way and that to catch the many shafts of colour, and, though Mother used to complain that opals brought bad luck, Vanessa never remembered her taking it off except when making pastry.

"These are nice," Vanessa remarked, noticing some roses on the kitchen table.

"I've made you a cake." Mother pointed to a linen tea cloth covering her work. "Lemon pound," she added, turning away to fill the kettle.

The sound of running water drowned Vanessa's 'thank you', as well as the whine of cats.

"Silly things!" Vanessa muttered as she fetched them milk and dribbled it onto their saucers. She tried holding them back with a foot but some of the milk landed on their faces and they shook their tiny heads, scattering milk droplets across the linoleum. Vanessa smiled as she placed the empty milk bottle on the counter and watched for a moment before going to her room.

Her suitcase was waiting next to her bed where Piglet, Tigger and Paddington Bear sat propped up against the headboard just as she had left them. On her dressing table, Mother or the housekeeper had arranged pink carnations that smelt of nutmeg. Vanessa smiled again and walked to her window overlooking Bellamy Boy's playing fields. Scattered across the fields, patches of frosty grass resembling clumps of silver tinsel remained untouched by the winter's sun. *Home*, she mused – the Headmaster's house in Dulwich. This at least had been home prior to Oxford, but there had been so many houses before. First they had lived in Nigeria and then she and Mum had come back to England while Father remained abroad. It was better, Vanessa mused, when it was just she and Mother in the days before the drinking started.

She turned from the garden and ran her fingers along the lined edges of the floral curtains. This was a young girl's bedroom, and she missed the room in Oxford with its serious books, newspapers, and ashtrays. But then she remembered Tayo's Christmas present and took it out of her bag to play. *Shulie-a-bop, shulie-a-bop,* she sang twirling to the music of Sarah Vaughan. She had promised not to open it before Christmas, but she couldn't resist these sorts of things and what a lovely present! Now she wanted to find him something and she remembered the photographer's shop on Upper Street. She would get him a print of Louis Armstrong or Sonny Rollins or, failing that, she could always look for a first edition of *The House at Pooh Corner.* Tayo had introduced her to some of his favourite writers so it might be nice to do the same, provided he didn't think Pooh was too childish. Vanessa was still thinking of presents when she heard her mother calling and hurried downstairs.

They were sitting at the dining table when Father peered suspiciously at his food and announced that the pie looked soggy in the middle.

"Mum, it's fine," Vanessa insisted, trying to stop her from scooping up the servings and running back to the kitchen but it was too late.

"So what does Oxford think of Harold Wilson?" Father asked.

"I don't know," Vanessa shrugged.

Father's breath smelt and he was stabbing peas with his fork and popping them into his mouth in a way that reminded her of an oversized child. She hated the fact that her father so easily irritated her. Had it been anyone else, she would have spoken eagerly of the new Prime Minister but she knew that Father scorned Wilson and the Labour Party. In any case, why couldn't he think of other things to discuss?

"There's so much more than Wilson, Daddy. There's racism in the Midlands, apartheid in South Africa, American civil rights... that's what Oxford talks about."

"Is everything okay?" Mother reappeared with a burnt-looking pie.

"Yes Mum." Vanessa nodded, thinking that if her father didn't like his pie this time she might scream, but he didn't say anything and Mother had started talking about preparations for the Christmas party, wanting to know who Vanessa was inviting.

"Better not be anti-apartheid people," Father grumbled.

"What do you mean?" Vanessa asked, sharply.

"Because I've invited my mining friends."

"You what?" Vanessa looked to her mother for support.

"Oh 'Nessa," Mother pleaded.

"But they're horrible men, those mining idiots! They own all the bloody mines in South Africa and make packets of money out of their black workers. How can you invite them? Do you know how many blacks die in the Kimberley mines every month?"

49

"Vanessa, I think you're being silly," Father snapped.

"Silly?"

"It's not nearly as bad as the press are saying, Vanessa, so don't be taken in just because you're filled with the rush of Oxford. And, frankly, if you look at the mess in the rest of Africa, South Africa is doing very well by comparison."

"Yes, thanks to all the blacks doing the work and being bloody exploited." Vanessa let her fork drop noisily to the plate, and pushed her chair back. "Look, I'm sorry Mum, I can't take this."

She ran upstairs and slammed her door shut before flinging the stuffed toys off her bed and jamming the pillow over her head. How dare he! She had always known of Father's white South African friends, but how could he invite them to a family party? What would Tayo and Gita think? *Oh sorry, here are my father's racist South African chums, you don't mind do you?* She sat up, wiped the tears from her face and took a deep breath. She considered for a moment telling her friends not to come but realised this would be what her Father would want and she wasn't going to do that. In any case it was Mother she wanted to introduce to her friends, not Father. But what if Mother got drunk?

"Bloody, bloody hell!" she moaned, banging her head repeatedly against the pillow.

Chapter 8

A manservant welcomed Tayo to Aberleigh and ushered him into a brightly-lit room abuzz with the animated chatter of people drinking as they mingled. Tayo looked for Vanessa but couldn't see her. Everyone was dressed in fine clothes and seemed completely at ease in the grandiose setting; enormous chandeliers hung from the ceilings and festive swathes of holly and ivy decorated the large bay windows. Waitresses in frilly white caps and starched aprons weaved through the room, balancing silver trays on their fingertips. One stopped to offer Tayo a *canapé*, which he accepted with a glass of wine and made as if to mingle, peering at flower arrangements or gazing at paintings until, to his relief, Vanessa appeared. She was wearing a midnight blue sequined dress that hugged her slim body all the way down to her ankles, where the material spread out in a circle hiding her shoes. She hugged him in greeting, which surprised him. "Come and meet my family," she said.

First she introduced him to her grandfather who had difficulty hearing but spoke at length about India, and when Vanessa was able to make him understand that Tayo came from Nigeria his eyes lit up as he launched into a series of stories about Lord Lugard and their family ties. While he enthused, Vanessa kept muttering apologies to Tayo for her grandfather's unabashed support of the British, but Tayo didn't judge the old man for his colonial fervour. The grandfather was simply a man of his times and it was clear to Tayo that he was generous at heart.

They moved on to talk to Vanessa's mother, whom Tayo

Sarah Ladipo Manyika

found charming and strikingly beautiful too. She chatted to Tayo at length about Nigeria, expressing how much she missed the country and its people, and wanted to know how he found England. If the evening had ended there, it might have been a perfect party for Tayo, but meeting Vanessa's father was definitely less than enchanting. It didn't help that one of his South African friends mistook Tayo for a servant.

The meeting with Vanessa's best friend also seemed peculiar to Tayo. Vanessa had always described Jane as shy, but Tayo had the strangest feeling that Jane was deliberately flirting with him whenever Vanessa wasn't around. But perhaps he was only imagining it. Sometimes shy people could be socially awkward, he reasoned. At any rate, Tayo was glad when the party was over. Vanessa had told him beforehand that he could spend the night at her grandparents' home and all evening he had been dreading sharing with one of the South Africans. As it turned out, he need not have worried. The house was big enough for him to have a room of his own.

The room was large with beautiful antique furniture but no fireplace so Tayo was thankful for the woollens he had brought along to wear beneath his pyjamas. The cotton pyjamas were hardly appropriate for winter, but his mother had sewn them, and he treasured them even though their once bright green and white stripes (colours of the Nigerian flag) had faded to a limey-grey. He also wore two lambs' wool cardigans, an extra pair of socks, some gloves, and his Balliol scarf. He did a few jumping jacks to get warm and then sat down with the intention of writing to his father. He stared at the paper in front of him, knowing exactly what his father would like to hear, but delayed while his mind wandered back to thoughts of Vanessa.

At least her mother seemed to like him, so that was a good sign. She had loved the thorn carvings and sherry he had brought as gifts, making room to display them on one of the tables. "Isn't he delightful," he overheard her saying to her husband, who of

52

course would not have thought the same. "In which case," Tayo muttered aloud, "I had better stop thinking about his daughter."

He stood up and, still feeling cold, took the blanket from his bed and wrapped it tightly around his shoulders. He removed a glove and wrote the date, remembering that this time last year he had been with Christine. He had not spoken with her for several weeks but knew that she and Ike would be spending the holiday together.

Dear Baba,

I am writing this letter to you from Aberleigh, the family home of a fellow student. I have learnt that it is the custom here for country houses to be given names.

Tayo paused, considering what to say next. The words 'fellow student' made Vanessa sound distant but he knew his Father might still question it. The fact that his son had not written for several weeks plus the sudden mention of a woman was likely to signal something to Father even though, for the moment at least, the relationship had been quite innocent. They had seen each other several times over the holidays but all that had taken place was friendly teasing and the normal flirting between the sexes. However, if Tayo was being honest with himself there was something more. The fact, for example, that she had been on his mind for much of the night and that he had cared about what her family thought of him. He was pleased to notice that her friends Mehul and Charlie were not there, not that this meant anything in particular, but he was glad nevertheless.

Miss Richardson is a student at Oxford who is interested in Africa and has invited a group of us to her grandparents' home for the Christmas celebrations. The home is spectacular – more than 200-years-old, with seven bedrooms, as well as stables, and servants' quarters. It belongs to Grandpa and Grandma Hume

(Vanessa's mother's side) who lived in India for many years. Grandpa Hume was in the Army as was his son-in-law, Mr Richardson, who later served in Sierra Leone and in our own country in the Northern province.

Tayo wondered what his father would have thought of the likes of Mr Richardson. He always spoke with pride of his years in the Native Administration, but surely it must have been irritating to serve younger British men who knew so little yet felt naturally entitled to power. For a moment, Tayo considered naming for Father some of the artists and politicians at the party, but then changed his mind. The more he named, the more he would have to account for later, and he had already made the mistake of telling his father that the former Prime Minister's grandson resided in college. Ever since, he had been hounded by questions as to the possibility of a visit to the Macmillan home. He was about to write something else when he heard the knocking.

"One moment please," Tayo called, jumping up as he pushed the blanket off his shoulders, throwing it back on the bed. He glanced at his watch. Midnight. Quickly, he removed his scarf and tugged at his gloves, wondering what to do with the rest of his layers, when the knocking resumed.

"Tayo, it's me," came the whisper.

He opened the door a crack.

"Oh Vanessa, I'm sorry. I didn't know it was you and...'"

He opened the door wider, wondering if he ought to ask her to wait while he changed but what would he change into? He had no decent pyjamas, not even a dressing gown, which made him realise why he ought to have heeded the British Council's advice on clothes to buy for England. Vanessa still wore her lovely dress that was now discreetly covered at the neck by a mohair stole.

"Can I come in?" she whispered again, pushing her face closer.

"Yes, yes of course. Come in," he stammered, feeling foolish for keeping her waiting.

They now stood awkwardly for a moment in the middle of the room while he thought of excusing himself and she tugged nervously at her stole.

"I hope you weren't too disappointed."

"Disappointed?"

"Well it's just that my father, especially when he's with those friends, can be dreadful."

"Don't worry." He smiled. "But come. Please sit." He pointed hesitantly to his bed, which somehow didn't quite seem the decent thing to do, but it was the only place to sit apart from the chair cluttered with his things. "Please, sit." He straightened the blanket. "If you'll excuse me, I'll just change into something more appropriate."

"No, really, I mustn't disturb you, and I see that you're working."

Tayo watched her as she moved back towards the door, stepping daintily so as not to make a noise on the floorboards. He guessed from the way she wobbled on her heels that she was not used to them; tall women rarely wore them. He smiled as she tried, unsuccessfully, to creep gracefully away until he remembered his own fluffy, green slippers bulging at the sides from the extra layers of socks.

"I must look ridiculous," he said, abandoning all thought of a change now.

"You look perfectly handsome, as always, Tayo." She smiled.

"And you, Vanessa, look like a lady of the night."

"A what?"

"No, I'm just being silly," he laughed. "Please stay." She sat on his bed and he moved the chair from the desk, placing it near the bed.

"Seriously though, you look lovely tonight, Vanessa. I mean you always look lovely but tonight even more lovely if that's possible."

"Oh, Tayo, stop!"

"So," he said.

"So," she answered. "I'm just embarrassed by my father."

"We all get embarrassed by our parents; it's normal," Tayo said. "Besides, if I were your father I think I would be wary of any young man near my daughter too!"

"Well, I'm sure your parents are wonderful," Vanessa replied. "Will you tell me about them?"

She wanted to know about his mother and so he told her what he thought she would find interesting about her profession as a cloth trader.

"And what does she look like?"

He replied that his mother was slender and that she routinely wrapped towels around her waist to make herself look bigger, which made Vanessa laugh. Skinny, he had to explain, was not considered beautiful, and then he remembered having seen Vanessa with a towel wrapped around her waist too, at Charlie's. He reminded her, which made them both laugh.

He was enjoying telling Vanessa about his family and found it easy to talk to her because she seemed genuinely interested in what he was saying. Even though she didn't understand everything about where he came from, she was so far removed from his culture and so intrigued by it that Tayo felt no need to embellish his childhood as he had sometimes done with Christine. He even felt comfortable enough to admit that his mother was one of several wives.

"Four?" Vanessa repeated. "I'm sorry, I didn't mean to sound surprised."

"No, you mustn't apologise, Vanessa. It is permitted and when my father became a Christian, well, he couldn't easily change his marital status."

"And did you live together in one place or in different locations? Do you mind me asking?"

He didn't mind because he liked the fact that she wanted to

learn more, except that now she was looking puzzled.

"I was just thinking," she explained, "that in one sense, you could argue that polygamy is not terribly different from people here in England marrying, divorcing, and then remarrying, only in one situation the marriages are simultaneous and, in another, consecutive. But do you think your mum's happy? I mean to have other wives around. Am I asking too many questions?"

"No, not at all," he smiled. "Yes, I do think my mother is happy; she's certainly very independent. In fact, you could almost say she practised a form of polyandry because she left my father for a time to be with another man. It was when I was a boy so I don't know the full story, but a year or two later she returned to my father. Maybe it happened because my father decided to make the family Christian. I'm not sure."

"It's so interesting. I'd love to meet your mother one day."

"Then you will, and she's also quite jovial, just like you," Tayo added. "And what else? I don't know. She carries the tribal marks on her face, like my father – three parallel marks on each cheek, from cheekbone to jaw. What are you thinking?" he asked, watching her smile lift in its sensuous way, a little higher on one cheek than the other.

"Oh, just that you will marry someone like your mother because isn't that what they always say? That a man looks for someone like his mother."

"And a woman? Does she look for someone like her father?" he asked, mildly-alarmed as he considered resemblances with Mr Richardson.

"I certainly won't. At least not someone as conservative as my father."

All this time she had been tugging at her hair so that now most of it had fallen in loose curls onto her shoulders, and more than ever Tayo wanted to touch her. He moved from his chair to the bed, close to where Vanessa had slipped her feet beneath the blanket.

"I almost wish that my mother had the polyandry option that your mother had," Vanessa added, looking more serious.

"Why?"

"Maybe it happens in all marriages at some point, and this sounds awful, but I just think Mother would be happier with someone else."

For a few moments she sat, silently running her pretty fingers along the embroidered edge of the pillowcase.

"You don't have to stop," he said softly.

She sighed as though she were tired, but then patted the pillow, forcefully.

"So, what suits Tayo Ajayi? You never told me. Polygamy or monogamy?"

He watched her, wondering whether she would share more, but the resolve on her face stopped him from probing.

"I note the absence of polyandry," he remarked.

"Somehow, I didn't think you'd go for that," she laughed.

"Oh, I don't know. I quite like the idea of getting other men to fix things round the house. I'm not good at that. But as for the sexual part," he laughed, "well no, I couldn't share my woman. I'm afraid I'd be too jealous. Monogamy, happy monogamy, I think that's what I would pick. And it would have to be a woman who is gentle and loving. Someone intelligent, able to put up with me, of course, and God-fearing. What do you think?"

"God-fearing or Tayo-fearing?"

"Now why should anyone fear me?"

"I don't know." She laughed. "But it's late and I should be going."

"Afraid?"

"No," she smiled. "It's been lovely."

She pulled her feet from under the blanket that bristled with static, and rubbed her bare arms.

"Lovely," he repeated, knowing that this was the moment to do something if he was going to do anything, but the fact that this was her family home and that her father was somewhere nearby made him hesitate.

She stood up, slipped her shoes on, and took the stole from where it had fallen next to the pillow.

"Don't get too cold," she said, placing her hand lightly on his shoulder.

He watched as she slipped quietly out of the room and tiptoed down the hall. "*What's wrong with you?*" Tayo muttered to himself, slowly closing the door.

"*O de!*" he cursed himself in Yoruba.

Chapter 9

On Monday they shared walnut cake at the Cadena; Tuesday, they ate chicken curry at the Taj Mahal restaurant; Wednesday they drank coffee in her room; and on Thursday they attended St. Antony's weekly seminar on African theatre. They had considered going to the Moulin Rouge on Friday to see Zimmermann's *High Noon*, but decided instead to stay in Tayo's room and listen to jazz.

Vanessa loved the smell of Tayo's room – a comforting mix of Old Spice, Brylcream, and Nigerian food. Occasionally, when they were not together, she would catch the scent on pages of Tayo's letters, or on clothing he had touched. His room was on the first floor of staircase XVI, large and sparsely furnished. In it was a bed with three neatly folded blankets – two green and one cream – and, at the far end of the room, a fireplace, boarded over and replaced with a coin-operated heater. The heating was always on when Vanessa visited and she suspected he rarely turned it off. He had told her that in his first week at Oxford he had nearly set fire to himself by sitting too close to the heater. The only other items of furniture were his old oak desk by the window, the sofa where she now sat, a wardrobe and a coffee table. On the floor were his football boots, and propped up against the bit of wall between the windowsill and desk was the room's only decoration: two colour postcards of ocean liners. Today she had brought him daffodils to brighten the room.

"Women can bring men flowers too, you know," she smiled,

sensing some hesitation on his part as she arranged them in an empty milk bottle. Already, the buds were opening and adding a bright splash of buttery yellow. She placed them next to the neat stack of books and papers and picked one up marked *A Handbook for Students from Overseas*. She looked at what he had underlined and smiled as she read aloud from a section entitled *Habits and Customs*.

"It says here that when two people meet and they wish to save themselves from the embarrassment of silence, they usually talk about the weather. Did we talk about the weather when we first met?"

"I believe we did."

"No we didn't!" She laughed, closing the book, and picking up another. "*The Interpreters*, by Wole Soyinka."

"SH-oyinka," he corrected.

"Any good?" she asked, watching him take the record player from its box on the floor and then, while his back was turned, she tugged at her skirt, which despite Pat's reassurances was, Vanessa now decided, definitely too short.

"Where do you buy all these Nigerian newspapers?"

"My father sends me some, and others I get from London."

"'*Preparations well underway for the first Negro Festival of Arts*'," Vanessa read a headline. "Wouldn't you love to go? Look." She held up the paper for him to see. "Everyone's going: Haile Salessie, Duke Ellington, Langston Hughes, Marpessa Dawn…"

"So let's go, and we'll sail the *Aureol*."

"You know, I think I might already have sailed that same ship when mum and I came back to England. I'm sure it had a yellow funnel, just like the one in your postcard."

"I knew it!"

"Knew what?"

"That you were the girl on the ship, the day I first saw the *Aureol* in 1951."

"Then it wouldn't have been me. Not in 1951."

"But your mother was lifting you up like this." Tayo demonstrated, flexing his muscles. "And I waved to you. Actually no, that wasn't it. I remember now. You blew me a kiss, and I sent you one back," he said, matter-of-factly, as he leant against his desk and rested the record against his knees.

"Tell me more, then." Vanessa smiled.

"Well, to set the scene, it was before the days of Father's Morris Minor so we took the bolekaja bus from my hometown in Ibadan to Lagos. These are the typical Bedford trucks, the type you find here in England carrying goods or livestock, but in Nigeria they're fitted with benches to carry passengers. Do you remember them?"

"No." She shook her head.

"Well, the buses are not very advanced which means that everything travels on them – people, children, goats, chickens, you name it. Combine this with hours of driving on dirt roads full of potholes, and you get some pretty irritated passengers, not to speak of the rude bus boys. That's how the buses get their name. Bolekaja literally means, 'Come down and let's fight it out.'"

She laughed, picturing the scene with Tayo on one of these buses, though it was hard to imagine him ever getting angry as she watched him playfully twirling his record in the air.

"When we got to Lagos, my father took me straight away to the ocean, and I screamed. I never expected the sea to look so vast and to sound so loud. I thought the tide and all that foam were about to swallow us up, but somehow Baba must have calmed me and we spent hours watching the water and the ships. The next day we watched the *Aureol* leave and you were on that ship, I'm sure of it. So you see, sea-sea, we were destined for each other."

He jumped up, causing her heart to skip a beat.

"And now that we have spent an evening going to Africa and

back, as your Christopher Robin would say, how about this, Miss Vanessa?"

She watched as he twirled the disc on his index finger and blew imaginary dust from both sides before placing it gently on the record player. Little things like this, the way he touched things and the way he moved, had the strangest, most thrilling effect on her. And there were other things too that she would normally never notice and admire, but with him it was different. His tidiness, for example, the way he organised his jazz LPs in one pile and West African Highlife in another, all neatly stowed away at the bottom of his wardrobe.

Initially it had been his gentleness and a sense that he was genuine that had attracted her and of course there had always been his looks, but now there were these conversations, the things he was teaching her, the way he listened. She loved his attentiveness and the way he made her laugh. There he was, happily singing along with Louis Armstrong and it didn't matter if he didn't like her Bob Dylan or the Beatles. He marched in exaggerated steps, still singing, "*Oh Lawd I want to be in that number, when the saints go marching in.*"

"You do put me in a good mood, Tayo."

"That's good. I'm here to please. *Omotayo*, remember? The man who brings joy. Come," he beckoned, "dance with me."

She watched as he pushed up his sleeves to reveal the fine muscles in his forearms, which again set her heart aflutter.

"I'll just watch," she said, knowing there was no way she could move with his ease or flair. She would end up stepping on his feet.

"Okay, as you please. If you don't want to dance then I'll just have to tell you the Satchmo story."

"No, stop!" she laughed, tossing a cushion at his legs. "You've told me that story so many times that I've memorised it! In 1961 Satchmo played on the Ikorodu Road at Bobby Benson's club. The place was packed and you were *sooooooo* proud to see a gifted American Negro inspired by the beats of Africa. So proud that you will personally write Satchmo's biography one day."

"I will," he laughed. "So you see, next time you should dance and then you won't have to listen to my stories. But, first, I'm making you coffee." He lifted the stylus back to the beginning of the song and marched off, humming.

Vanessa smiled to herself as she waited, remembering the first time that Tayo had talked to her about Satchmo's visit to Nigeria and she imagined herself as the reporter. She had always wanted to be a foreign reporter in Africa, but now she wasn't so sure – Malcolm X had been so critical of white journalists there. Tayo returned with the coffees and asked about her day, so she told him about the little things – the struggles with her work and horrible college food.

"I'm sorry," he said, looking concerned and then offering more of his mother's food.

"You're such a love." She wriggled to the edge of her seat, touched by his concern. Africans, she had noticed, were in the habit of saying sorry even if something was not their fault. And then he looked down at where she had tapped his knee and she blushed.

"What's the essay that's causing you all this headache?" he asked.

"American slavery, secession, and the old Lincoln-Douglass debates," she answered, clasping both hands tightly round the mug. "The topic is interesting, but it's not *modern* history. I keep thinking about Malcolm X and Martin Luther King, as well as everything that is happening in South Africa – you know, real modern history."

"So you must write about these things, Vanessa. Find a way of putting them in your essay, and then submit more articles to the newspapers."

"Do you think so?" She clasped her mug a little tighter,

watching bits of cream bob up and down in the circle of coffee, and wondered what he was really thinking.

"Of course you should write. You have a flair for writing, Vanessa, and you already have your own unique voice."

She smiled, gazing at him for a safe moment. She loved the way he pronounced her name. '*VA-nessa*', with the accent on the V, making it sound strong and exotic.

"And now I have a new song for you." He took her mug and placed it next to his on the desk. "Listen to this." He shook another record out of its sleeve.

"Who is it?"

"Listen."

"Ella?" she tried.

"No."

"Lena Horne!"

"No," he smiled.

"Who then?" She jumped up and snatched the sleeve from his hands.

"Hey!" He laughed, chasing her back to the chair.

"*What a Little Moonlight can do* – Billie Holiday," she read the label, holding it up high out of his reach. "But it doesn't sound like her – it's happy," she said, handing it back. "Let's hear it again."

He lifted the stylus and placed it carefully on the record. She thought he was going to join her on the sofa, but instead he moved the coffee table, and brought his chair closer to hers.

"So which Billie Holiday songs do you remember?" he asked.

She felt the heat rising in her cheeks. "I can't really remember the titles, but there were several songs Mum listened to when we were living here and Father was still in Nigeria."

"It must have been lonely for her."

She nodded. One day she would tell him about Mother's problems, but not now.

"Will you show me a photograph of your mother?"

"Of course."

He stood up and took an envelope from his drawer and then, choosing one of the photographs taken on the day he left for England, began pointing out who was who. Vanessa nodded, taking the black-and-white print from his hand for a better look. In the picture, Tayo's head was tilted, looking up and smiling as though there were something interesting on the roof of the photographer's studio, while his brother Biyi kept an eye on the little sister. Biyi was handsome too and wearing a smart checked shirt unbuttoned at the neck. His little brother, Remi, was the only person staring solemnly into the camera, and he wore traditional clothes like his mother and sister. His tiny hand rested on his mother's lap, next to her jewelled fingers and wrists. His mother wasn't smiling, just looking into the camera with her head tie (or *gele* as Tayo called it), which stood tall and made her look regal. 'What a proud-looking mother,' Vanessa thought. His sister, Bisi, was grinning at the photographer, too young to be flirting, yet it looked like that was precisely what she was doing.

"And your father?"

Tayo passed her another picture.

"Your photographers must instruct everyone not to smile," she laughed, noting the seriousness in the father's face. Three tribal marks ran deep across each cheek. Tayo didn't resemble his father at all, only the eyes with the thick eyebrows.

"Any more?" she asked.

"That's it."

"Oh come on!" She tugged at the envelope.

"It's only a football photograph, and one of Christine, who is related to our family," he explained, letting her look for herself.

"I didn't know that." Vanessa felt relieved, staring at Christine's large dark eyes and the perfectly arching eyebrows. Her skin was smooth and her hair swept up high in a Sophia Loren style. She could easily have been a model. "How is she related to you?"

"Sort of like a cousin," Tayo replied, standing up to change the record.

After a while, she placed the photographs on his pillow.

"Tayo, can I ask you something?"

"Anything you like."

"Do you think I could be a journalist?"

"Absolutely! Besides, you are a journalist already, and a fine one at that."

"No, but I mean a real one. Could I write about Africa? I mean, not so much could I write, but would I be accepted?"

"Why not? Of course you would. Vanessa Richardson," he said, writing her name in the air. Africa Foreign Correspondent. I can see it already."

"Even if I'm white?"

"And what's wrong with being British?"

"Well, it's just that with all this talk of indigenisation..." she trailed off. "I do understand and I know it's important."

"Vanessa, my friend, Africa needs as many good journalists as it can get – African and British. There is so much to be done in our continent, and you would be perfect."

She turned, accidentally brushing her leg against his as he sat down beside her.

"What will you play next?" she asked, trying not to blush when he stroked her knee.

"What would you like?" He reached for her hands.

"Anything," she whispered, as he gave her hands a gentle squeeze before letting go.

"I'll surprise you, then." He stood up to change the record and stretched out an arm. "Come," he whispered, this time offering his hands.

Nervously, she reached for him, and he pulled her up. Her heart was thumping and her feet shuffled clumsily as he wrapped one arm around her waist and then the other, moving her away from the chair with the first notes of Ellington and Coltrane's *In a Sentimental Mood*. She rested her head against his chest and closed her eyes, allowing her body to sway a little to the music. He kissed the top of her head and, after a while, let go of her waist. He placed warm hands against her cheeks and lifted her face to his. She wanted to kiss him, but her heart was pounding so loudly that she found herself turning away out of embarrassment. Gently, he placed her head back on his chest and kept on dancing.

Chapter 10

Simon suggested that they spend Easter in Paris. His Uncle Rupert owned an apartment that they could use while he was away holidaying in Guadeloupe. Simon would take his girlfriend, Nina, and Tayo could take Vanessa. Tayo liked the idea but doubted whether Vanessa's father would let her spend a week away from home in the company of men. He need not have been worried – English fathers were either not as strict as their Nigerian counterparts, or their daughters more cunning.

The apartment was located in the fashionable 9th arrondissement, close to the Place de la Madelaine in an affluent area of the city where women wearing furs and carrying miniature dogs strolled the Place Vendome and Champs Elysees. The women amused Tayo for he could tell that being seen was just as important to them, if not more important, *tout simplement*, as what they purchased. What would it be like, he wondered, to sit and watch their comings and goings? And what would his mother make of them? But he and Vanessa never stayed long enough to observe and, except for a visit to the Opera and an evening of coffees and mille feuilles at the Café de la Paix, they spent little time in the neufieme.

Instead, for the first few days, they walked through the Jardin des Tuileries onto the Seine and over to the left bank, which was Vanessa's favourite part of the city. Paris was a place Vanessa knew well, having visited many times as a child and on their walks she recounted for his benefit the history of Paris, explaining to him the origin of the Ile de la Cite and the distinctive architectures along the Seine.

It was Tayo's first visit to the continent and each day he found himself marvelling anew at its beauty. It made him want to travel to as many European countries as possible before returning to Nigeria, and especially to the famous cities of Vienna, Prague and Amsterdam. At the same time, and in a strange sort of way, Paris reminded Tayo of Nigeria, even though in its appearance it was quite different to anything back home. The buildings were old, the diet rich in dairy products, and the climate cool, but in its feel there was definitely something reminiscent of home. It might have been the bustle of Paris, the incessant talking and the way people argued openly and loudly on the streets. The bureaucracy was also excessive like home and there were many Africans – French-speaking ones. Vanessa had bought him his first writing journal to record his thoughts, which he began doing on their first day.

Today I cannot stop smiling. I imagine walking with you forever, hand-in-hand, strolling through the Jardins de Luxembourg. It seems like we could laugh and talk, and never run out of things to say. This afternoon, as we sipped our cafés au lait at Les Deux Magots, and as you charmed the proprietaire with your fluent French, I watched you with such pride. I love you Vanessa, so much that I think of nothing else. Tomorrow we will visit new places, but it hardly matters where we go, just to be with you is heaven.

The next day, however, was not so romantic for while he and Vanessa were out on the streets of Montmartre, a Congolese man approached them and asked to take a photograph.

"I will make a beautiful picture. You give me your address, Mademoiselle, and I send it to you."

'Rubbish,' Tayo thought. It was obvious that the man had other intentions, and yet Vanessa gave him her address! Tayo was quiet for the rest of that afternoon and doubly annoyed because Vanessa could not see for herself what was bothering him. It grew into a long simmering argument that lasted all day and was only resolved the following morning as they walked to the Sorbonne, down the Rue Des Ecoles, in search of Presence Africaine.

Presence Africaine was a tiny bookshop, filled with books by African and Caribbean authors. Tayo thought, not for the first time, about Christine and how much she would have liked the place. Out of guilt, he bought her a copy of the Presence Africaine Revue with special essays in tribute to Malcolm X. He also bought some work by James Baldwin, which he and Vanessa read together on a park bench nearby. And this was the pattern of each of their days: long stretches spent wandering Paris followed by evenings with Simon and Nina. They lived the bohemian life, eating baguettes with Brie and saucisson, and drinking red wine as they debated world politics. They spoke frequently of America – Malcolm's tragic death and Vietnam. Vanessa and Simon argued adamantly against intervention while he and Nina played devil's advocate. On the last night they talked for hours on the subject of society and who was best placed to critique it. Vanessa suggested that only those who had travelled away from home could really see their countries for what they were, which led to a long discussion of Herodotus and De Tocqueville.

Tayo wondered, as they spoke, how he would perceive Nigeria once he returned. Would he see things more clearly? And what, as a foreigner, were his thoughts on England? What pearls of wisdom might he have to offer? They stayed up late discussing these questions, but still got up early the next morning. They were to visit Versailles on their last full day in France and were packing a picnic. They were almost ready to leave when the telegram arrived. Christine was dead. Suicide.

It had been an overdose and the body was found only several days later by the cleaning lady. Ike was the one who gave Tayo the details, telling Tayo that relatives had come immediately to take the body away and clear out her room.

"Why did she do this?' Ike kept asking. "Why?" Tayo did what he could to reassure him, telling him that these were questions no one could answer, but inside he asked the same questions and more. Everyone believed that things between him and Christine had ended long ago but, in reality, it had only been a few weeks before leaving for Paris that Tayo had stopped visiting Christine. She had sent him several notes that he had chosen to ignore and now he felt devastated.

Even though there was nothing in the notes to suggest desperation, Tayo felt that had he responded to her notes it wouldn't have happened. She had told him so many times that she felt caught between two lands, never fully belonging to England or Nigeria, but he had never taken it seriously, always thinking that she was the strong and privileged one. But now he could see it clearly – the peripatetic lifestyle contributing to her anxieties at Oxford and amplifying her desire to please her family with academic success. But the taking of her life, how could she have done this? Why hadn't she talked to someone? And why, *how*, had they all failed to realise the depth of her despair?

Additionally he asked himself why had he not been honest with her and said that he wasn't ready for a serious relationship instead of making up excuses that he knew she hadn't believed anyway? Why hadn't he been more of a man and told her that at the time he had loved her for God's sake! And now he was caught up in another web of untruths. He had lied to Vanessa about Christine, telling her that Christine was related to him. Tayo clasped his hands tightly behind his neck and pulled his head down to his knees. He still had her notes to him, but he couldn't bring himself to re-read them. Yet the phrases were branded in his mind.

Bolaji tells us you are busy with your new girl.

Please, spare a few moments for your old friend.

The notes were sitting on his desk, and next to them the journals that he had bought for Christine when they had been in France. He flicked through them, tears welling in his eyes as he realised that she might already have been dead when he had bought them for her. And then he thought of Vanessa who would by now be in France again, and he thought of how patient she had been with him as he grieved for Christine. "She's not what you think," he found himself mumbling as though Christine were with him. "Vanessa's not just any white woman."

He was supposed to be packing his things to spend the summer with his cousin in Bradford, a trip he had planned months before, but he couldn't bring himself to start. Instead, he sat before his empty trunk grieving for Christine, missing Vanessa and staring at the Nigerian newspaper cutting sent by his Father.

Christine Arinze, who died of sudden illness while studying abroad at Oxford University.

May her soul rest in peace. April 4, 1965.

"Rest in peace, rest in peace," Tayo whispered.

Chapter 11

Vanessa worried about Tayo, not knowing how best to comfort him after Christine's death. She had hoped that he would return to France with her, but he seemed keener to spend the summer with his cousin, which she could understand given that this was his only family in England. In the meantime, although she had been dreading the time away in France with her parents, things had not been quite as bad as she feared, at least not in the beginning. It helped that Grandma and Granddad were not there at the same time, and that the weather in St. Jean was heavenly. There was also Madame Pagnole's Provencal cooking which could never be underestimated. Jane had come to join them for a few days too, so all was going well until Mother received the letter from Nancy Murdoch. 'N' for notoriously nattering, nitwit Nancy who wrote to inform them (never asking, always announcing) that she and her husband would be visiting over the Bastille holiday. Father was delighted (typical). Mother was furious.

Mr Murdoch had been Father's friend of many years. They met in 1945 while taking the summer course at Oxford in preparation for colonial service. It was there that they both learnt their first few words of local African languages as well as acquiring some knowledge on tropical medicines and diet. Mr Murdoch was subsequently posted to Tanganyika while Father had gone to Nigeria, but they had stayed in touch over the years.

Whenever the two got together they drank, smoked cigars, and reminisced about the good old times and their chums in the Corona Club. But it was not such a jolly time for Mother, who was left entertaining 'nattering Nancy'. Unlike some talkative types with whom one could '*umm*' and '*ahh*' without paying much attention, Nancy's chatter was of the intense type that demanded responses. She spoke incessantly about herself, which was why, when Father refused to say no to the Murdoch's, Mother insisted upon inviting Uncle Tony, who conveniently happened to be in France at the same time, as a way of balancing things out.

Father disapproved of his brother-in-law just as much as Mother objected to Mrs Murdoch, so this made them even. Uncle Tony was far too unconventional for Father – he had never held a steady job or married, and rumours circulated about his preferring men to women. Moreover, his politics embarrassed Father, especially in front of people like the Murdochs, who shared his conservative views. Uncle Tony was not a Communist Party member (his taste in clothes, art, and wine precluded this), but he sympathised with the Left and considered himself a late Fabian. Father also begrudged his brother-in-law for having had the opportunities that he would have liked; namely, being born into the upper class and achieving a place at Cambridge University. To make matters worse in Father's eyes, Uncle Tony had had the effrontery to squander his opportunities, dropping out of Cambridge and associating with people Father deemed socially and politically unsavoury.

On the day before Bastille, the Murdochs arrived on time but Uncle Tony missed his train and, because Father wouldn't go back to the station, Jane went to fetch him instead. Father had wanted to start the meal without Uncle Tony too, but Madame Pagnole would hear nothing of the sort. To Father's chagrin, Madame Pagnole exerted considerable authority over the home in France. She had been chef to the Hume family since Mother and Uncle Tony were children, and when it came to meals she was boss. She had a voice that carried like thunder and a girth to match, with the result that nobody ordered her around, least of all Father, whom she disliked. And Madame Pagnole had a soft spot for her little "Antoine," so much so that the menu was chosen according to Uncle Tony's favourite dishes– *foie gras, Coquilles St. Jacques* with black truffles and, of course, the famous Pagnole *tarte aux poires*.

During the meal, Jane and Uncle Tony sat together at the dining table, wisely paying no attention to Father, who was scowling like a little boy at the far end of the table. 'Oh la la-la-la', Vanessa thought to herself. At least there was something undeniably happy about Jane, which was a recent change. She still didn't say much in large groups, but Vanessa now noticed a quiet confidence that could be sensed even when she wasn't talking.

Vietnam was the topic of discussion with Uncle Tony describing his participation in recent anti-nuclear testing demonstrations. Not surprisingly, Father grunted his disapproval, but that didn't stop Vanessa from asking questions. Did Uncle Tony think that America would be forced to withdraw their troops? She tried several times to ask the question but, true to form, Nancy Murdoch, in collusion with Father, kept interrupting. Mr Murdoch said nothing when his wife talked, either because he was too intimidated or more than likely because his wife embarrassed him.

"Do you know that the number of black children in our English children's homes is on the rise?" Nancy spoke in her affected high-pitched voice, making no attempt to link her comment to anything said before. "And did you know that the brown children are the hardest to find families for?"

'And did you know,' Vanessa thought as she watched Nancy's lips, 'that you have chunks of green spinach lodged between your teeth?'

"And why is that?" Jane asked, the only one kind enough to indulge the woman in conversation.

"Well," Nancy paused, "many parents won't take the brown ones for fear of what others might think. If the children are *properly* black of course, there's no mistaking the mothers. But with the brown ones…well, people gossip, you know. Few women want to be mistaken as mothers of…" Nancy paused again. "*Mulattoes*," she whispered hurriedly, as though the word itself were dangerous.

"That's just stupid," Vanessa scoffed, riled by Nancy's conspiratorial tone.

"*Fromages!*" Mme Pagnole announced, arriving with another course.

"Well you can't blame them, 'Nessa," Father said, covering his nose as he pushed away the plate of Munster and Camembert.

"Why not?"

"People will think it rape," Nancy answered, peering dubiously at the cheeses and opting for the date garnish.

"Oh, that's ridiculous!" Vanessa insisted.

"I think 'Nessa's right," Uncle Tony added. "There are probably very few rapes; its just people being too racist to deal with the results of their actions, or should we say passion."

"Precisely," Vanessa nodded.

"*Et ha, c'est bien!*" Mme Pagnole exclaimed, happy to find dents in her cheese. She had returned with the salad.

"Well, you can't just blame the English for being racist, you know." Mrs Murdoch raised her palms meekly. "The blacks are just as bad, if not worse. They reject them too. It's terribly distressing, but at the end of the day we just need to find these little dearies a home, don't we?"

"So 'Nessa, darling, how is Oxford these days?" Uncle Tony asked.

Vanessa smiled, knowing that her uncle felt the same way as she did about Nancy Murdoch. Everything about the woman was irritating: her high-pitched voice, her supercilious tone, her feigned generosity, and the green in her teeth.

"She's having a jolly time, aren't you, Vanessa?" Father answered.

"And what's this I hear about you writing for the Oxford newspapers?" Uncle Tony asked.

"Oh, it's just a few things for *Isis*."

"So, you're a writer now?" Nancy interrupted. "How delightful! I've always thought it a super career for a woman – something that you can do when you have children. You must also learn to type, darling."

Vanessa rolled her eyes.

"Vanessa's very interested in Africa," Mother added. "She supports all their independence movements."

"Well, she might not be supporting them for long. Wait and see if they last," Father added, dryly.

"Jonathan, please." Mother tapped the side of her glass again.

Vanessa shook her head, wishing she could disappear from it all. Mother had been doing so well, but now with Nancy's stupid comments and Father's equally stupid remarks, she was back to her drink and it was only going to get worse.

"So, tell me more, darling," Uncle Tony urged, offering cigars. "Cuban, Lizzie?"

Mother declined.

"Jane?" he added with a wink.

Vanessa watched with curiosity as Jane accepted. So this was the new Cambridge Jane!

"Tell me more about your writing 'Nessa," Uncle Tony probed, thinking she had been silenced by Nancy.

Vanessa mentioned a few of the articles, including the one that she was most proud of, which critiqued American foreign policy as it pertained to their previous discussion.

"Rather silly if you ask me," Father mumbled.

"Well, nobody's asking you," Mother replied, pouring another brandy, as Mme Pagnole entered with the prized *tarte aux poires*.

"Vanessa has lots of foreign friends up at Oxford, especially from our colonies," Father continued, ignoring the tart that brought a round of applause from everyone else.

"*Ex*-colonies you mean! Madame Pagnole, this is *delicieux. Fantastique!*" Vanessa smiled.

"*Bien se nourrir pour bien se porter.*" Mrs Pagnole winked.

"Ahh, Gisele." Uncle Tony was the only one who could call Madame Pagnole by her first name. "What do you think? Should Vanessa become a writer?"

"*Il faut d'abord qu'elle aprenne faire la cuisine.*"

"And why must I learn to cook?"

"*Parce-que,*" Madame Pagnole paused, looking mischievously in Father's direction, "*Savoir faire la cuisine, c'est savoir controller les hommes.* You cook, you control the mens," she said, laughing at her own translation, which made everyone laugh except for Father, who kept on talking.

"We've had quite the foreign lot to visit, haven't we, Elizabeth? One feels rather obliged to show them the world. It's very civilizing for them really."

For many years, Vanessa thought that this was just Father's way of speaking, that he spoke condescendingly on most subjects without really meaning to do so. This was also how Mother explained it, but Vanessa no longer believed it.

"Didn't we meet some of them at the Christmas party?" Mr Murdoch asked. "There were Indians I believe, and a coloured man, wasn't there?"

"Yes, that's right," Father replied. "They must make special concessions for them to get into Oxford these days. They're still bright for Africans mind you – future ministers and leaders of their countries."

"Oh really, Jonathan, don't be so stupid!" Uncle Tony replied.

"Well, I'm simply telling you what I observed at Oxford," Father continued.

"I hardly think a summer course counts as having gone to Oxford."

"Please," Mother pleaded.

"Well, some of us did go to Oxbridge," Tony insisted.

"And dropped out," Father added.

"Will you two stop it!" Mother's voice was raised.

"As I was saying," Father continued, "we've had quite the foreign lot to visit, including the Nigerian chappie at Balliol. Now there's a bright fellow for you, with good manners, reading PPE at Balliol, and he's Yoruba of course. They've always been the most straightforward. With the Hausa you can never tell what they are up to, and the Igbos are always so sly."

"Oh, Daddy, you can't say things like that!"

"Why not? They would tell you the same thing if you asked."

"Actually, I recall that chap looking rather like your gardener in Jos," Nancy remarked. "A lovely young man. Why ever did you sack him?"

"Because he was an idiot," Father snapped.

"Oh dear! I always thought…"

"Nancy," Mr Murdoch glared at his wife, cutting her off in mid-sentence.

"Jonathan's the idiot," Mother muttered, recklessly filling her glass without looking.

"Oh, for Christ's sake, Mum!"

"So tell me, 'Nessa," Uncle Tony winked again at Jane, "Are Oxford women still being treated as second-class citizens and what about –"

"Jonathan's the bloody i-di-ot," Mother interrupted.

"You're the one that looks idiotic, Elizabeth," Father snapped. "You and your beloved gardener. Did you ever tell him you were a drunk?"

"Oh, I say!" Nancy exclaimed.

"You say what?" Mother shouted, glaring at Nancy and then at Father. "Don't you remember the gardener's name? He had a name you know." She banged the bottle back on the table.

"Mother!" Vanessa pleaded, but she was already up and marching unsteadily, but determinedly, out of the room.

*

"Well, that was quite some drama for one night," Jane remarked as she and Vanessa went to their room after helping Madame Pagnole clear the plates.

"I can't believe my mother," Vanessa muttered angrily to herself.

"You shouldn't let it bother you, 'Nessa. Nancy's enough to drive anyone to drink. But you've got to tell me, who is this chappie from Balliol? 'Very nice chap'," Jane imitated Father's accent.

"Oh shut up!" Vanessa tossed a pillow at her.

"So let's have a look at that photo again." Jane hopped from her bed to Vanessa's.

"Why?"

"Because I want to see it, silly! Come on. Not all of us are lucky enough to have handsome boyfriends, or even a boyfriend at all. And have you done it yet?"

"Done what?"

"You know…" Jane cocked her head and raised her eyebrows. "Oh, don't be such a prude."

"I'm not being a prude!" Vanessa picked up the fallen pillow, and lobbed it back at Jane.

"Yes you are."

"No I'm not."

"Promise then to tell me all about him and I'll tell you a secret."

"What secret?"

"Promise?"

"What secret?"

"Promise?"

"Okay, yes. Promise." Vanessa nodded impatiently.

"We, as in me and your uncle, did it on the way back from the station."

"Did what?"

"Had sex."

"You what!"

"You're so dramatic, 'Nessa. This isn't Victorian England. It's the 60s for God's sake."

"You and…"

"Your Uncle Tony."

"But he's not that way in…" Vanessa stammered.

"Inclined? Oh yes he is!"

"Oh God, Jane! Is this serious?"

"Of course not 'Nessa! Tony's far too old for me, though I must say that older men really have that touch. The way he –"

"Jane! I don't want to hear."

"Well, if you don't want to hear then tell me about your boyfriend. What do you two get up to?"

"Obviously nothing compared to you, but we do things."

"Like…" Jane rolled her hands in continuous circles for more detail. "It's not like you to be lost for words, Vanessa."

"Oh Jane, what does this mean for you and Tony?"

"It doesn't mean anything, 'Nessa. Read some Freud. It's just sex. Speaking of which, is it really true what they say about size?"

"I have no idea!" And with that Vanessa pushed Jane off the bed.

"Okay, so what did your parents think of him?" Jane asked, jumping back. "Oh, come on 'Nessa, don't be so cross."

"They like him."

"But how about what nattering Nancy was saying? Wouldn't they worry about the way people would view your children?"

"It's just a skin colour, Jane."

"*I* know that and you know that, but your father's not exactly the most liberal of thinkers."

"Liberal enough to marry against *his* parent's wishes, so I don't see how he could object. Anyway, who said anything about marriage?"

"Of course you will." Jane thumped the mattress with her hand. "Oh Vanessa, you're smitten. I can already imagine you married to him. He'll be the next Nigerian Prime Minister, and you'll be living over there in one of those fancy mansions with servants fanning you and bringing you food. You'll have all those lovely brown children running around. The local papers will carry the headlines. Prime Minister… what's his name again?"

"Tayo Ajayi." Vanessa smiled, momentarily forgetting her annoyance.

"Prime Minister A-ja-yee and his wife Vanessa A-ja-yee," Jane announced, wriggling under the covers, "visited by Drs Jane and somebody so-and-so. Sounds good *n'est-ce pas*?"

"More likely Professor Ajayi than Prime Minister Ajayi. He wants to teach."

"Well, that's a shame. Never mind, I'm sure he'll be somebody important one day. A Chancellor perhaps, and won't that be nobby!" She rolled onto her side. "Hey," she rolled back, "let's go and see Jean-Pierre and Olivier tomorrow. They ought to be back now."

Vanessa shrugged her shoulders. She wasn't as excited about them as she might have been a year ago. It was Tayo she dreamt of. Perhaps he would be a Chancellor one day or a professor lecturing in the university. Perhaps she would do the same. Or perhaps she would write for one of the national newspapers. They would live on campus or in the city maybe. She imagined shopping in the outdoor markets and at weekends enjoying long walks by the beach and nights of music and dance. She wondered what Tayo was doing at that moment without her.

Hopefully he wasn't meeting women. She didn't like it when he flirted with other women and especially with coloured women. It didn't help that whenever Christine's name was mentioned he became withdrawn, and when she remarked on it he accused her of not understanding his culture, which made her angry because she was doing all that she could to understand.

"So, let's say, just hypothetically, if I marry Tayo, would you definitely come to Africa and visit me?" Vanessa peered over Jane's shoulder.

"Jane?" she whispered, but Jane was fast asleep.

Chapter 12

Le Carrelat
06230 St. Jean-Ferrat
France

18th June, 1965

Dear Tayo,

    *How could you possibly think that you were boring me? I want <u>lots</u> of letters (*beaucoup de letters!*) and even longer ones, but make it less polite and formal next time. Tell me how much you've been missing me and how much you dream of me – otherwise I'll start to wonder what you're up to with those northern lasses!*

    I do wish you were here, darling. The weather is beautifully warm, just as you would like it, and we spend most of our time outdoors. Most days I cycle to the nearby town of Beaulieu to the outdoor market where we buy fresh breads, pastries and smelly cheeses (I know you're not a fan, but just wait till you come). In the afternoons I visit the local cafe and sip my café-au-lait, while fending off all the French men (ha ha!), and then I gaze across the Cote d'Azur and dream of you.

    And in between these dreams, I've been reading the books you suggested, starting with Chinua Achebe's Things Fall Apart *and* No Longer at Ease. *I enjoy them and think I might review one for* Isis, *so you'll have to help me. Achebe has such a wonderful way with descriptions! Do you remember the scene in* No Longer at Ease *when, in the words of Obi, Achebe describes the dancing women with waists swivelling as effortlessly as oiled ball bearings? What a wonderful image! I'm looking forward to discussing his writing with you when I see you. I only wish that Achebe's stories were not so tragic, but perhaps the tragedy highlights the dilemmas of post-independence, which brings me to your Perham review.*

I feel so flattered that you sent me the review and asked for my opinion. What do I think? I think it's a fab! I don't have much to add except that reading Achebe made me wonder whether it might be worth mentioning somewhere in the piece that Africans themselves are sensitive to the difficulties inherent in the new postcolonial world.

I also have a few more minor suggestions. First, for the purposes of Spear *magazine and its West African readership, I think you ought to provide background information on Dame Margery. Mention that she is an Oxford don and that her family has a lengthy history within the service. By the way, Father says that Perham was "a royal pain" for the Colonial Service and much more provocative than we give her credit for. Also, I think you should consider structuring the review more tightly around what I see as your principle criticisms of Perham's work.*

1.   An underestimation (dismissal almost) of Africa's pre-colonial history – a little like Trevor Roper.

2.   Failure to acknowledge the potential of Africa's new leaders (e.g. Senghor, Kenyatta, and Nkrumah).

3.   The belief that independence was granted too swiftly to African states (here is where you might reference Achebe).

I've also corrected one or two grammatical errors – you will see them marked in red. Well done and Tres Bien!

Reading your review has made me think more about what we discussed vis-à-vis my own journalistic writing. Perhaps I should write more, and especially this year with no exams. If Isis *is still looking for an Arts Reviewer, I'll apply for the position and, if I'm accepted, be prepared to accompany me to films, exhibitions, and jazz. I'm off to lunch now with Jane and some French men, so you'd better write soon! Loads of love, kisses, hugs and anything else you dare to imagine.*

Nessaxxxx

6 Aberdeen Road
Bradford

30th June, 1965

My dear Vanessa,

Thank you so much for your letter and I'm glad to hear that you're having such a splendid holiday. Now as for those men at the café, I hear that French men can be quite romantic so don't let them woo you with their sweet talk and philosophy! Remind them that you have a sweeter man waiting for you in England and, in the meantime, I will do my best to ward off all these northern lasses.

So here I am in Tunde's small but cosy house with the evenings to myself when Yusuf and Tunde are working. I realise more than ever how fortunate I've been to receive a Balliol scholarship. Most African students spend long hours working to make ends meet, and I wonder how they manage to pass their exams with so little sleep. Tunde, for example, works from 10.00 at night until 6.00 in the morning at the local bakery. Yusuf also takes night shifts, at the hospital. There are apparently many Africans working as orderlies, and most are assigned to the geriatric ward where others are not so willing to work. I find this sad because in Africa old people are respected and their families look after them. We never put them in homes so maybe that's why Nigerians always staff these geriatric wards, and I hear that the matron also favours Africans because she used to live in Nigeria as a missionary.

Northern England seems very different to the South. People are friendlier on the whole, although one does occasionally see those signs: 'No Dogs. No Irish. No Coloureds'. It's disappointing, but the Africans here don't seem too bothered – they know they are here for a limited time.

Yesterday, I accompanied Tunde to the bakery. One of his

mates was sick, and I offered to take his place loading bread. It was an interesting experience and it gave me some insight into Bradford society. I found that the Pakistanis and Indians are the ones working the ovens, which is the hardest and dirtiest job, because the ovens get very hot and messy. Many of them don't speak English but they have a translator by the name of Samir, who loves to talk politics. The Africans (mainly students, all of whom speak English) have the slightly better task of loading freshly baked breads, scones and teacakes onto the carts and wheeling them to the loading zone. This, by the way, was my job. The least strenuous job of all, which is packing the goods and loading them onto the dispatch trucks, is reserved for the English. So that's the pecking order: Pakistanis and Indians on the bottom, Africans in the middle, and English on top.

Last week I visited York. Have you been? It's full of history and I enjoyed walking along the old Roman wall. There is also the Minster, which is magnificent. At times, when I see things like this, I wish that we had similar marks of history in West Africa because so few visual reminders of our past remain. This is when I realise how important it is for us to record and preserve our oral histories for future generations. But, by now, you must be tired of this letter that has become longer than intended, although you did ask for a long letter! Oh and I mustn't forget to thank you soooo much for reading my Perham review and with all the helpful feedback. I've entitled it: An African's Response: Reflections on Dame Margery Perham's Colonial Reckoning. What do you think? I miss you dreadfully Vanessa, but I'll sign off for now and await your reply.

Kind regards to your mother and father.

Yours truly,

Tayo

Chapter 13

Tayo's cousin, Tunde, lived in a small terraced house close to St. Luke's hospital. It was the sort of house known as 'two up, two down', with a living room and kitchen on the bottom floor, two bedrooms upstairs, and a toilet outside. Bathing was done in a bucket (generally in the kitchen) or at the public baths down the road. Tunde had one of the upstairs bedrooms and Yusuf used the downstairs living room as his bedroom. Normally there were two other Nigerians who shared the second bedroom, but because they were out of town on this particular weekend, Yusuf and Tunde decided they would have a party. Yusuf and Tayo spent the afternoon clearing out his room for space to dance. They took the mattress away and lifted the wardrobe into the hallway so that the room looked like the lounge it was designed to be. As they worked, Yusuf muttered to himself about how unfortunate it was that Tunde refused to have drinks at the party, which he blamed on Tunde's new church. Tayo said nothing, but he had also noticed that his cousin seemed a little over zealous at times. He put away the carpet sweeper and began to help Yusuf sort through the mess of records strewn across the floor.

"He thinks parties are ungodly, and worries about drinkin' and smokin'," Yusuf added.

"What's *drinkin* and *smokin*?" Tayo laughed. "Have you become a Yorkshire Yusuf?"

"Yorkshire Yusuf, Yoruba Yusuf, Yankee Yusuf – pick any you like as long as it gets me the girls." Yusuf laughed. "It's just too bad there's gonna be no boozing tonight," he sighed. "Hey!

What's wrong with Cilla Black?" Yusuf grabbed the vinyl that Tayo had tossed to one side. "What do you have against her? The English girls love it, you know, and yours truly," Yusuf paused to take a bow, "aims to please the ladies. Anyway, what do you people listen to at Oxford? Beethoven? Opera?"

"Ahh, come on. We have all the latest stuff."

"*And you drink too isn't it*? Don't tell me you don't drink at that university of yours."

"Of course we drink. Now where's the Highlife?"

"Hold your horses, Oxford man." Yusuf hopped over discarded records. "Here. I keep them in a special place. Dairo, Bobby Benson, Sunny Ade... Just name it – I have it." He fanned out the sleeves between his arms in demonstration but too quickly and all the records fell to the floor. "Ahh shit," he laughed, bending down to gather them up and inspect each for damage. "Arinze," Yusuf muttered peering at a name on one of the sleeves. "Hey, wasn't there an Arinze at Oxford?"

Tayo nodded, hoping Yusuf would leave it at that.

"It was that Igbo woman, wasn't it? Someone said it was suicide and not an illness like they were saying in the papers."

"Who said that?" Tayo frowned. "Look, my friend, I don't know." The last thing he wanted was for Yusuf to ask if he knew Christine, so he steered the conversation back to Yusuf. Was Yusuf intending to marry his current girlfriend?

"Oh no," Yusuf exclaimed. "But don't get me wrong, I do like Joyce. We dance, we go to the pictures, we have a good time; there's nought wrong with an English lass for a bit of fun, but marriage, that's different. When I'm ready, my friend, it's going to be a one hundred percent Nigerian woman. Yes, most definitely, and a good northern Muslim one too. I don't care what Spear is saying these days about Nigerian women. The fact remains that, at the end of the day, and in the middle of the night," he winked, "they are the best and..."

Tayo shook his head, impatiently.

"No, no, no. Listen to me, Tayo. Nigerian women know how to care for us, how to cook our food, and maintain the culture for our children. That's right. But the English women… *dem no fit do dat*. Besides, have you seen English woman after they reach 30-years-old?"

"What do you mean?"

"Tayo, come on, don't tell me you don't know what I mean. *Haba*! After they pass 30, they look old. *No tell me say you no dey see am*? They get all those wrinkles." Yusuf scrunched up his face in demonstration. "And their bottoms just go flat like ironing board; whereas our African woman remains young and smooooth and curvy, man."

Tayo laughed as Yusuf dusted the surface of his cheeks with his fingertips in exaggerated gestures.

"But Nigerian women are no use for girlfriends. *I no fit take Nigerian girlfriend*," Yusuf insisted, eyeing himself in the mirror above the mantelpiece.

"Why?"

"Because it's too much palaver. *Wallahi! Dem just go dey talk wedding, wedding, wedding. But white woman, eh henh – dat's where man fit relax well-well!*" Yusuf grabbed his crotch.

"You're foolish." Tayo laughed in spite of himself.

"But it's true. Don't tell me you don't know white women."

"Of course, but I don't agree with your stereotypes."

"What stereotypes? White is nice for us. Black is nice for them. It's exotic, that's all. Pure, one hundred percent ex-o-ti-cism."

"Okay, maybe the first time with a white woman is something new… well, just because it's new. But after that, there's no difference. You love the woman for who she is, not for her colour," Tayo insisted, recalling a similar but less jocular debate with Christine.

"Tayo, my friend, you're fooling yourself. Why do you think they like you? *Because you get Oxford mind? And no tell me say you no tink white woman be kule like expressway. And you treat am different to African one now, no be so?"*

"I don't."

"Anyway, as for me, I'm gonna marry a Nigerian. It's my patriotic duty. And then, if I want, I can even marry up to four. *Yes now!* And they're gonna be natural ones too. No make up. No wigs. No mini-skirts."

"Haba Yusuf, you wan go back for caveman age?"

"Look, I have the right to marry four women, and it's the same for you." Yusuf stepped away from the mirror. "Look at your father. *How many wives he get? Plenty no be so?* And he's happy. His wives are happy."

"That's his business."

"So you go marry English woman?" Yusuf laughed. *"This Oxford don brainwash you, ba?* And what about Master Tunde?"

"What about what?" Tunde asked, standing in the doorway, with an armful of paper cups and plates.

"How many wives you go take, and English or Nigerian?"

"What do you mean '*how many*'? One, of course," Tunde replied. "The Bible says a man shall take one wife. *Genesis chapter 2, verse twenty-four.*"

'Uh-oh, here we go' Tayo thought, exchanging a knowing look with Yusuf. 'The Lord spare us!' But Tunde had already launched into scripture.

"Therefore shall a man leave his father and mother and cleave unto his wife and they shall be one. It doesn't matter what nationality, as long as my wife is born again."

"But what about Abraham and Moses?" Yusuf asked. "Didn't they have plenty of wives?"

"Only two, and that was in *Old Testament* times." Tunde squeezed the paper plates hard against his chest.

"And what's wrong with *Old Testament*?" Yusuf persisted.

Tunde stood in silence, gazing bewilderedly at the now

squashed stack of cups in his arms, so that Tayo felt obliged to intervene on his cousin's behalf.

"Yusuf, those were in the times before Jesus Christ. Things have changed since then. Don't you even know that?"

"Ahh, that's your Christianity," Yusuf laughed. "*Na* too confusing for me. Anyway Tayo, what about that French lady writing to you? You didn't read it to us. Who is she now?"

Tunde sighed loudly and left the room.

"Don't vex him with his religion," Tayo whispered, punching Yusuf on the arm. "And she's not French. She's a good friend, whom I've accompanied to…"

"Good friend? *Girlfriend*, you mean." Yusuf laughed, striking back with a jab in the ribs. "Don't use those fancy-fancy Oxford words with us. 'Accompanied,' what does that mean? Accompanied to the sack? Anyway, I'm off to change my shirt, and don't accompany me-o!"

Alone in the room, Tayo straightened the records that still lay scattered across the floor. "Such a joker," Tayo mumbled to himself, thinking of Yusuf's nonsense talk, yet perhaps he was right about some things – but not about race. Tayo reasoned to himself that if he behaved differently with Vanessa than he did with Christine it was because they came from different cultures. And the same thing would apply to any other woman from a different culture – Oriental, Russian, or any other woman not from Nigeria. But how did Vanessa see things? Were Yusuf and Christine right to say that English women only liked black men because they were 'exotic'? Though why was he troubling his head with all of this? Tonight he wanted to have a good time – dance and enjoy some sweet vibes.

*

Joyce, and her two friends Norma and Jean, were the first to arrive. They wore matching pink mini-skirts with high heels, which reminded Tayo of the three Supremes, except that these Supremes were white and carried wicker baskets of food instead of tambourines.

"Now we're ready to party!" Yusuf announced, clapping his hands while Tayo saw to the women's baskets and carried them to the kitchen.

"*Mo mbo*," Tunde called from upstairs.

"Oh – what language was that?" Joyce asked. "Is it Nigerian?"

"Yes," Tayo smiled.

"I've never heard *you* speak it." Joyce turned accusingly to Yusuf.

But Yusuf didn't hear. He was too busy peering into the baskets.

"Custard pie. Scotch egg," Yusuf mumbled. "Cheese Straw. Swiss roll. Treacle tart. Ah-ha! Now *that's* what I'm talking about. Sausage rolls."

"Yusuf," Joyce shouted.

"Bloody hell, woman!" Yusuf jumped, one hand hovering guiltily over the sausages. "Why are you shouting?"

"I said I haven't heard you speak Nigerian."

"Nobody speaks *Nigerian*, you daft thing," Yusuf laughed.

She waited for an explanation, but none was forthcoming. The boys from the bakery had arrived, and she had lost Yusuf's attention to Samir, who wanted to know what they were celebrating.

"It's a party for my cousin," Tunde explained, "and also in honour of Gambia's independence."

"But you chaps aren't from Gambia."

"Yeah, but we're all African," Yusuf replied, ushering people back to the front room.

"And India's our inspiration," Tayo added. "We're hoping for an African Nehru."

"Well, stop hoping," Samir laughed.

"Why?"

"Only wish for your Nehru if you want trouble. You want religious divisions? You want poor people to remain poor and power to stay within one family? If that's what you're after, then by all means pray for a Nehru. No disrespect to the deceased, of course."

"Oh, come on," Tayo raised his voice against Samir's. "Look, the man might have failed a little with the economy but you can't accuse him of siding with landed interest, or for condoning religious differences. Read his autobiography, and you'll see what he has to say on religion."

"Why should I read his stuff when I lived it? And you think his daughter will make things better?"

"Aren't women always cleverer than men?" Tayo turned to Joyce, who had been leaning against the kitchen counter listening. The others were busy arranging food, but Joyce seemed to have taken an interest in what they were discussing.

"So, why doesn't Yusuf speak Nigerian too?" she asked, picking up a knife and a cake.

Tayo glanced at Samir and then back to Joyce. Where was Yusuf when he was needed?

"There are many languages in Nigeria, Joyce. Yusuf speaks Hausa, and I speak Yoruba."

"How many languages?" Joyce asked with serrated knife now poised above the large Victoria sandwich.

"Hundreds."

"Crickey!" She stabbed the cake and sliced it rapidly into triangular servings. "Yusuf never told me that. He's taking me to Africa after we're married."

"I see," Tayo nodded, wondering just how many girls Yusuf had promised that to. Samir had left them talking and the music had started. "Come ladies, I think you've worked hard enough. Let's join the party."

The front room was crowded, and Tayo recognised only a few

people. Some were from the bakery, others from the hospital, and Mr and Mrs Winter came from across the road. Tunde was introducing Tayo to others when Yusuf announced the first dance.

"Distinguished ladies and gentlemen," he boomed, "welcome to our party and let's see some dancing. The first is ladies' choice and, please, don't all rush for our Oxford gentleman because there are others in the room, too. Yorkshire men, Yoruba men, Yankee men, you name it!" Yusuf laughed, winking at Tayo.

Soon Tayo was twisting and jiving to Sam Cooke's *Saturday Night*, and enjoying the attention of several women. Booze appeared from somewhere (contrary to Yusuf's prediction) and the dancing improved. Yusuf was demonstrating the wild jitterbug better than Elvis, and then showing all the girls how to do the twist to Highlife. He concocted fancy Hausa names for the two-step and the cha cha cha, and called himself a cool cat after Victor Olaiya's band. It made the girls laugh and soon the whole room was spinning from side-to-side, arms in the air, skirts swishing back and forth. Girls reached for Tayo's hands. He held one, and then another, until at some point in the evening he found himself standing in the hallway with one hand pressed against the wall, and the other wrapped tightly around a woman's waist.

"Easy does it," Yusuf winked, brushing past them to open the front door, and then there was a shout and a thud and something struck hard against Tayo's jaw.

"Don't you bloody touch my sister," someone swore.

Tayo spun around, and caught the next punch just as Samir arrived to intervene.

"You bastard," Tayo swore, tasting blood.

"Who said bastard? I'm gonna teach you a lesson, just you wait!"

"Yeah," Tayo shouted angrily, "why don't you ask your sister who started it," but by then the girl was nowhere to be seen.

"Hey-hey-hey, what's all this nonsense?" shouted Tunde.

Someone had switched off the music and people had begun to

leave, squeezing past and muttering hurried goodbyes.

"Time you niggers hopped back to your jungles!" the man sneered.

"Shut your bloody mouth. You wanna fight? Come!" Tayo beckoned, stepping forward, but Yusuf blocked his path.

The man kept shouting as others pulled him back and pushed him outside.

"Yeah, go ahead and call the police if you like!" Tayo jeered, pushing Tunde out of his way. "Look at that." Tayo pointed angrily to his jaw. "This bloody idiot just walks in and starts the fight. Let him call the police."

"Nobody's calling the police," Tunde said, angrily picking things up. "Let's tidy this mess. Party over."

"And what are you looking so pleased about?" Tayo glared at Yusuf, standing in the hallway grinning.

"You still want to marry an English girl?" He laughed.

Tayo swore at Yusuf as he fingered the swelling on his lip and was about to swear again when he realised Yusuf had stopped grinning and was urgently waving for him to run. The front door was open and the man was back – with friends.

"Which one is it?" someone shouted.

"That's him. Scared, are we?" he sneered.

"Tayo!" Yusuf shouted, desperate this time.

"Who's scared of you?" Tayo looked the man in the eye, ignoring his friends with him, and the bottles that emerged from coat pockets. He braced himself as one of the men rushed him. A fist rammed into his stomach, taking the air from his body and he fell against someone's foot. Yusuf and Tunde were shouting as he clasped his head and then there was silence.

"What's going on?" Tayo gasped, opening his eyes to see men in uniform.

"Get up," the policeman barked. "All of you, down to the station for questioning."

Tayo closed his eyes and winced in pain. Tunde and Yusuf

were trying in vain to convince the police that this was their house, but the thugs had fled and now they were being handcuffed and bundled roughly into a police van.

On the short ride to the station, Yusuf sat silently, his body rigid with anger, while Tunde tried explaining to the police that it was not their fault Tayo told Tunde to shut up, but Tunde wouldn't listen so by the time they arrived, Yusuf and Tayo were ready to fight both the police and Tunde.

"Look, this is ridiculous!" Tayo shouted. "I'm a policeman's son and I know we have rights."

"What rights?" one of the officers asked, looking bemused. "And no use asking for a superintendent; it's just the four of us."

"We do have rights," Tayo insisted, trying to gesture with his hands, forgetting that they were handcuffed. "You can't do this! I'm a student at Oxford and I know people who could make your life miserable."

"Do you now?" the officer laughed, grabbing him roughly by the arm and pushing him into an empty cell.

"You racist pigs, the whole lot of you!" Yusuf shouted.

At first, Tayo was too angry to be worried about what would happen next but, as the hours passed, fear crept into Tayo's mind with the realisation that he had no control over events. Here they were, three black men locked up in separate cells. It didn't matter what sort of families they came from, it didn't matter that they were educated, it didn't even matter that he was at Oxford. Tayo stared at his empty cell, imagining various morbid scenarios and then trying to think of a solution.

It would have calmed Tayo to know that Mr and Mrs Winter had seen everything that had happened and would come to the station the following morning, but Tayo had no way of knowing this at the time.

Chapter 14

When Tayo returned to Oxford he decided not to tell anyone about the fight in Bradford. He definitely didn't want to tell Vanessa, but she noticed his chipped tooth, which left him little choice but to tell her something. So he told her that a fight had started between two drunkards and he, acting as Sir Galahad, had intervened. But Vanessa seemed to have a sixth sense, which was the only explanation Tayo could find for why she had started nagging him so much. Sometimes it was the way he spoke to other women, sometimes his football, or at other times it was his social life. She told him that his Nigerian friends made her feel excluded, but he wondered how she could possibly feel excluded in her own country. She complained that she and Tayo didn't spend enough time together, and yet everyone knew that the final year was tough. And if she really wanted to spend time with him then why hadn't she wanted to come to this wedding? Yes, she would be coming to join him later, but that wasn't the point.

"Morning," someone said, drawing Tayo from his thoughts as he sat waiting the arrival of the bride.

"Good morning." Tayo smiled at the young woman who sat next to him in the pew.

He was about to introduce himself properly when she turned to face the altar and made a sign of the cross. She then knelt on a prayer cushion in such a way that her skirt rose above the back of her knees, revealing a shapely pair of legs. Tayo closed his eyes and listened for some moments to the organ music thinking that maybe he ought to pray too, but her legs were distracting him. He looked instead at the altar and the sanctuary where the choirboys sat behind the lectern, looking angelic in their white robes and ruffed collars.

The church was otherwise dark and musty until an unexpected ray of sunlight pierced the stained glass windows. Tayo smiled to himself, thinking of the sunshine coming all the way from the groom's home in Kano and bursting through the English clouds to make a guest appearance in Finchley, North London, for today's service. Unfortunately this sun was a frustrating winter one, bringing plenty of light but no heat. Tayo looked at the woman next to him and contemplated conversation, but the organ music stopped and everyone's eyes turned towards the back of the church. They all stared in anticipation, but the organist had not stopped to signal anything in particular and soon resumed another piece. As Tayo listened he felt a sense of relief and awe – relief because it was not him having to take the vows, and awe at the solemnity of such occasions. He reflected that this wedding was the most surprising of any he had attended and he surmised that the bride must have fallen pregnant. This at least would explain the speed of arranging it, but there was no one to confirm his hypothesis. Tunde was not around and the only other person to ask was Yusuf himself, who now stood at the front of the church smiling broadly.

Tayo stared at the groom, looking for signs of nervousness. There were no obvious indicators, but Tayo knew that beneath the smiles Yusuf was anxious. Sitting in the congregation on the bridegroom's side were many of Yusuf's Bradford friends and on the bride's side were women dressed in the traditional Nigerian wedding lace. It surprised Tayo to see that Joyce had so many Nigerian guests seated there when he would have expected English people. A hush then fell across the congregation and everyone turned again to face the back of the church. This time the veiled bride appeared like an angel beneath the arch of the church doors.

Tayo looked again, squinting to make sure he wasn't seeing things. The bride was black! He glanced at the service sheet and reread the names – Yusuf Abubakar and Joy Williams. *Joy* not Joyce. Tayo looked around to see if anyone else was shocked, but nothing showed on people's faces. Who was this Joy? Williams was not a typical Nigerian name but this was less puzzling to Tayo than the fact he couldn't recall meeting anyone named Joy when he was in Bradford, just a few months ago, and yet Yusuf was smiling broadly as though he had been planning this day for years. Vows were taken, rings exchanged, and nobody stood up to give reason or just impediment why the two should not be joined together in Holy Matrimony. And so it was that Yusuf, the ladies' man, became a married man. The organ started its wedding march and the happy couple walked down the aisle followed by the congregation.

Outside, people threw confetti as the church bells rang out. Tayo stood watching, amused by the cameramen who dashed about trying to capture each joyful expression; and for a moment he could have been back in Nigeria. He had missed this – the fancy ways women tied their *geles*, and the starchy rustle of wrappers and agbadas. He had also missed the smiles, the loud imperious voices and perspiration. Of course, now that the sun was out, the reception would start late, but it was bound to have started late anyway. He wondered what the reception would be like, remembering the chaos of those back home where he and his brothers would compete to manoeuvre their way into the VIP queue. He was laughing to himself at his childhood antics when someone tapped him on the shoulder.

"Vanessa!"

There she was, dressed in the fine lace wrapper and buba that they had borrowed from a friend in Cowley. The pale blue material with its silver thread sparkled against her skin and drew attention to her smiling eyes. Then it dawned on him that he was in trouble. How was he going to tell Vanessa that the bride was not Joyce, but Joy? And especially after all that he had been saying about how common it was for Nigerians to marry Europeans. He wouldn't be able to blame his mistake on the fact that he didn't know Yusuf that well either, because Vanessa was under the impression that Yusuf was a close friend. That had been his line for being so upset over her decision to skip the service. There was no other way then but to tell Vanessa that he had made a mistake.

"What?" Vanessa exclaimed.

"I know, I can't believe it myself, but I must have misread the invitation. I thought it was Joyce, but it's Joy. So maybe the relationship with Joyce wasn't so serious after all."

"Not serious? But Joyce was his girlfriend!"

"Shh, please," he begged, aware of how close they stood to the bride's family. "Come," he urged. He could hear that the band had started up in the church hall, and he would take her to the reception where they could talk in private.

Men dressed in brilliant white agbadas waved them into a noisy room smelling of fried rice. Wall heaters turned to maximum and glowing orange made the hall feel too hot, even for Tayo.

"You look beautiful," Tayo whispered as they found their way to a table. He said it again, but she still didn't answer.

"Come." He took Vanessa's arm. "You should have seen people in the church. Lots of people looked shocked when Joy came in. We're bound to find out what happened sooner or later."

Vanessa said nothing, but by now the bride and groom had arrived and people had started showering the couple with pound notes.

"It's a tradition," Tayo explained, "to bless the couple by placing money on the bride and groom. Come, let's make our contribution." He stretched his hands through the huddle of well wishers and tucked two pound notes into Joy's head tie that had become so laden with notes that a few fluttered to the floor.

"Congratulations, old chap." Tayo patted Yusuf on the shoulder.

"Now you've finally met the woman I've been telling you about – my Yoruba queen." Yusuf beamed.

'What woman?' But of course he could not say this in front of the bride. Instead he nodded enthusiastically and greeted the bride.

"It's very odd," Tayo whispered to Vanessa.

"What were you saying to the bride?"

"I was wishing her the best from us – a happy and blessed marriage. *Ire a kari o*, literally translated, means 'may the blessings of this joyful occasion be spread among your still unmarried friends'." He slipped his hand beneath the tablecloth and tried running his fingers down Vanessa's skirt, but she stopped him with an angry movement.

"Gosh," he said, surprised by her reaction, but others had joined their table so nothing more was said.

Food was served – *jollof, amala*, goat stew, *egusi*, and many more dishes that Vanessa would normally have asked Tayo about, but she had her back turned, chatting to others. He did the same and then later pretended to be listening to the speakers while mulling over the meaning of her silence. He had expected her to be surprised by the new bride and maybe a little cross with him for making the mistake, but not angry, not this angry.

"What's wrong, Vanessa?" he whispered, trying to cajole her out of her silence, but she wouldn't be drawn so that when the orations eventually ended, and the dancing began, Tayo didn't bother to ask her to join him. He didn't feel like dancing on his own, but he would be dammed if he was just going to sit there and not at least appear to be enjoying the music. A part of him considered asking the pretty woman who had sat next to him in church, but he couldn't. No mattered how annoyed he was with Vanessa, he would never do something like that. He moved closer to Vanessa and let his arms swing loosely as he sang along to the words of Sunny Ade, but even this did not bring a smile to her face. She wasn't even looking at him. Suddenly, there was a loud crash from the far end of the room. A woman was angrily flinging plates off a table and Tayo's heart sunk when he looked over and saw Joyce lurching towards the newlyweds. The band stopped playing.

"You bastard! Bastard!" she screamed, flailing her arms as others attempted to restrain her.

For a few minutes everyone stood in shock until someone led her out of the hall. '*Na drink, drink,*' people muttered, but they knew it was not simply drink.

*

Vanessa and Tayo shared a stuffy train carriage back to Oxford, just the two of them – he sitting on one side, and she on the other, silent. Tayo tried to start conversation by joking about Nigerian weddings and the drama that came with them, but Vanessa wouldn't be moved.

"And that crazy woman," Tayo added, in a final attempt to coax Vanessa into talking. Really, he felt sorry for Joyce and ashamed of the way he had avoided her, but he couldn't have risked anything more going wrong in front of Vanessa. Things were bad enough already.

"Vanessa, you've been silent all afternoon; surely it's not just because of the wedding?"

"I'm fine," she answered coldly.

"No, you're not."

"Yes, I am."

Tayo watched as she continued to stare out of the window, occasionally combing her hair with her fingers.

"Of course something's wrong."

"Well, why don't you tell me then, Tayo?" she said, turning to glare at him.

"Tell you what?"

"Tell me why you lied."

"Lied?"

"Well, let's start with Christine, shall we?"

"Christine?"

"Yes, Christine. Your old lover, the one you were supposed to be related to. Remember? I'm not stupid, Tayo. Charlie told me a long time ago that you two were lovers, but I never believed him and now it's so bloody obvious. You and all your bloody Nigerian friends just use white women, don't you?"

"And you choose to listen to Charlie? Are you in love with him or something?"

"Oh, for Christ's sake, stop trying to turn this into something else. Do you really think I couldn't figure out who that poor woman was? You use us and then dump us for black women when you want to get married."

"Well, you obviously don't understand me or my culture."

"Oh, so it's culture again, is it? Bloody culture!" she shouted. "What a nice little excuse. And what do you call me dressing up like this in your Nigerian costume? Don't you think I'm trying to adjust, to show you that I can fit in?"

"Is that supposed to impress me?" he said, ignoring the fact it had. "And it's not a costume, it's our national dress."

"Fine. National dress. Attire. Call it whatever the hell you want. Happy now? Ready to tell me the truth? Or is this also cultural? Perhaps you don't call it lying in your culture."

"You think that's funny?"

"No, as a matter-of-fact, I don't think lying is funny."

"Vanessa, how many times do I have to tell you that I don't know what happened between Yusuf and Joyce. I really didn't know her well and perhaps this marriage was arranged and…"

"And *you*?" she cut him short. "What happened between you and Christine?"

"Nothing."

"Nothing! How the hell can you say that?"

"For goodness sakes, Vanessa, the woman's dead. Can't you show some respect, for once? And all this swearing!"

"Show some respect! What's that supposed to mean? You lied to me, Tayo! You told me you were related to her. Why don't *you* try a little respect?"

"Vanessa, someone's going to stop the train because of the way you're shouting."

"Let them! I don't care."

Tears were now streaming down Vanessa's face, which further alarmed Tayo. If someone did stop the train to investigate, saw her crying and then saw him and his colour...

"Vanessa, please don't cry. I love you, Vanessa. I don't care about nationality, race or whatever; all of that means nothing to me."

He moved to sit next to her and tried to hug her but she wouldn't let him. After a while, though, he was able to draw her close, and eventually she grew calm and stopped crying.

"*Moremi*," he whispered, blowing at the little bits of confetti that refused to be dislodged from her hair.

"No!" She burst into tears again. "Don't *Moremi* me. Stop bloody trying to turn me into a Nigerian."

"Fine!" He let go of her waist and pushed her away. "Forget this," he shouted, stood up and left, slamming the carriage door behind him.

Chapter 15

The following week, Tayo had tried patching things up, but the arguments persisted. He felt that the pressure of study was partly to blame for the friction between them, which was why he was looking forward to the holidays. Maybe then they could sort things out. But several days before Vanessa changed her mind. "I think we should spend Christmas apart," she suggested and, even though she said it without conviction, Tayo wasn't in the mood for discussion. If time apart was needed, so be it. He was tired of arguing. He hadn't wanted to discuss his problems with the Barkers either, but because they had been expecting both he and Vanessa to house-sit while they holidayed in Tuscany, he had to say something to Mr Barker, who then took it upon himself to suggest that Tayo be more patient and a little more sensitive when it came to women. Tayo listened out of his respect for Mr Barker but on this occasion did not find his advice helpful.

When the Barkers left for their holiday, Tayo set himself a strict schedule, using Mr Barker's study on the first floor. For good measure Tayo took down the *egungun* mask that was propped up in one corner of the desk. As a Christian he was not supposed to believe in the power of such things, but he wasn't going to take chances. The British might be safe messing around with festival masks, but not him. He also removed Mr Barker's journals that lay strewn on the windowsill, dusted their faded covers, and stacked them neatly to flatten the curling corners.

The room was cluttered with history books, but the desk faced the window, away from the mess, overlooking the back garden where he would often find himself staring and thinking of home. And sometimes he would think of nothing in particular as he watched the sparrows hopping across the lawn, pecking in search of worms. Eventually he would look back at his books and, if he still could not concentrate, he would stand up and wander around the house. He never grew tired of browsing the Barkers' bookshelves. In addition to history, Mr Barker owned a large collection of musical scores, mainly classical, and some jazz. Tayo remembered his first visit with Vanessa to the Barkers and the way in which Mr Barker had spoken to her at length about his collection. Tayo remembered feeling a little envious about their intimate *tête-à-tête* on a subject that he didn't know much about.

There were other books in the house in German, French, and Italian, which were Isabella's – an impressive assortment of European and Russian literary greats, including a complete collection of Dostoevsky and Tolstoy. Tayo admired this vast assortment of books and the way the Barkers had decorated their house with a mix of Italian and English paintings, as well as the African bronzes and carvings that Mr Barker had collected over the years. Tayo imagined owning a house like the Barker's one day – a home tastefully decorated and filled with books; a home which could be shared with friends in the same way as the Barkers shared theirs. Isabella liked beautiful things, just like Vanessa who had transformed his own rooms with her thoughtful touches – the silver candlestick holders, the Spanish mirror, and the warm cashmere blanket that she had given him only last week.

On New Year's Eve, Tayo awoke feeling particularly homesick. He thought of Tunde and Yusuf in Bradford, and Ike and Bolaji in London, preparing for the night's parties, and he pictured the scene back home in Nigeria. Women would be pounding yam, and palm wine would be flowing while the irresistible beats of Highlife and Juju would be calling dancers to their feet. He began to feel that everybody except him would be in the party spirit and so, to rectify the situation, Tayo took out his favourite Dairo vinyl and filled the house with his music. Then, on the spur of the moment, he decided to cook. By mid-morning, he set off to buy a chicken from the Covered Market.

When he arrived at the market stalls, he realised he didn't know what spices his mother used, so he asked an Indian woman for advice. She sold him two powders carefully sealed in wax paper: one marked cumin, the other turmeric. Tayo smiled to himself at the thought of a culinary adventure but, as soon as he got back to the house, the novelty of the idea had worn off. He had never made stew in his life, so what did he think he was doing? Trying to be a modern man? Everyone knew that women were the natural cooks, not men. Besides, even if his chicken were a success, what joy would there be in eating alone?

He thought of the time two years ago when Christine had prepared a banquet of his favourite food. She had cooked yam with *egusi, gari* and *akara*, and had invited all the African students in Oxford, as well as a few cousins from London. And that night, after they had cleared everything away and were all alone, they had started kissing. But it was still too painful to remember these things so he tried to concentrate instead on looking for something in which to prepare his pasty-white bird. He looked everywhere, but found no black pots of the type his mother owned, so he decided to use the largest stainless steel pot. Now what? How was he going to know when the chicken was properly cooked? None of Isabella's recipe books contained a chicken stew recipe. There was chicken soup, *coq-au-vin*, chicken *vol-au-vents*, coronation chicken, but no chicken stew, which meant he would have to guess.

He had just finished chopping the bird into irregular chunks, two of which managed to slip off the breadboard and sail across the kitchen floor, when the doorbell rang. "Oh no," he sighed. This would be one of Isabella's friends sent to check on him. He must make sure nobody came into the kitchen and saw the mess. He opened the door expecting Fiona or Anne, but instead there was Vanessa, and in his excitement he forgot that his hands were slimy with chicken. As he reached to kiss her, she turned her face and the kiss landed clumsily on her cheek.

"Come in," he said awkwardly.

She sniffed the air and so did he.

"Yeeeah-oh!" He panicked, running back to the kitchen. He pulled the pan from the ring, tipping it dangerously and nearly scalding himself. He stood helpless wondering what to do next. Vanessa, who had followed him in, was smiling.

"Mr Ajayi," she smiled, "what are you doing? And what does 'yeaho' mean?"

"It means 'oh bugger'," Tayo laughed, "and this is my lousy attempt at cooking."

"But who are you cooking for?" The smile vanished from her face. "Were you expecting someone?"

"Only you, Vanessa."

"Me?"

"Yes," he said, tossing her a tea towel. "And now you can dry the dishes."

"But I'm not staying," she added quickly.

"Then I'll have to entice you with a cup of tea," he said, knowing without looking that she was smiling. She could say what she liked; he knew her well enough to be sure she had not come all this way simply to say hello. He filled the kettle, switched it on and returned to the stove to fiddle with his pot, while watching her from the corner of his eye. The heat from the oven had misted the kitchen window, and she had taken off her cardigan. Static made her blouse stick to her body and, each time she tried to pull it away, the material leapt back, clinging more tightly to her breasts. He smiled and stepped closer, pretending to need a spoon in one of the drawers near where she stood, and when he brushed against her back she stopped what she was doing. He waited for a moment before gently pulling her hair from her shoulders to plant a line of kisses down the back of her neck. Slowly, she turned towards him, and quickly he lifted her up onto the counter, knocking over one of Isabella's teapots. They tugged clumsily at each other's clothes. Nothing else mattered, not the teapot, not the whistling kettle and not the angry chicken spitting bubbles from its ill-fitting lid.

*

That evening they devoured a box of Ritz cheese crackers, a jar of Heinz pickles and the rest of Isabella's Christmas fruitcake. They were clearing the plates when Vanessa reached for his arm and made him sit.

"Tayo, we can't keep doing this. Making up and patching things over."

"I know," he said, but he wished she hadn't brought it up, not now at least, not after what they had just shared – not on New Years Eve. "But you said you wanted a break and now you've come back, and we've done all this, so I'm confused."

"I didn't want a break. Couldn't you see that?"

And then she stood up again and began gathering the plates.

"No wait, Vanessa." This time he reached for her arm. "I'm sorry for being insensitive, and I'm sorry for burying myself in my work."

"But it's not about work; Tayo, it's about the way we talk to each other. It's about the way you're always so critical of my views. Yes, you are, Tayo. Every time we talk about religion, or women's lib, you've always got something negative to say. It's as if I'm always saying something wrong."

"But can't I tell you how I see things?"

"Yes, but don't judge me at the same time."

Did he judge her? Maybe she was right. Perhaps in an unconscious way he did judge her. He thought a lot these days about how his family would view Vanessa. He had also wondered how she would feel in a context where everyone was expected to believe in God, whatever God, at least *a* God. Back home, women were expected to put children before profession and do the womanly things like cooking; something he knew Vanessa did not agree with.

"Aren't you going to say something?" she asked.

"Okay, perhaps I do so unconsciously, and if I do then I'm sorry, but it's because I think of home, and when you talk about women having professions and no children…"

"Is that it? You think I don't want to have children?"

"I don't know."

"Then why don't you just ask me? You never ask. How am I supposed to know what you think if you never talk? Just because I defend a woman's right *not* to have children doesn't mean that's my own choice. *Of course* I want children."

"You do?"

"Of course I do, silly you! Come," she tugged at his arm, dragging him away from the chaos in the kitchen, leading him to the lounge.

"I love you, you know."

"How much?" he teased. "How much do you love me?"

"Too much," she smiled, holding him tightly. "I'll find some music and then I'll show you just how much. And you can make a fire."

She chose Nina Simone and before he had found the matches she was already dancing towards him.

Love me or leave.

He reached for her, but she pushed him away.

"Vanessa," he pleaded, trying again to hold her, but she wouldn't have it. She sang in a whisper, flirting with him until she drew close enough for their hips to touch and only then did she let him rest his hands on her waist. She kept on dancing, lifting her hips from side-to-side as she led the way, backwards, to the sofa.

Chapter 16

The New Year brought with it an unexpected visit from Tayo's uncle and the first chance for Vanessa to meet someone from Tayo's family. They were all to have afternoon tea at the Randolph Hotel, which was where Vanessa now waited for Tayo and his uncle. She sat in the lounge next to an open fire feeling uncomfortably warm but this, she guessed, was where Tayo would prefer to sit.

While she waited, she watched people around her serving themselves tea from fat china teapots and sampling scones and cakes. This was Oxford's finest hotel, but Vanessa did not care for the musty, stuffy feel that came from the large upholstered armchairs and the carpet in sombre shades of green and mustard. The walls were wood-panelled and several large chandeliers hung low from the ceiling. She wondered what Tayo's uncle would think of the Randolph and, more importantly, what he would think of her. This wasn't just any old family friend, but Tayo's favourite uncle and, while she looked forward to meeting him, she worried too.

Tayo had once told her (though she suspected he had now forgotten) that in his culture one never introduced a girlfriend to family unless the relationship was serious. So this was a good sign for her, but what if she disappointed his uncle? What would Tayo think of her then? Everything had been going so well since the New Year and she desperately wanted it to stay that way, especially now that Tayo only had a few more months left at Oxford. Secretly she hoped he might propose before leaving.

Nervously, she ran through her list of greetings. "*Ekaasan. Salafia ni*," she practised, hoping that the pronunciation was correct, when Tayo arrived with his uncle.

"*Ekaasan. Salafia ni*," she said, curtseying as she had seen other Nigerian women do.

"Vanessa, my dear, lovely to meet you," the uncle said, in such a reassuring way that it made her feel immediately at ease.

Tayo's uncle was taller and younger than Vanessa expected, and more effusive too.

"Splendid!" he exclaimed when the waitress brought them their Darjeeling tea, scones, sandwiches and cake. Uncle Kayode had insisted on ordering everything.

"Now Vanessa, do tell me, what does one begin with? Scones? Sandwiches? Or cakes? I've never known. And does one put cream on these things first," as he indicated a scone, "or jam?"

"Whatever catches your fancy, I think." She smiled.

"Ahh, but everything catches my fancy and that, my dear, is the problem," he said, laughing as he peered eagerly at the top tray. "Now, here we have a most exquisite collection of gateaux, a little almond marzipan, shortbread, some macaroons, petit fours, and what do you suppose this is?" He pointed to a rectangular slice. "I think it ought to be something German to render the platter a true representation of Europe. A Bavarian torte, or some such thing, wouldn't you say? But just look at these other two trays – so quintessentially English!"

"And crust-less sandwiches like the ones we were served at school cricket games," Tayo added.

"Indeed." Uncle Kayode winked conspiratorially at Tayo, "For what is good for the English, must also be good for their protégés abroad, and especially at those elite institutions like Fiditi Boys. Vanessa dear, did this chap ever tell you about the first-class schools he attended?"

Tayo tried to interrupt, but had no luck as his uncle kept

boasting about his nephew's school and then proceeded to describe, in some detail, his nephew's sporting prowess.

"I wasn't captain of every team sport," Tayo laughed.

"Well, nobody's talking about silly sports like table tennis or hockey," Uncle conceded, before saying something more to Tayo in Yoruba while waving his hands in the air as though chasing those sports away. "But look, let us partake of this wonderful spread." He opened a scone and spread it generously with a layer of clotted cream. "I don't think that anything beats warm English scones with a dab of butter, a dollop of cream, and strawberry jam. So I say, what's the good of touring dusty old barracks when some other occupation would allow me to travel, and visit my nephew and his charming young lady over this most civilized afternoon tea. Enough of army life!"

"Are you really thinking of leaving the army, Uncle?" Tayo asked.

"Indeed I am," his uncle nodded. "Engineering is what I'm considering and I would do it at the Institute Francais du Petrole in France. What do you think, Vanessa?"

"Why Engineering?" She asked, surprised that he would ask.

"Ahh, now that's what I like – a woman who asks questions," he said, leaning forward in his chair to explain. "The future of Nigeria is no longer in its army as some of us used to think, but in the oil business. Of course there are many places here in Britain where I could study, but who can turn down an offer from France – *ce pays de liberte, egalite et fraternite*."

"Ahh, *vous parlez francais?*" Vanessa replied.

"*Mais oui!*"

"I think that's enough of the French," Tayo interrupted.

"You're right," Uncle Kayode smiled. "In any case, that was really the limit of my French, I'm afraid, but Tayo, didn't your mother teach you French?"

"Does my mother speak French?" Tayo looked surprised.

"Why of course! How do you think she conducts her

business? Let me tell you, Vanessa, Tayo's mother is a most successful trader along the West African coast. Tayo hasn't told you this, has he? She regularly visits Benin, Dahomey and Ivory Coast, and is Chief of all the textile traders in Ibadan – which is a very revered position in our Yoruba culture."

"But Uncle," Tayo protested.

Vanessa smiled at Tayo, who was looking shocked but he had stopped protesting because it was obvious his uncle was enjoying telling the stories and Vanessa was enjoying listening.

"But do tell me something about you now, my dear. Tayo tells me that you write beautifully, so tell me about your writings and some of the artists and writers you admire."

She began to talk, not knowing how much of her work would really interest Tayo's uncle, but he listened closely, letting his cup of tea go cold while she spoke. It was only when Tayo reminded them that his uncle had a train to catch that they noticed how much time had passed.

"How unfortunate," Uncle Kayode grumbled. "With Vanessa's talk of women's issues, I was going to impress you both by telling you more about my recent encounter with Anais Nin."

"Anais Nin!"

Uncle Kayode nodded, smiling at Vanessa's surprise.

"Then we can't possibly end the conversation," Vanessa insisted.

"So come with us to the station and I will tell you about the lovely Anais."

"The lovely Anais," Vanessa smiled to herself, wondering how much Tayo knew about Anais and what he thought of his uncle, who was apparently not at all embarrassed by this writer of erotica. She knew little about Anais Nin herself, but enough to find it surprising that an African man, whose training had not been in the arts, would not be critical. With an uncle like this, Vanessa felt certain that she would love the rest of Tayo's family.

Chapter 17

It came as a surprise (or rather shock) when Tayo received the invitation from Mr Richardson. It was an invite to lead Mr Richardson's school assembly with a lecture on Nigeria. Tayo had given many talks about Nigeria while at Oxford, often to schools and sometimes to churches, but this request was the most important thus far. Not only because of the reputation of Bellamy Boys' School, but principally because the invitation came from Vanessa's father and it couldn't have come at a better time since he had just heard that he had received a first-class degree and won a graduate scholarship. There was a time when Tayo told himself that he didn't care what Vanessa's father thought of him, but that had never really been true. It was certainly not true now that his relationship with Vanessa had grown more serious, which was why Tayo took a lot of time and care in his preparation for the talk. He made sure he had all the necessary facts and practised his delivery out loud so that on the day it would go well.

"What do you clever boys know about Nigeria?" he began.

A flurry of little hands went up.

"Nigeria is near the desert."

"The people don't wear clothes."

"Boys play with animals."

"It's boiling hot."

Tayo thanked each boy for his contribution, thinking how wonderful it was that children spoke openly, making his task of correcting the stereotypical views easy. Instead of presenting a simplified version of what he usually said to adults (an overview of Nigeria's history, its topography, its main industries, and political parties), Tayo began with his childhood, telling them what it was like growing up in Nigeria. His stories held the boys' attention, and his talk was a big hit.

"Bravo," Mr Richardson said at the end, patting Tayo on the back as he led him to his study.

It was a room that reminded Tayo of Mr Faircliff's study. It had that same musty smell of old books and papers, and the same neat row of trophies and shields displayed in glass cabinets. Even some of the decorations, the Nigerian gourds and masks, were similar to those that hung in his old Headmaster's office in Ibadan.

"Do sit down." Mr Richardson waved for him to take a seat in front of the desk.

Tayo sat and watched as Mr Richardson lit his pipe. He felt pleased with how things had gone and expected a discussion on its value for the boys.

"What are your intentions with my daughter?" said Mr Richardson, catching Tayo completely off-guard.

"My daughter seems very enamoured with you," Mr Richardson added, not waiting for Tayo's reply. "And you of her, I imagine."

"Well, yes, sir. I…" Tayo fought to find the appropriate words but found himself simply staring at Mr Richardson.

"You see, Tayo," Richardson continued, taking his pipe from his mouth, "in many ways you and I are quite similar, aren't we? I was fond of a woman from a different class in the way that you seem fond of a woman of a different race. My wife, as you know, is from the upper-classes, and her family didn't approve of me. You understand, don't you?"

Tayo nodded, deciding it was easier to let Mr Richardson talk, for it was obvious that he had things he wanted to say and probably didn't want to hear a response anyway.

"Well, Mrs Richardson and I married, but our families have never entirely accepted our marriage. Now with you and Vanessa, if you ever were to think of marriage, you would face an even greater challenge. One that is, I fear, insurmountable. I hope you understand it is my duty to warn you of this and that I have a responsibility to my daughter's happiness. You must certainly be aware of the difficulties of a cross-racial union."

Tayo nodded again, stunned by what he was hearing. So Mr Richardson thought that he wanted to marry his daughter? And now he was talking about the challenges that mixed race couples faced, with half-caste children. How presumptuous of the man!

"And Vanessa is impetuous, you see," Mr Richardson continued, "and has a tendency to dash into things. Not long ago she got all hot and bothered about Lumumba, wanting to go to the Congo. Really, she is most naïve. Always jumping into things, like her mother at that age. Do you understand what I'm saying?"

"Yes," Tayo nodded, "what you are saying is that I must not think of marrying your daughter."

"What I am saying, young man, is that the challenges would be great and, as someone who is older and wiser, I must advise you against the idea."

And that was how it ended, except of course that that was not how it really ended. Tayo still had the journey back to Oxford and an ensuing conversation with Vanessa, who was eager to hear how things had gone.

"How was it?" she asked, slipping an arm around his waist as they walked back to college from where they had met in town. "You're quiet? What's the matter?"

"Nothing," he said, still not knowing where to start or what to tell her.

"Oh, come on, something's wrong; I can tell." She stopped and turned to face him just as a policeman cycled past.

"All right, Miss?" he asked, propping one foot on the ground.

"Yes!" Vanessa snapped.

The policeman hesitated, looked Tayo up and down, and then pedalled away.

"What's the matter? Tell me."

"I'm fine, Vanessa. Let's go."

"No, not before you tell me. Well, what is it?" she insisted, reaching for his hand and pulling him towards her.

"I just..." He stopped as she touched the side of his face.

"Tell me," she urged.

"Today your father..."

"My father what?"

"Could we talk about this later, Vanessa?"

"My father said what?"

"Okay. Your father told me that he didn't approve of us."

"What do you mean? He's always said good things..."

"He hasn't," Tayo said crossly without meaning to, but he was tired of her being so naïve. Did she really think her father liked him? And now she was looking innocently at him, gazing into his eyes and threading her arms around his waist. He held her briefly and then moved from her grasp.

"Vanessa, we can't be together when your father is so opposed."

"What do you mean? Tell me what he said – exactly." She held out her hand and he took it reluctantly.

"He said it would be difficult for us, that the cultures would be too different and that one day if we were to... well, it would be difficult if we had children."

"Well, who cares what he says!" she replied. "All that matters is that we love each other."

"But relationships are also about family, Vanessa."

"And I would sacrifice my family for you, Tayo."

"Vanessa," he took her hands, touched by her love that he knew was genuine. "You know I wouldn't let you do that. We must respect your father. You are young and Nigeria is not a calm place these days. Perhaps it's God's will."

"Oh bloody hell, don't bring God into this," she said, letting go of his hand. "So now you think I'm too young? You think I don't know what I want?"

"Not too young Vanessa, but just too independent sometimes. Look Vanessa, it's late, I can't think straight, and…"

"Too independent? It's you, Tayo, who needs to learn some independence. You won't confront these things, will you? You register something, block it out of your mind, and never deal with it. My father is racist. It's simple. Don't you see that?"

"But Vanessa, you just told me that your father didn't mean it…"

"Well, of course I'd say that. It's much easier to pretend, isn't it? But I'm tired of that and wish you'd stand up to it. Don't just turn the other cheek with my father, or the policeman, or…"

"You wanted me to confront the policeman just now, and your father? And tell them what? That they're racist? *You* confront them Vanessa if it's so easy."

"And it's so easy for you, isn't it Tayo! You never wanted to marry an English girl anyway. That's still what it is, isn't it? Why don't you just go and find a nice subservient Nigerian girl who will do exactly what you say and agree with everything you want."

"Well, nobody is talking about marriage anyway," Tayo said roughly, and then immediately regretted it.

"Ma'am?" The policeman had returned and was jumping off his bicycle with baton in hand. "Do we have some trouble here? Hands off her!"

"I'm perfectly fine – just bugger off, will you!" Vanessa replied.

"Excuse me?"

"She's okay. We are together," Tayo replied.

"I wasn't asking you," the policeman warned.

"I'm okay, for God's sake. Leave us alone!" she shouted.

Her shoulders were shaking, and Tayo took off his coat to wrap it around her. The policeman watched, but Tayo didn't care. He took her in his arms to comfort her, to comfort himself.

It had started raining as Tayo walked back to college and only then did he realise that he had left his coat at Vanessa's. Usually he would have sprinted to outrun the shower, but the damp and drizzle had already seeped through his clothes the way English rain always did. "*No point in running,*" Tayo mumbled to himself. Maybe Vanessa was right. He should have stood up to her father and argued with him instead of giving in. Tayo flicked the rain from his face and picked up his pace. If Vanessa really thought he couldn't stand up for himself, he would soon prove her wrong.

"I love her," Tayo spoke to the rain. Damn the rain, damn her father, and damn every racist in England. For once in his life he was going to act on impulse, and prove to Vanessa that he was capable of being a man of action. No one – not society, not her father – was going to stop him from proposing now.

He ran the rest of the way back to college and stood panting for a few moments as he fumbled in his trouser pockets for his keys. He opened the little door that led into the porters lodge and ducked, but still hit his head against the top of the doorframe and swore silently.

"Ah, Mr Ajayi," the porter called out, "glad to see you. I've just popped a telegram under your door. Stayed here to make sure you got it."

"Thank you," Tayo nodded, walking faster to reach his rooms.

Porters rarely worked late at night, especially not during the summer when college was empty so Tayo was worried. He jogged the last few yards and found the slip of paper sticking out from under his door.

Baba is in hospital, recovering. Return home immediately. Mama.

Chapter 18

Allahu Akbar!
Allahu Akbar!

The shrill voice of the muezzin pierced the morning's silence with calls to prayer, jolting Tayo from sleep. He rolled over on his mattress and stretched his arms high above his head onto the cool cement floor, brushing his hand against the transistor radio. He reached for Vanessa but she wasn't there. It took him a few moments to realise that he was back home in the small room normally used as storage space for rice and millet that had been cleared out so he could have his own room. Everyone else, with the exception of his father, would be sleeping in crowded quarters. The older boys shared one room as he had done when he was young, and the girls and babies slept in their respective mother's room. The whole of upstairs had been given over to Baba and Tayo could hear him calling. It reminded him of the days when he was the one to fetch water for his father, polish his shoes, or take him tea first thing in the morning. Now it was the younger ones, wife Amina's children, who cowered at the sound of Baba's bellowing. His father was a disciplinarian and a firm believer in corporal punishment. It was an approach that made children obedient, but at what cost, Tayo often wondered. Somewhere else, he heard a woman scolding a child for taking too long to get ready and he wondered which wife it was and whether she had been the one to sleep upstairs the night before.

These days it bothered Tayo to think that his Father preferred the attentions of the younger wives to his mother. When Vanessa had asked him how things worked between wives he'd hardly given it a thought, but now he wondered. His mother seemed her usual jovial self, but maybe it was all a facade? He sometimes wished he could talk to her about her life, but there was never a moment when she was alone. Now, for example, she was outside chatting to the other wives as they drew water for morning baths. The standpipe was close to his room and the metal buckets clanged noisily against his wall. The smell of paraffin used to light the outside fires had already seeped in and that, combined with the sticky heat of the new day, made him get up.

He wiped his brow and stretched his arms again before reaching for his briefcase in search of some paper. Soon his brothers and sisters would be knocking on the door begging for more stories about England, and there would be guests to greet, places to visit and people to see, so he needed to write to Vanessa quickly before being caught up with the day's events. As he took the paper from his case, he noticed two separate black lines running from his suitcase to the ceiling. Ants. What could there be in his case that had drawn them? Earlier he had cleaned it of the melted Black Magic chocolates that were supposed to have been gifts for his brothers and sisters. Tayo sighed as he brushed them away, watching the black dots scatter, then regroup, persistent in their march. As a child he would have played with them, throwing them off course with chalk, but he didn't have time for that now.

"Remi? Tope? Bayo?" Tayo heard his father bellow and guessed that he was standing at the top of the stairs, having spotted one of his children, but unable to remember their name. Sure enough, he then shouted *"Ki ni won pe e paa paa?"* which made Tayo laugh. It was a phrase he remembered well from his own childhood. Even then, when there were fewer names to commit to memory, Baba invariably forgot who was who and would bark in that same gruff voice, "What do they call you anyway?" There were so many children in the house these days;

so many that Tayo could not keep track either.

He had even found it hard to recognise his own immediate brothers and sisters at first. Bisi had grown tall and thin like sugar cane and brother Remi, who was just a boy in 1963, was now a young man, stylishly sporting the latest Nkrumah haircut. They had all been at the airport to welcome him home, dressed in their finest, and some of the women were dancing as he came through customs. There was so much that he wanted to describe for Vanessa.

29th July 1966

My dear Vanessa,

I miss you so much and can't wait to see you again soon. I have been trying to write ever since I arrived in Ibadan, but each day I am besieged by family and friends. I barely have time to myself, so I am rising early this morning to write before time is whisked away. How are you? And your mum and dad?

Tayo paused, thinking of his last encounter with Mr Richardson. He despised the man for his bigotry and yet, now that he was back at home, Tayo could see that convincing his own family to accept a white woman might prove more of a struggle than he originally thought. Yesterday, when a family friend announced that their son would be marrying an English woman, Father had been sceptical. "How will the woman fit in?" he had asked, in a tone that Tayo found eerily similar to Mr Richardson's. The only difference being that Father's main objection lay in the fact that the woman's parents were divorced while Richardson's objections were based on race.

Both seemed wrong to Tayo, but there was at least one relative who had been enamoured by his talk of Vanessa and this was Uncle Bola. Tayo smiled, remembering yesterday when they had sat together in the shade of a mango tree, chewing kola nut and sipping coconut milk, for Uncle B had given up drink in the time Tayo had been away. But while his uncle's interest in booze might have diminished, his interest in women remained as strong as ever, so when Tayo showed him photographs of Oxford, Uncle Bola spotted Vanessa straight away. He insisted on keeping the photograph, staining it red with the residue of cola nut. *"Bring de lady come my house when she come Nigeria,"* he said, beaming a toothless smile. Tayo was thinking of how he was going to describe his uncle to Vanessa when he heard people calling loudly, running up and down the corridor.

"Brother Tayo! Brother Tayo!" The knocking sounded urgent, and Tayo stood up quickly to answer the door.

"Brother Tayo. *E kaaro,*" brother Remi said, hurriedly dispensing with what was usually a much longer string of greetings.

"Kilode? What's going on?" Tayo asked.

"They say *'Na coup',*" Remi answered, waving his hands like a crazy man.

"Coup? What coup?" Tayo dropped his pen, and tucked his singlet into his trousers as he ran with Remi to the front of the house. Normally, at this time of the morning, the front courtyard would be quiet but now a crowd had gathered with women and children, neighbours, street sellers, and even the cripple who sold groundnuts two streets down. And there in the middle of the crowd was someone he almost didn't see because of the commotion.

"Modupe!" he exclaimed, his jaw dropping as he saw the size of her stomach. "I didn't know," he said, walking towards her and hugging her clumsily.

"Yes," she smiled, "and this is my husband, Olu." She pointed to the tall man standing next to her.

Tayo did not recognise the man and felt suddenly grateful for the chaos around them. Baba stood in the centre of the crowd clutching his radio as he spoke with Dele, the neighbourhood drunk.

"What is it?" Tayo asked, anxiously pushing his way to where his father stood. "*E kaaro Baba,*" he added, remembering he had not yet greeted his father.

"Dele is telling us they tried to kill Ironsi last night," Baba replied, and then everyone started talking at the same time with Dele repeating what had just been said, others disputing the facts, and Modupe's husband blaming it all on the Northerners. Tayo took a good look at Modupe's husband this time. Suit and tie, Barclays Bank tie even, but ugly nonetheless, and not very educated by the sound of it. What did Modupe see in him?

"Dele, what did you hear exactly?" Baba was asking.

"*I hear the shots-oh. Pa-pa-pa-pa-pa.*"

"What shots? Are you sure? What were you drinking?" Baba shook his hands in exasperation.

"*No sah! Na shots, real ones-oh! I no dey lie-oh. Yes sah, na shots. They wan kill am.*"

"So what do we do?"

"What about the BBC, what are they saying on the radio?" Tayo asked, surprised that his father was looking to him for advice.

"Nothing," Baba replied, twiddling the knobs back and forth. "Go inside, go inside! Go on," Baba shouted, suddenly irritated by the children who had grown bored and were playing clapping games.

The women hurriedly ushered the children back into the house, leaving the men in the courtyard. Modupe left too and Tayo watched her go. He didn't care for her husband but at least she looked happy and that was all that mattered. But still he felt a twinge of sadness and jealously too.

"It's not a good sign that they're playing military music," Father muttered as the men gathered anxiously around. "This is something we learnt from the first coup."

"What of Uncle Kayode?" Tayo asked, suddenly remembering.

"No word," Baba replied, looking around as though hoping Uncle Kayode might just appear.

"Listen," Dele shouted.

The music stopped and the wives and children came scuttling back in time to hear an announcement by Brigadier Ogundipe.

'As a result of some trouble by dissidents in the army, mainly in Ibadan, Abeokuta and Ikeja, the National Military Government has declared a state of emergency.'

"'A state of emergency'? *Na waa-oh!*" Dele jumped up, excitedly.

"Shh!" Baba ordered, straining to hear the voice on the radio.

'Military Tribunals have been considered and accordingly set-up. Curfew has been declared in the affected areas from 6.30pm.'

"Curfew!" someone shouted. "Curfew!" "Curfew!" others echoed.

"They say the situation is under control, didn't you hear?" Baba barked.

Tayo could tell by the way the veins stood out on Baba's neck that his father was anxious. Nobody knew what was going to happen. Tayo, like everyone else, kept his ear close to the radio, waiting to hear more but there was only music and, when he looked up, he found that everyone was watching him.

"Let's not panic," Tayo muttered and then, because people still stood waiting for him to act he suggested, with an authority that surprised even himself, that they return to their homes.

Chapter 19

All the daily papers carried news of Nigeria's *coup d'etat*, but it was several weeks before Vanessa received Tayo's telegram letting her know that he and his family were well. He didn't say when he would be back, but she hoped that it would not be long. She thought often of their last day together when she had gone to see him, not knowing until she arrived that he had received a telegram calling him home. She remembered offering to help him pack and how he had responded by pushing the suitcase aside and reaching for her instead.

"Come," he urged, pulling her gently towards the bed. He didn't seem to care that it was the middle of the morning when anyone might pass by. "Shhhh," he insisted, pressing gently against her lips before locking the door. "Better?" he smiled, peeling off his shirt as he joined her on the narrow bed that creaked with the added weight. And soon neither of them cared if anyone heard them or the noise of the bed as it thudded grudgingly against the wooden floors.

"You won't leave me, will you?" Vanessa whispered when they lay exhausted side-by-side.

"Never," he said, wrapping his arm more tightly around her waist. "I love you, Vanessa."

Vanessa had picked March as the month when Tayo would surely be back, but, instead, March marked the time when his letters stopped. She wrote, phoned and sent telegrams but still no reply. And then one day, feeling utterly distraught and not knowing what to do, she heard that he had been in touch with Balliol. Why had he not written to her! And of all times to leave her feeling abandoned, he had chosen the weeks just before her exams. But one week later she received the long awaited letter from Tayo.

Dear Vanessa,

Please forgive me for taking so long to write to you. I have tried to write this letter so many times over the past few months but each time it seems as if the gods have conspired to stop me. First it was the news of the coup, which by now you must know all about, and then of course the start of the civil war, but in between all of this came my father's second heart attack. It has been a very difficult time for my family, but Father is pulling through and I now feel an immense sense of relief. We were also worried about Uncle Kayode in the midst of all of these political events and I will tell you more about it when I see you, but at least he too is safe and well at this time. I don't know when I will be returning to Oxford but I am hoping that it will not be too long. I have been in touch with the college and they have shown great understanding. I miss you so much Vanessa and I do hope that you understand the reason for my silence during this time. I may not have written, but you have been on my mind every single day. I have so many half-finished letters that I started to write to you. I'm re-reading one now in which I described to you the way that people have grown up and things have changed. The buildings that I once thought of as large now look so small next to the new construction (offices, banks, hospitals, and schools). And then there is also the heat that I had forgotten. You know how much I hate the cold and yet this heat is too much! Even the food is spicier than I remember. And you mustn't laugh, but I really think that England has blunted my taste buds. My younger brothers tease me, calling me 'oyinbo' (that's how we refer to expatriates) for forgetting how to take pepper in my food.

I think of you all the time and, when I look at things, I try to imagine what you would see. I am even using my sense of smell, like you. Rain, for example, like the smell of sea meeting earth – so sweet and comforting. And all the wonderful aromas of cooking. This morning akara is being fried in the back of the house where the cooking is done, and in the front of our house, there is always the delicious smell of roasted corn. A woman sits out there in the street with her open fire, turning the cobs by hand and selling them to bystanders.

Vanessa re-read his letter, over and over again, feeling terrible for him and wretched for what she had done. Getting drunk out of anger had been bad enough, but going off with Charlie to spite Tayo was worse. She knew that Tayo would never do anything like that and if he ever found out... Luckily, nothing much had happened with Charlie and at least one thing was now clear to her. She wasn't going to keep waiting for Tayo to come back. She would go to Nigeria and nothing, not even the Biafran war, was going to stop her. Telegrams were exchanged and two weeks later she flew to Nigeria.

When she landed in Lagos the first thing she saw was men in green fatigues with fat, black belts and oversized boots patrolling the tarmac with guns slung carelessly across their chests. It brought home to her the fact that here was a war and the danger of her coming to Nigeria at such a time, especially since Tayo had sent a telegram asking her to postpone her trip. She stood for a moment, trying to take it all in, the heat, the blinding brightness of the sun, the people all around and then she saw him across the tarmac. Tayo, in a crisp white shirt and sandals, looking cool and devastatingly handsome, and just as quickly as she had thought about the war she forgot it.

They checked into a hotel. Tayo said they would stay in Lagos for a few days before traveling up to Ibadan to meet his family. It was a small hotel with ceiling fans and private bathrooms. It was perfect and romantic, but first Tayo wanted to show her around. They took a short walk through Lagos and everywhere they went people turned to stare. Children followed them chanting 'Oyinbo pepper' which made her smile. She told Tayo that she felt like the Pied Piper, but Tayo seemed less charmed by the train of followers. More than once he tried shooing the children away, becoming more impatient with them the longer they followed. Vanessa had never known Tayo to be impatient, but this was now his country and she sensed that he was trying to protect her; she felt touched by his concern.

She stared at all the beautiful people, some wearing western clothes, others in more vibrant local attire. Hundreds of them: running, dodging, walking and bicycling, as they weaved their way in and out of the busy roads full of polluting lorries and imported cars that honked and beeped incessantly. Market stalls were everywhere with their rusted tin roofs and women sitting outside, spread out on mats or perched on upside-down buckets, whistling for business with their products piled high in front of them. People laughed and shouted, sometimes all at once.

It was all so wonderful to Vanessa but best of all she was here with Tayo. Late that afternoon they returned to the hotel. She wasn't hungry, but Tayo insisted that they go to a restaurant, where they ordered rice and plantains. He ordered for her the mildest things on the menu and yet her eyes still streamed from what the owner claimed to be merely 'small-small pepe'. Tayo laughed at her valiant efforts to eat, reminding her of the time had she had coughed her way through the food at the West African Society in Oxford.

He laughed most when they spoke of Oxford but became more serious when they talked about family and the war. She noticed that occasionally Tayo would stare off into space. She knew he was worried about his father and the state of his country, which was why she agreed to go dancing, even though she was exhausted, knowing that the music would relax him.

They went to Bobby Benson's, the legendary Bobby B's, where a local band was playing *juju*. Tayo was his loose and playful self, and this time she joined him, letting go and not feeling self-conscious even though, as the only white woman, everyone was watching her.

Back in the hotel there was no electricity but it didn't matter – they fell into bed where they were serenaded by crickets and frogs. There, in their dimly lit room illuminated only by candlelight and enveloped in the piquant smell of insect repellent, they made love.

Vanessa woke up early the next morning to find herself alone in bed. Tayo was already up and pacing by the window. She watched him for some moments, admiring the curves of his body and his muscles that stood out on his ebony skin, which had grown even darker in the months away.

"What is it, Tayo?"

He jumped in surprise.

"Nothing, my love." He turned to her and lifted the mosquito netting to get back into bed. "I've just got to buy a few medicines for my father," he said, kissing her lightly on her forehead.

"Can I come?"

"Why don't you stay? I'll be right back."

After he left, she took a long bath and then wandered around the hotel grounds, stopping to buy some *akara* from a street seller. She was thinking of venturing further when she gripped her stomach in pain and hurried back to their room. The next hour was spent sitting on the toilet and cursing for having ignored Tayo's advice about eating from the streets.

"Did you find the medicines?" she asked sheepishly when he returned.

"No." He shook his head.

She was about to tell him what had happened when she saw the anxious look on his face.

"Tayo, what's wrong? Something's not right."

He stared past her, looking pained. "I didn't buy the medicine, Vanessa. I just went out for a walk to clear my head, but it didn't help."

"What is it?" She offered her hand, but he wouldn't take it.

"Vanessa, I don't know how else to say this, but…"

"What? What is it Tayo?"

"I've had an affair."

"You what!"

For a second she felt relief that she wasn't the only one who had done something wrong, except that hers could hardly be called an affair.

"And it's worse Vanessa, it's worse. The woman is pregnant."

She stared at him in shock.

"I'm sorry Vanessa, I just don't know what else to say. I didn't mean to Vanessa. It didn't mean much…"

"I come all this way for you to tell me this!"

"I tried to tell you to delay your trip."

"Because of the war you said."

"I just wanted it to go away somehow."

"Well, it's not going away. What are you going to do?"

"I don't know."

"You don't know! How can you not know?"

"All I know 'Nessa is that I love you."

But by then she was gone, slamming the door behind her, only vaguely aware that Tayo was running after her. The heat was making her dizzy, stabbing pains had seized her stomach, and somewhere off in the distance someone was playing Otis Redding's *Sitting on the Dock of the Bay* …

II

Some years later

Chapter 20

1970. Dakar, Senegal.

"Put your head down. In Wolof we say *sëgël*," Salamatou explained.

"*Tennel se bop,*" Vanessa repeated, lowering her head so that Salamatou could braid her hair at the back.

Salamatou started tightly at the scalp, and within seconds Vanessa could feel her fingers flying down the strand of hair.

"*Tennel se bop,*" Salamatou repeated, fastening the braid with a small white bead.

"*Alors*, now let's hear the days of the week."

Vanessa smiled. Salamatou was determined to teach her Wolof, and she felt grateful.

She had learnt more Wolof with Salamatou in a month than in her whole first year in Dakar.

"*Altine, Talaata, Allarba, Alxames,*" she began, stopping on the word for Thursday.

"*Non. Regarde!*" Salamatou held the braid she was plaiting with one hand, and bent over to show her how to position her lips. "*Ce n'est pas difficile,*" she insisted, pointing to her throat with the comb.

Vanessa listened carefully. To her ears, it sounded like "Allah may."

"*Alxames,*" she tried again and started to laugh. "It's difficult!"

"*Non, ce n'est pas difficile!*"

"*Aiyee,*" she squealed as Salamatou tugged at her hair. "*T'es pas gentille, toi!* And are you sure I need cream?"

Salamatou rubbed more Vaseline along the hairline.

"I have greasy hair, you know. Grease. *La grise.*"

"*Si, Si* – you need it," Salamatou insisted. "*Il te le faut.* Believe me."

"Okay," Vanessa nodded, smiling to herself at the way Salamatou could be so stubborn about such things.

"Is it paining you?"

"No, it's fine," she replied, even though her scalp felt like it was on fire. But she wasn't about to admit it, certainly not when little girls routinely had their hair braided and never complained. She tilted her head to better see the children playing hopping and clapping games outside. It was a bright sunny Dakar day, and the children were happy. Beyond the main road, others would be diving off rocks into the brilliant blue waters of the Atlantic. Vanessa thought of writing an article on children's games in Senegal and comparing them to English games of hopscotch and skipping. She wished that all children could be as happy as these, remembering her interview with Flora Nwapa and the heartbreaking stories of Biafran orphans.

"You not talk? *Tu parles pas?*" Salamatou asked.

"I'm watching them." Vanessa gestured in the direction of the children.

"That's why you need to marry and have one of your own – like this one, your godson." Salamatou twisted her hips for Vanessa to see.

"Fast asleep." Vanessa smiled at the tight little bundle. All that was visible of Suleiman were the tufts of hair on the back of his head and two pink feet sticking out from under the wrapper that Salamatou used to hold him to her back. The cloth stretched tightly round his back and bottom and was tied in a secure knot beneath Salamatou's breasts. What a beautiful child, and yet the father had never seen him. Jean-Luc had promised Salamatou that they would be married. He had sworn to take her back to France, but as soon as she fell pregnant he had abandoned her, not wanting to be the father of a half-caste child. If Jean-Luc could see his son Vanessa felt certain he would change his mind. But Salamatou refused to discuss the subject. She said that if Suleiman wanted to meet his father one day he could do so, but until that time she would manage just fine on her own. And that was Salamatou. If she felt sad or sorry for herself, she never showed it, and Vanessa understood. She looked at Suleiman again, and imagined him as her child. She and Tayo could have had a child like Suleiman, this gorgeous mocha brown baby.

"So how is Abubakar?" Salamatou asked.

"Ahh!" Vanessa slapped the air dismissively with one hand. The truth was, though, that there had been a time when she had quite liked him; Abubakar had been generous and a good companion, and she had learnt a lot from him. They had taken long walks together down the *Route de la Corniche*, discussing African politics. She was grateful to him too for introducing her to people who helped her find the stringer jobs, as well as her contacts with the local paper, *Paris-Dakar*.

"You know you could have been his *deuxieme* wife," Salamatou remarked.

"No way," Vanessa exclaimed, pulling her head forward so that Salamatou lost her grip.

Salamatou laughed, pushing Vanessa's head back into place.

"Cultures are different, *non?* Maybe two wives is too hard for your culture."

"And you? Would you be a second wife?" Vanessa challenged, knowing already what Salamatou would say.

"No, but I am not a Muslim," Salamatou replied.

"Nor am I."

"But you're don't practise the Christianity either so *ca-va, non?*" Salamatou joked.

"No," Vanessa insisted.

"*Bon alors*, you should marry Edward," Salamatou suggested.

"Edward?"

"*Oui!*"

"*Aiy* Salamatou, you never give up. You are almost as bad as him!" Vanessa laughed.

"But he is good, *non?*" Salamatou insisted.

"Yes, he's good, but I am happy as I am. *Toute seule*," Vanessa said, reflecting on her life in Dakar, where she was doing what she had always dreamt of: writing about African art and culture. She wrote about that warm edge of life, which was Africa's laughter, the celebrations, the rituals and people's generosity. Nobody who came to Africa would miss these things. In the mornings she wrote and after lunch she took the articles to the Reuters office to be telexed to London or Paris. In the late-afternoons she did things such as this – chat, sip mint tea, and watch the world go by.

"So you never had a lover before you come to Dakar?" Salamatou asked.

"*Si,*" Vanessa replied.

"Then what happen? He go with another lady?"

"I'm not sure. Well, maybe." It had been two years since she'd last heard from Tayo. After she'd left Lagos he had written to her several times, but she had not replied. His letters hadn't said whether or not he was going to marry the woman. And he hadn't mentioned the baby.

"*C'est un Anglais?*" Salamatou asked.

"*Non*, Nigerian," Vanessa replied.

"Ahh, *les Nigerians, ils ont de l'argent avec le petrole, n'est-ce pas?*" Salamatou rubbed her fingers together. "Why you are not together? Did he ask you to marry?"

"No. It just didn't work. *Cela n'a pas marche.*" Vanessa shrugged her shoulders. She still couldn't talk about it.

"*Alors, il faut te trouver un mari. Quel est le genre que tu preferes?*" Salamatou asked.

"You mean, what do I want in a husband?"

"*Oui,*" Salamatou nodded.

"How about someone like Sembene."

"Sembene?" Salamatou asked.

"Sembene Ousmane."

"Ahh, mais you know him, *non*? So you have to show him you love him," Salamatou said excitedly.

"No, I was only joking," Vanessa laughed. "He is very handsome, but not the man for me. Too many women like him. Far too famous."

"So that says you still love the Nigerian?" Salamatou reasoned, holding the mirror for Vanessa to view her finished hair.

Vanessa laughed.

"*Alors?*" Salamatou asked.

"It's beautiful. *C'est tres jolie.*"

"*Non, non, non.* I don't talk about your hair! I speak about your man. You love him still, non?"

"Who?"

"*Le Nigerian.*"

"*Ouff.* It's finished. *C'est fini. Jeexna!*" Vanessa added, remembering a word Salamatou had taught her.

Salamatou laughed. "*Non.* You say *jeexna*, for example, if you finish with something, like I finish to plait your hair. But if you finish with a man, it's more better to say *sanu diggënte jeexna.*"

"*Sanu diggënte jeexna,*" Vanessa repeated.

She said it so well and with such conviction that they both started laughing, and it was good to laugh, but later that night

Vanessa went back to her flat and cried. It was the first time in many months that she had cried about Tayo.

Chapter 21

1984

Tayo sat in his armchair with his eyes closed and feet resting on his leather pouffe as he listened to Coltrane's *Love Supreme*. He looked forward to Sunday mornings when the house was quiet and he could reflect in peace. He stood up now and walked to the bookshelf in search of an exemplary text. Last week his publishers had phoned to congratulate him on his manuscript. They were planning a sizeable print run of his history of Nigeria, the largest, they said, of any third-world history book, and naturally he felt pleased. All that remained to be written was the preface, but what did one say in a preface? He flipped through several books and then traced his finger slowly along the mahogany bookshelf in search of one of his favourites, and there it was – *The Open Society and its Enemies*. He wondered how often a preface was overlooked in a reader's eagerness to hurry on and read the rest of the book. And here was Popper's preface, two in fact, in the edition he owned. Tayo nodded to himself, dwelling for a moment on the line that spoke of the need to break from the customary deference shown to great men. He reached for pen and paper and carried his selection of books to his desk.

For years now, Tayo had been writing about Nigeria's problems. He believed that greed and mismanagement were the root causes of oil corruption and a broken civil service. He also believed that the West, through the World Bank in particular, exacerbated his country's problems, but he was cautious with this argument knowing its potential to detract from what could be done at home. He was also determined never to treat Nigeria's problems as insurmountable and, in 1984, when others were saying that the country's many cultures and ethnic groups were never meant to co-exist, Tayo disagreed. He had no patience for the afro-pessimism mentality, which he saw as lending credence to the many racist historians of Africa. Instead, he firmly maintained that in spite of his country's numerous coups and despots, events could still change for the better. History, as Popper argued, was not deterministic and he would acknowledge him in his preface, alongside colleagues and friends, not forgetting family of course.

The book would be dedicated to Vanessa and to his father 'for being a tireless civil servant in pursuit of a better Nigeria.' Tayo shifted in his chair, sensing that something had fallen from his trouser pocket. He reached down, expecting to retrieve Naira notes, but instead found a sheet of paper in his wife's handwriting. It was yesterday's shopping list scribbled on medical paper advertising an unpronounceable medication. "Wretched pharmaceutical companies," he muttered to himself. Wouldn't it be nice if companies handed out free medicines instead of useless bits of paper promoting fancy experimental drugs; this was yet another of Nigeria's problems – the questionable role of multinationals. He read the shopping list:

Maggi cubes
Corn oil (large size)
Tomato puree
Treetops squash (mango or lemon)
Ribena
Bournvita
Lipton's tea
Quaker oats
Margarine (Flora)

Baby bell Dutch cheeses (Pick coldest)
Dairy Lee cheese
Walls' ice cream
Golden syrup (not local brand!)
Omo
Lux, and 1 packet Imperial Leather

Not many husbands helped with domestic chores, but Tayo felt it only fair. After all, his wife worked out of the home just as much as he did, more if counting her night shifts. Like most professionals, they employed a house servant and gardener, but some things they preferred to take care of themselves. Most Saturday mornings, she gave him a list and he would do the Kingsway shopping, while she haggled with the petty traders selling fresh fruits and vegetables in the car park outside. She enjoyed bargaining and was good at it; he was not, hence his relegation to Kingsway.

Usually after the food shopping she liked to stop at Challenge Christian bookshop, and he used this time to browse arts and crafts displayed in the stalls across the street. She didn't like him to buy from these traders, whom she claimed inflated their prices for tourists, but occasionally he chose something small, some glass beads or a leather bag, for his daughter. He knew the prices were high, but they were still far cheaper than the imported trinkets sold in Kingsway's household section. He never made a fuss about this to his wife, but he didn't like it when Nigerians shunned local products, preferring to import all manner of things like Quaker oats and golden syrup bearing the royal stamp of approval: *By appointment to her Majesty the Queen.* Tayo shook his head at the hypocrisy of it all, wishing his wife could see things his way, yet he knew he was being unfair, petty even, to criticise her. Life was hard and, if she wanted her few overseas luxuries, so be it. She worked hard for them.

Tayo stretched his arms out in front of him and interlacing his fingers extended further to loosen his muscles. Yesterday, after shopping, he had gone with Kwame and David to the abattoir to buy half a cow. Kwame White and David Wiseman were neighbours who, like them, lived in the new university homes on the Bauchi road in identical four-bedroom bungalows with sizeable back gardens. They had spent a pleasant afternoon at Kwame's house cutting the meat and portioning it into plastic bags for the women to freeze, but today Tayo was feeling the after-effects of their hard work. Every arm muscle ached, which made him doubly glad for the day of rest.

It seemed that the older he got the more he looked forward to the peace and quiet of Sunday mornings. Did he miss going to church? Not really. He still believed in God, or at least in the existence of a supernatural being, but he had grown disenchanted with organised religion. He disliked the newer charismatic services, and found it embarrassing to watch people crying and confessing their so-called sins in public. He viewed the speaking in tongues with great suspicion and did not care much for St. Mark's congregation, where it seemed that church members worried more about displaying the latest fashions and newest German automobiles than in humbly worshiping God. His family had taken offence at his assessments, reminding him that he hardly attended services, therefore, they reasoned, how could he know what congregations were like. So Tayo had learnt to keep his views to himself and, while his wife and daughter worshipped at church, he played his records and read the papers.

These days he listened less to Highlife and the swinging jazz of his youth and more to the serious jazz of artists like Coltrane, which was the music that kept him company now as he started to read the local papers. He bought *Punch* and *New Nigerian* out of habit and always with the hope of finding something worthwhile in between the excess of advertisements, obituaries, memorials and other social announcements. The more serious international paper, *The Weekly Guardian*, he saved for last. It kept him abreast of international news with a selection of articles sourced from *Le Monde, The Guardian,* and *The Washington Post.*

Tayo realised that he must have drifted off to sleep. The papers had slipped from his lap and the family was back. Kemi eagerly waved her Sunday school colouring in front of his face.

"Do you like it, Daddy?"

"It's beautiful," he smiled, preparing to add it to his already large collection of fishermen, shepherds, and babies in mangers.

"Not the colouring! My autograph." She pointed to her name scribbled in joined-up letters.

"I see."

"I'm going to save it," Kemi said, whisking the paper from his hands and skipping off to her room.

"Miriam?" Tayo called, wondering where she had gone.

He stood up and went to the bedroom where he found her changing out of her Sunday clothes into a looser fitting dress. He slipped his arms around her waist, hoping for a few minutes of intimacy, but Miriam wriggled free, intent on getting dressed. Tayo sighed, wondering why he bothered. There had been a time when she would lean back in his arms, and be affectionate and playful. He thought of those times as he went to look for a jacket.

It was a tradition in the Ajayi household to have lunch at Yelwa Club one Sunday a month, which was one of the few surviving country clubs established by the British in colonial times. It was located on the outskirts of Bukuru, a thirty-minute drive from the Ajayi home. Tayo frequently took younger lecturers, and sometimes students, to the club for a peaceful drink or a stroll around the grounds. He liked to play squash there too, but Sundays at Yelwa were always reserved for the family, and today they would be meeting the Abubakars. On their drive to the club, Tayo had hoped to listen to the news, but he was out-voted. He never seemed to win when Miriam and Kemi were both in the car.

"Lets play the Wombles music," Kemi clamoured from the backseat. "Please Daddy! Please Mummy! Pleeeeeease!"

So they listened to the Wombles for a while until Tayo could stand it no longer and Miriam changed the cassette to one of her American gospel tapes. Tayo didn't mind gospel, but found the musical arrangement irritating when it hopped haphazardly from slow to fast tracks. Albums should either be fast or slow Tayo mused as he swung the wheel to avoid a pothole. They had taken the Jos-Miango road, passing the Nasco biscuit factory, Trebor Sweets, and the Coca-Cola bottling plant. Most of these factories were closed at the weekend, but a few factory chimneys still spewed their dirty gases, staining the blue sky, brown.

"Are you okay, Miriam?" he asked, knowing that the factory emissions made her nauseous. She had wound up her window and was caressing her stomach.

"I'm fine," she replied, sliding a hand onto his knee.

He squeezed the hand and gently massaged her fingers. Miraculously, after all these years, Miriam's belly was full again with a child. So many miscarriages and now this. He squeezed her hand once more. Seeing her happy made him feel better and he thought of the unborn child. When people asked him if he wanted a baby girl or a baby boy he would always say that he hoped simply for a healthy child, but of course he wished for a boy. With a son he could play football and build model ships. His boy would be studious like his daughter, but also a sportsman. He had already thought of names: Adeniyi Oluwakayode Pele. Adeniyi after his father and Pele, of course, after Pele. He had even thought of adding Segun to the names in honour of his own country's footballer, Segun Odegbami. And wasn't that the beauty of giving many names to one's child? Except of course that they couldn't *all* revolve around sports.

When they arrived at the Club, Tayo parked the car in the

shade of frangipanis. It was the coolest spot and close to where they would eat.

"*Ranka dede*," Ibrahim called out in greeting as they entered the lounge.

"*Sanu*," Tayo replied, smiling to himself at the waiter's exuberance.

"*Make I go get drink sah?*" Ibrahim asked.

"Yes, the usual." That meant a Dubonnet for him, Fanta for Miriam and a Sprite for Kemi.

In Tayo's seven years of coming to Yelwa Club, little had changed. The sweet and spicy aroma of curry always hung in the air, accompanied by the clatter of pots and pans from the kitchens in the back. Then there was the put-put sound from people playing pool in an adjoining room and the steady whirr from overhead steel fans that blew a gentle breeze. The décor too remained the same – velvet settees, leather-topped side tables, withering cacti and African violets in clay pots. There were also two oversized pictures hanging from the wall: one of Her Majesty the Queen, the other of President Shagari. Through the open doors Tayo could hear faintly the excited sounds of children playing by the pool. Miriam and Kemi stood up to go outside while he waited for the drinks. He watched them leave and then gazed for a moment at the President's picture. Others had preceded this President behind the same glass frame, and Tayo hoped that sooner rather than later this one too would be replaced. While he had celebrated Nigeria's return to civilian rule, Tayo now believed that the only way to bring his country back to its senses was to install the military, not forever, but for a short while to restore law and order.

"Professor Ajayi, my honourable good friend," Yusuf's voice rang out across the lounge.

"My honourable good friend," Tayo answered, standing up to greet Yusuf, whose stomach was what greeted people first these days – a decidedly large and unorthodox Muslim beer belly.

People joked that Yusuf's size came with the good life. He had recently been appointed District Manager for NEPA, while his wife held a senior position at National Television. However, life for the Abubakars was not as easy as it looked from the outside. They had lost their first two children to sickle cell anaemia, and for a long time didn't know whether the youngest would suffer the same fate. Thankfully, Isaac and Dari were healthy. Yusuf embraced Tayo tightly in his *danshiki*, and then moved on to greet others whom he recognised in the lounge.

Tayo marvelled at Yusuf's temperament, always jovial, and seemingly at ease in any setting; by the time Yusuf had dispensed all his greetings the whole room smelt of his cologne. He had made his mark. Yusuf knew everyone in Jos from the Lebanese, Indian, and British, to the Nigerians. One minute he could be heard speaking Pidgin, then Hausa or English (with the Yorkshire accent he had never lost), and even some Yoruba these days depending on who happened to be around. And it wasn't just linguistics that Yusuf juggled with so smoothly, but everything, it seemed to Tayo, right down to the clothes he wore. Today it was a *danshiki*, but he might just as easily have donned a safari or a three-piece suit.

Yusuf had the sort of personality that Tayo associated with those best attuned to life in Nigeria – that seamless ability for social metamorphoses, which Tayo sometimes envied. Yusuf's cultural juggling did not come naturally to Tayo, and Miriam was always reminding him of the fact saying that he was far too English in the way he dressed, in the music he listened to, and in his preference for speaking English rather than Yoruba. He took it as teasing even though it sometimes felt like a series of rebukes, as though Miram held it against him. And it wasn't just Miriam, but his brothers and sisters (even Bisi) who told him he had too much *oyinbo* mentality for his own good; yet, for all his so-called Western thinking, he refused to leave Nigeria to live abroad. Nigeria was home for his soul, if not entirely home for his mind. His friends and family maintained that, in the past, he had been more carefree but he disagreed. Except for his approach to religion, he remained the same. It was society, he told them, not he that had changed.

"Look at you, my dear, you're looking splendid," Joy complimented Miriam, spotting her as she returned with Kemi through the back doors.

"Is that so? But I'm tired *sha*," Miriam replied, grasping the sides of her abdomen.

Her stomach was big like a watermelon, and it made Tayo anxious. He worried, as he had done when she was carrying Kemi, that her slender frame would not withstand the pregnancy.

"How many months is it now?" Joy asked.

"Five," Kemi answered for Miriam, before dashing back outside to play with the other children.

Tayo remembered how Miriam had at first wanted to keep it a secret from Kemi until it became visible. He did not hold strongly to these cultural beliefs but played along for Miriam's sake; although in the end there was little they could hide from a curious six-year-old.

"Professor Ajayi is a very lucky man," Yusuf chuckled, grasping Tayo again by the shoulders. "You're looking stunning, my dear Miriam."

'As does Joy,' Tayo thought wistfully, finding Joy carefree and sensuous in the way that Miriam used to be.

The one o'clock gong sounded, and Tayo led both families to the long table where waiters in white suits and red cummerbunds were serving the guests white basmati rice and bright yellow curry. It was then self-service from a line of silver trays, each with its own condiment – shredded coconut, green pickles, purple onion rings, sultanas, tangerine segments, sliced banana, and tomato. Soft white rolls were brought to the table with shavings of butter floating in ice water to keep them from melting.

"You know there's going to be a coup soon," Yusuf announced when everyone was seated.

"But until the BBC says so, it's all rumour," Tayo asserted, smiling to himself at this unconscious borrowing from his father. He remembered Baba saying it on the weekend of Nigeria's second military coup, and Tayo had wondered then whether Baba really believed that the first accurate news would come from the BBC, or whether he had made the announcement to distract the men from their anxieties.

"We just need a strong ruler," Yusuf broke into Tayo's thoughts, "someone who can bring discipline to this country. Corruption. That's the problem with this place – corruption. *Wallahi!*" Yusuf pounded the table with his fist. "We need a dictator. Like Rawlings. Even Idi Amin," he added, shaking his arm to straighten the Rolex that hung loosely around his wrist.

"How about Jimmy Carter?" Kemi suggested.

"Please Yusuf, don't exaggerate," Joy said, ignoring Kemi's question.

The Abubakar children spoke only when spoken to, and Tayo worried that he and Miriam had spoilt Kemi. Baba would certainly not have stood for so many interruptions, and yet Tayo knew he should not compare. He had never wanted to be as strict as his father.

"No, I'm serious," Yusuf insisted. "I'm telling you that unless this country is ruled by force, we're all doomed. Yes now, force! Just look at our property. Did we tell you, Tayo, what happened when we went to Florida last year? When we returned from the US, there was no cement in our place. You know, our place where we're building our small-small palace. No bricks – no nothing. The workers were stealing it and then carrying it to their villages to build their *menene*. So I sacked them, all of them. *Wallahi!* Look, Nigerians are just too corrupt," he insisted.

"It's true," Tayo nodded. "This business of corruption is so bad. When I travel these days I'm embarrassed to show my passport."

"Precisely," Yusuf stabbed the air with his fork. "You see, you watch everyone passing so smoothly through those immigration places in Europe, but when they take your Nigerian passport, the way they look at you – it's an insult. That's why I got myself a British passport. Yes now! The end justifies the means isn't it so?" Yusuf chuckled.

"Was Jimmy Carter a dictator?" Kemi persisted.

"No, he was a democrat. *But not a Naija democrat-o,*" Yusuf laughed.

"I know he's a demo…"

"And did you hear about that Professor of Economics?" Tayo interrupted.

"No. Which one is that one now?" Yusuf laughed in anticipation.

"Last month," Tayo began, "the university passed on a candidate to the committee stage, this fellow from Oxford, Innocent something-or-other. I wasn't involved in the recruiting, mind you, but I just wanted to meet the applicant – a fellow Oxford chap and all that."

"Of course. We all know your reputation, Tayo," Joy smiled. "Always looking out for younger colleagues. Isn't that so?"

"Well," Tayo shrugged nonchalantly so as not to appear flattered.

"*Haba,* Tayo, you're too humble my friend," Yusuf insisted.

"Anyway, I called Innocent to my office," Tayo continued, "and straight away I knew something was fishy about the chap. He was sort of shifty-looking and telling me he didn't have much time to talk. And then I asked him which college he attended at Oxford. Do you know what he said?"

"What did Mr Innocent, innocently say?" Yusuf asked, already laughing.

"Oxford College!"

"Why is that funny?" Kemi insisted.

"So then I thought, let me just have some fun with this Innocent chap," Tayo continued, "and I asked him, 'Did you read Economics at Oxford?' Of course I knew this couldn't be true because, as you know, there's no Economics course at Oxford, only PPE. But this man just nodded saying, '*yes, yes, yes*'. And then…" he paused, trying not to laugh, but Yusuf and Joy were laughing so hard that it made it difficult not to do the same. "And then I said, so was Marks one of your tutors? 'Of course,' the chap replied. 'Yes, Karly Marx,' he added. So there I was even giving the foolish man the benefit of the doubt asking if he knew Daniel Marks, and the chap thinks I'm talking about Karl Marx." Tayo struggled to keep a serious face. "So then I ask him if he meant the one who died in 1883. And what did he say? 'Karly Marx junior.' Can you imagine?"

Yusuf's loud laughter, punctuated by fists pounding on the table, now had the whole room going.

"Come on Tayo," Yusuf spoke in fits and starts, "you exaggerate too much, but I like this story-o!"

"We simply need a God-fearing man in power," Miriam remarked, her words landing like a fly swat against their merriment.

"Well, we need someone who is not corrupt." Tayo wiped his eyes. "That's what we need. Someone like Awolowo." Why, Tayo wondered, did Miriam always insist on a God-fearing man? He had nothing against the suggestion itself, but the predictability of Miriam's responses and their simplicity annoyed him even more than their daughter's interruptions.

However, when he had first met Miriam it had been that very simplicity, her youth and her unwavering faith in God that he had liked. So why did these things now bother him? At least she hadn't joined the Aladura church or any of the cults popping up like anthills all over the country. He would never dismiss religion or faith, but he wished she were more questioning, or could at least engage with other people's ideas – the way Joy did, for example. There was so much that he wanted to do, so much he wished to change in his country, yet Miriam showed very little interest.

In the early years it hadn't been like this; they had discussed things together, she had read literature and taken an interest in the courses he taught, but now she confined her reading to the Bible and Christian pamphlets. He could not but wish she had never fallen pregnant all those years ago. And then all the trauma and heartbreak of losing the baby had made things even worse. Doubly tragic. But no, he wasn't being fair. They had both decided to try to make it work and maybe it had worked as well as could have been expected. Meanwhile, Yusuf was still talking and teasing Tayo about Awolowo. *"I'm telling you. Awolowo is corrupt, no be so?"* Yusuf turned to Ibrahim, who had begun to clear their plates.

"So oga, when you go be President?" Ibrahim asked looking in Tayo's direction.

"Me? You wan make I die? Neva!" Tayo laughed. *"Make you bring me some of dat your fruit salad."*

"And do you have sherry trifle?" Yusuf requested.

"Yes sah. We also have Bird Eye costad and ice cream."

"Eh-henh, then make you bring all of dem."

"Yes sah." Ibrahim dashed off to join the rest of the amused waiters, who stood idly in a line at the back of the room.

"Ah-ah, look at this man, our Black American brother!" Yusuf exclaimed, pointing to a new arrival.

It was Kwame, who had come with some friends for lunch. Tayo stood up and they chatted for a while.

"So how do you know Kwame?" Tayo asked, once the desserts arrived and Kwame had left.

"We play tennis. The man's an Arthur Ashe, you know."

"I didn't realise he was *that* good."

"Shows how little you know about your university colleagues.

He used to be a Black Panther too."

"Well of course I knew that," Tayo smiled.

"He's a good man, so dedicated to our country," Yusuf mused.

Tayo nodded. They were all close friends now, but he remembered when Kwame first arrived at the university and was suspicious of him. It was only when Tayo told Kwame about his admiration for brother Malcolm and the fiery Oxford debate of 1964 that Kwame grew more relaxed in his presence. Perhaps, Tayo mused, Kwame, like Miriam, had found him too English and not quite African enough.

The children, as always, had finished their ice cream in seconds and were eager to play in the pool so the women took them away while Tayo and Yusuf stayed behind to drink tea and continue their conversation.

"Karly Marx Junior and Professor Innocent," Yusuf repeated, shaking his head and laughing. "Did the man even know any economics?"

"Who knows!" Tayo laughed as they stood up. "But the man was smart enough at least to try bluffing his way into university."

They walked slowly across the courtyard, past the building where the annual horticultural show took place and where Scottish dancing was taught on Sunday evenings – the last vestiges of colonial days that seemed destined to stay.

"Now Tayo, remind me again, when is the baby due?"

"We're told the last week in August."

"*Inshallah*. Good. Very good." Yusuf stared ponderously at his snakeskin slippers. "So, are you still considering that job at Birmingham University?"

"Yes, still deciding."

Tayo didn't need Yusuf to remind him that it was an attractive offer. It was a chance to teach in the African Studies Centre while completing his own research towards a PhD, yet he was reluctant to accept. Of course life would be better in England, offering a more conducive academic environment, and greater financial security, but he felt an obligation to remain in Nigeria if for no other reason than for his students.

"And what does Miriam say?"

"She thinks we should go."

"You know you owe it to your family. You must be very careful, Tayo, how you criticise the government these days."

"I take it Miriam told you to say that?"

"Look, my friend, you think we don't read your articles in the paper? You have to be careful Tayo, I'm telling you. These guys aren't the small-small thugs we used to fight in Bradford. These ones have guns and armies, my friend."

"But you know as well as I do that this government is corrupt."

"Yes, and that's why I say we need a dictator. I don't want any of my friends losing their jobs for the sake of politics, and I'm not even going to mention losing your life."

"So what do you propose?"

"Look, Tayo, you're right to blame our leaders, but they don't work alone. They dance with Western governments and oil multinationals, and each one of them is taking a slice of our national cake. I don't need to tell you that."

Tayo shook his head and sucked his teeth in irritation.

"But Yusuf, change has always come from individuals and we first need to fix our problems at home before thinking of changing The World Bank and all those people. Remember Nehru and Gandhi, Martin Luther King."

"Look, Tayo, you know I can't talk book like you, but I can tell you one thing for sure – in this, our country, don't make waves alone. Why don't you go into business instead? Take a break from the teaching."

Tayo glanced at his wife sitting with Joy by the side of the pool, and sighed. He resented people who criticised the government and yet did nothing to change the status quo. Admittedly, Yusuf was not as bad as Ike, who had joined the government talking about the need for change from within while changing nothing. Yusuf wasn't that bad, but the suggestion to go into business was silly, and Tayo had heard the line too often. He was fed up with it and, if anything were to drive him back to Europe, it would be this growing lack of respect for the pursuit of knowledge. He did sometimes wonder if he should have stayed in Europe in the first place, forging a serious career there many years earlier. And not just for his career. Other things might have been better too.

"You have a good family," Yusuf repeated, as though he had read Tayo's thoughts and decided to challenge them.

"As do you," Tayo muttered, watching his daughter dive under water and out again.

"Look Daddy!" she gasped. "I'm doing synchronized swimming like the Olympics!"

"I can see that," Tayo smiled. "Show me some more!"

Kemi treaded water and raised her hands high in the air. "Does it look good, Daddy?"

"Beautiful," Tayo smiled. Sometimes when he saw Kemi it seemed impossible that she had grown so big. It felt like yesterday when he had held her in the palm of his hands and now look at her – a potential Olympic swimmer.

"Oh, I almost forgot. I brought you some papers," Tayo added, taking them from his briefcase so Yusuf could borrow them.

Yusuf thumbed approvingly through the *Weekly Guardians*.

"And when you've finished, I'd like that article back." Tayo pointed to one he had circled.

Yusuf studied the paper and read the title aloud. "'African authors write back'. Do you have a mention in this?"

Tayo nodded – his children's stories were mentioned. They were gaining greater international acclaim these days too, but that wasn't why the article was important to him.

"*Hey, make you treat my papers properly! Don't bend 'am*

now!" Tayo ordered, stopping Yusuf from rolling the paper into a tube.

"*Na just paper now,*" Yusuf protested.

"It's not just paper, my friend. It's the person who wrote it."

"Vanessa Richardson," Yusuf read the name without recognition.

Tayo nodded, thinking for a moment that he would remind Yusuf of who she was but the wives had joined them and the moment had passed.

Chapter 22

That evening, after Kemi and Miriam had gone to sleep, Tayo went to his study to read. He started with what lay on his desk, some academic journals and Ngugi's *Petals of Blood*, but soon he had put down his reading and was looking in his drawer for something else. The object was a tattered diary, which had found its way to Tayo in 1979 via his father's old address in Ibadan. The address on the inside cover was the only address, indeed the only bit of writing still clearly legible in Vanessa's old diary, yet he kept these torn and yellowing pages and would look at them from time to time. There was nothing new to read and usually he would end up dreaming about what might have been. What might have been had she stayed with him in Nigeria or had he gone back to Oxford or joined her later in Dakar. And then a door creaked, followed by the sound of flip-flops slapping gently against the concrete floor. It was Kemi on her way to the toilet.

"Vanessa," Tayo whispered, turning back to the journal and thinking that had it not been for his mistake, had he known, had *they* known that the pregnancy would not hold… but what was the use of wishing now. It was all in the past. Now Vanessa was a well-known writer and one of Africa's most loved journalists. So much for him believing she would never fit into West Africa; of course she did. He reached now for the photograph that sat on his desk and used his sleeve to dust it off. What if he had married Vanessa regardless? But he couldn't have left Miriam when she was pregnant and, besides, his whole family loved Miriam, which made it even harder. Miriam had looked after Father when he had his stroke, and because Baba always attributed his speedy recovery to her nursing, she became an honourable member of the Ajayi family even before he married her.

What had happened with Miriam was done on a whim, in a moment of weakness. She was the one who had come to him after Baba's operation, comforting him when nobody else thought to do so. He had been touched and felt that he owed her something, so he had taken her out for a drink and met with her a few more times in the weeks that followed. And then... even though he hadn't meant to and hadn't even really wanted to, he slept with her. She was beautiful and religious and it just sort of happened, despite the religion or maybe because of the religion which made it seem all the more unlikely. And then she fell pregnant and he felt he had no choice; yet had he known...

"What are you doing, Daddy?" Kemi asked, causing Tayo to jump and knock over the photograph.

She stood in her Snoopy nightdress, which read, 'Love is the whole world.' Her eyes were squinting beneath the glare of the bare yellow light bulb dangling from the ceiling.

"Just working, baby," he answered, watching as she started rubbing one foot rapidly against the inside of her standing leg.

"I need to spray your room for mosquitoes."

She dropped the foot and wandered closer to his desk, yawning. He reached quickly for Ngugi's novel, and placed it on top of the journal.

"You work too much, Daddy." Kemi smiled, picking up the wedding photograph. She removed the cork backing and straightened the print before pressing the frame back together. "There." She smiled, propping it back on his desk.

"And you should be sleeping, my baby."

"But I can't sleep Daddy, I'm too excited about the holidays. I can't stop thinking about it."

"All the more reason to try. That way time will go faster. Before you know it, we'll be off to Lagos."

"Okay," she said, walking towards the door, "but Daddy," she stopped and turned back, "will you tell me a story of when you were a child? Just one! Please?"

He smiled, knowing already the one she wanted to hear.

"Come then, baby. Come and sit on my lap and I'll tell you a story." He pushed his chair away from the desk and she hopped onto his knee.

In 1951, there was a little boy...

"Was it you, Daddy?"

"Yes," he smiled. "Now, are you sitting comfortably?"

"Yes," she nodded.

"I'll start again then."

Once upon a time, in 1951 there was a little boy called Omotayo, who was visiting Lagos for the very first time. The boy came with his father from Ibadan and this was their second day in Lagos.

Kemi smiled and occasionally giggled as he told her of how he had been forced to sit patiently in church waiting for the service to finish before he could run outside and see the fine ocean liner called the *Aureol.*

"And who else gets impatient?" Tayo smiled, tickling Kemi's tummy.

"Stop it, Daddy!" Kemi shouted. "Tell me the story!"

"Shh! You'll wake your mum." But it was too late.

"Ah-ah! You two!" Miriam exclaimed.

She stood by the door shaking her head.

"Look, we've woken Mummy now."

Miriam smiled and walked to where Kemi sat on Tayo's lap. She rubbed her eyes sleepily.

"Just finish your story and come to bed, both of you," she said, kissing them, one after the other, on the forehead.

"Come," Tayo called, pulling her by the waist a little closer. "There's room in the armchair for you two," he said, tapping the side of her large tummy.

"Come to bed," Miriam smiled, massaging the back of his neck.

Tayo dropped his arm behind Miriam's back where Kemi could not see what he was doing and lifted Miriam's cotton nightdress to caress her naked thighs.

"Hey!" Miriam whispered, moving away.

"I'm coming soon!" Tayo called after her.

"Daddy!"

"What?"

"Finish the story!"

So Omotayo was standing there, waiting and praying to see the ship again when suddenly his father seized the boy's hand, and lifted him up. "THE AUREOL," Omotayo screamed excitedly. On his father's shoulders he could see the entire ocean. He watched people running on deck in white shirts and shorts, and he wondered how the ship knew which way to drive. Would it get lost? Who would find it then? Omotayo lifted a hand from his father's head to wave at the passengers. Then the church people started singing and he joined in with words he didn't understand but still sounded good to him.

My Bonnie lies over the ocean,

Please bring back my Bonnie to me.

It was then that Omotayo saw something that made him jolt and nearly lose his balance. His father said children couldn't go on ships, but look! There was a child just like him, held up by her mother. It must be the maiden voyage!

"Was that me?" Kemi interrupted.

"No," Tayo laughed. "You weren't born yet."

"Was it Mummy then?"

"Listen," Tayo smiled.

Omotayo wished with all his heart that the maiden were his friend. That way they could sail the seas together and see all the countries, the pirates, other ships, and the sharks – everything. He would protect her, and they would find gold-and-fleece for their families. He felt very sad that he wasn't going on the ship, and slumped on his father's shoulders. "Baa mi. Igba wo lemi n'lo?" When can I go Baba? he pleaded, and rubbed his eyes to stop the tears from falling.

"And the little girl was Mummy!" Kemi jumped in to finish the story. "And when you were grown up you went on the boat to England, then you came back and you married Mummy, and we all lived happily ever after."

"Yes, darling." Tayo hugged her tightly. "Yes."

Chapter 23

In July of 1984, the Ajayis flew to Lagos as they always did for the summer holidays. They would spend three weeks with Uncle Kayode and his wife, using their home as a base from which to visit Mama and Remi, as well as other relatives in Lagos and Ibadan. In years past, visits to kinfolk were endless, but Uncle Bola and Uncle Joseph had now died and many other relatives had moved away. Bisi was living in Ghana with her three children, and worked as an accountant in Abuja. Aunty Bayo had left Nigeria shortly after her divorce, which had been messy because of Uncle Kayode's affair with Helene. Apparently the affair had begun in 1963, which was not long after Uncle Kayode's marriage to Bayo. Tayo wondered sometimes how the relationship had started and what had made his uncle so sure about Helene. And what had made Helene so certain that Uncle Kayode wouldn't later find another woman to replace her? But these were not things one asked, not even to a heterodox like Uncle Kayode.

Uncle Kayode had left the Nigerian army shortly after the Biafran war and gone to France to complete his engineering training – just as he had said he would when they'd had tea together at the Randolph. Tayo presumed that it was during this time that his uncle lived with Helene in France, and then returned with her to Nigeria after his studies. They were married in 1974 and moved from the old house in Yaba to Victoria Island.

Uncle Kayode held a senior position with the oil

conglomerate Elf, while Helene worked from home as an artist. For a few years, Miriam had refused to stay with Uncle Kayode out of a sense of loyalty to Aunty Bayo, who had been her mentor at nursing school but, with time, Miriam, like the rest of the extended family, came to love Helene, and it would have been hard not to. Helene was one of those rare expatriate women who embraced Nigeria and adopted its cultures to the point where it was easy to forget she was French. She even spoke English with a Yoruba accent rather than a French one. Often, when Tayo was with Helene, he thought of Vanessa and allowed himself to fantasise – he and Vanessa living happily together in a beautiful home such as Kayode and Helene's.

The house was a five-minute walk from the ocean and it was such a striking building that it had once featured in a prestigious design magazine under the caption, 'Beauty in the Heart of Darkness.' Uncle Kayode never liked the caption, but it certainly didn't annoy him enough to stop displaying several copies prominently throughout the home.

Like most properties in this most expensive part of Lagos, none of the beauty was visible from the outside. A 10-foot-high concrete wall, laced with loops of barbed wire, encircled it, hiding it from public view. Even when the guards let people through the imposing steel gates, little of the actual house could be seen from the front; leafy palm trees and thick bougainvillea obscured the building. Always, when they arrived at the Ogundeles', Kemi would announce that this was the sort of house she wanted when she grew up. And because the Ogundeles had no children of their own, they spoilt her.

"When I have a house it will be just like Auntie Helene's," Kemi would say. "Maybe not so big, but it will have lots of art." And there was certainly an abundance of art in the Ogundeles' home, which sometimes reminded Tayo of the Barker's home in Oxford. Helene, like Edward, had collected paintings from around the world as well as sculptures and bronzes from across West Africa. On this visit, as a special treat for Kemi, Helene had invited two local artists to the house to talk about their craft. One was a carver and the other a bronze sculptor. Of course Kemi had been thrilled, and Tayo had watched with amusement as his daughter badgered the artists with questions.

The carver, a man by the name of Akin, had brought a small collection of his works, including some statuettes of former colonial officers. The inspiration for these, he explained, came from a great uncle who enjoyed recounting stories, particularly about his boss, named Lugard. When Tayo heard this, he could hardly contain his excitement. Might this be Lord Lugard? Many books had been written on the legendary British High Commissioner to Nigeria, but never from the perspective of Nigerians who knew and worked with him – so if this old man could still remember stories, it was certainly very exciting.

When Akin offered to take Tayo to see the uncle, Tayo jumped at the opportunity. Miriam was less keen, complaining that Tayo was not spending enough time with them, but Tayo argued that this was a once-in-a-lifetime experience that he wasn't going to miss. Besides, since the uncle was an old man, he may not be around much longer.

"And isn't your mother also old?" Miriam retorted, reminding him that his trip would delay their planned visit to Ibadan.

"But what difference does a day or two make?" Tayo would not be dissuaded.

The next day, Tayo set off with Akin, on the four-hour drive to the old man's village of Atan. They left early in the morning, avoiding the worst of Lagos traffic and the accompanying street vendors who stuck to cars like magnets, thrusting everything from boxes of rat poison to French perfumes through open windows in hopes of a sale. As they drove out of

Lagos beyond the lagoon and the freeways, the landscape changed to one of dense rainforest, which gradually thinned as they progressed northward. It was the rainy season and mounds of rich, red earth lay by the side of the roads. For miles around, the landscape showed no sign of habitation. Only a few people walked by the side of the road, some of them children who waved excitedly at the passing cars. What a beautiful country, Tayo thought, admiring the vast open space.

They drove by roadside bukas that sold bush meat and firewood, and once they stopped to buy some peanuts and dodo ikiri, which they ate in the car as they continued on their journey. The drive was peaceful, except for the occasional crazy driver who would overtake on bends. Mostly these were lorry drivers transporting farm produce, some of which would drop off the sides of the trucks as they sped by. The vehicles sported popular phrases painted on the back and sides in bright, florid letters, large enough for even the short-sighted to read – *Allah Saves, Jesus Saves, The Almighty Saves* – as if this would guarantee them safe passage. Akin was playing some juju music on the crackly car radio and after a while they began to speak of Akin's plans to move to Europe. He intended to spend just a day in the village before driving on to Illorin for an exhibition of his work, with the hope of meeting a rich European or American sponsor.

They arrived at the village in the middle of the day when the sun was fierce and people sought shade from their work in the fields. The old man had gone out, so Akin went to find him, leaving Tayo to wait at home. He sat on the grass beneath a tree drinking warm Coca-Cola and eating shelled groundnuts given to him by the woman of the house. After a while some young boys returned from school and started playing football close to where Tayo sat. They used Sprite bottles as goalposts, reminding Tayo that he had done the same as a child, and his mind then wandered on to other memories of his childhood.

He recalled having to wake up early when the cock crowed to do his chores around the house, then bathe and eat. In those days everybody walked to school so they needed a hearty breakfast that their mothers cooked. Sometimes it was Quaker oats, corn porridge, beans with yam, or sometimes *akara* and, if it rained, Father used to drive them to school in his Morris Minor; otherwise they went by foot along city paths and across the Ogunpa River. During the rainy season, Tayo remembered that the river would sometimes rise so high they would have to remove their shoes and school uniform, place them in a canvas bag on their heads, and then wade through water that was occasionally chest-high. School ended early in the afternoon, as it apparently still did since these boys were out playing. Perhaps they also stopped at roadside *bukas* on their walk home to buy refreshments such as groundnuts, oranges and coconut milk before coming home to play football.

As Tayo continued to watch he thought again of his future son and felt remorse for being impatient with Miriam. Pregnant women were entitled to be irritable, and he shouldn't have dismissed her concern for his mother. How many husbands could boast, as he did, of a wife who loved and cared for his mother just as much as her own. He would have to apologise when he got back and now, as he waited, he picked up a twig and drew a grid in the sand with three headings.

F (for family) *W* (for work) *O* (for other)

Beneath family he wrote the word, *time*. For all his denials to Miriam, he knew that he had been spending too many hours working and not enough at home. There were also other things to change. He had fallen into a bad habit of cutting Miriam out of discussions by referring to topics or people with whom she was not familiar. He did it as a way of asserting his intellectual interests because Miriam rarely asked about them and, when she did, he found her questions superficial. But he knew that to talk above her, to simply make her more aware of what she didn't know, was not the way to solicit interest, and certainly wasn't strengthening their relationship.

No doubt there were also things she would like to share with him. Perhaps, for her sake, he ought to make an effort to attend church again and in this way they would share more in common. Perhaps it might make him less nervous about growing old with her and, even if it didn't, it would surely be good for the children. Children were, after all, the one thing he and Miriam did share in common, and always would.

On the work front things were going well. Being Chair of the Department of History was a considerable achievement for someone his age. He was proud of his staff and of the projects he had started, but he still needed to find ways of limiting his administrative duties in order to devote more hours to research.

Other? What should he write here? He should perhaps increase his physical activities now that he had officially entered middle-age. And then there was the perennial question of what he had achieved at this supposed halfway point of his life. In one sense he knew he had every reason to be proud of being Chair, but he was Chair of a department that was chronically understaffed. As a result, neither he nor his colleagues had been able to make their mark as scholars in the wider world of academia. The government had promised a review of higher education but these were empty promises. Ike was one of the Ministers of Education, but had done nothing. Tayo remembered their last encounter on a flight to Abuja, during which he had challenged Ike on the situation of their country but he had refused to discuss his party's policies, instead saying that Tayo was unreasonable in his expectations. But it was Ike, as far as Tayo was concerned, who had lost his way.

Tayo was still thinking of Ike when Akin returned with the uncle.

The uncle was indeed elderly, as Tayo had been told, and

looked frail, but he had a youthful twinkle in his eye as one might expect of a storyteller. Greetings were exchanged, and soon others from the village arrived to sit with the uncle and Tayo. They talked about the village and the season's crops, while the women pounded yams and washed pots nearby in preparation for the evening meal. A bowl of water was brought for the men to rinse their hands, and then two large steaming plates of pounded yam and *egusi* soup were placed in front of them. The men took turns, rolling balls of yam between their fingers and dipping them in the stew with its large pieces of chicken that rested at the bottom of the pot. More meat than usual, Tayo guessed, in honour of him as their guest. They ate by the light of two kerosene lamps that attracted flying ants, which folded their wings and began crawling round and round the base of each light. Once the meal was finished, Tayo hoped to ask the uncle some questions, but the old man had started a game of *ayo* with his friends and it was soon time to sleep. Tayo resigned himself to waiting until the next day and went to sleep recalling all that he could from a recent publication of Lugard's diaries.

By the next morning Tayo was keen to begin talking but, by then, word had spread to a neighbouring village that a professor had come, and visitors besieged the house. Men and women came with their children, or photographs of children, wanting to see what the professor could do to guarantee them places in universities. There was little Tayo could do except show interest and concern and by the end of the day he was exhausted. He wished that Ike and all the other government officials could see the desperation in these people's faces. The only hope for them was the future of a son or daughter, and that was tenuous. Tayo tried not to be downhearted, but it was hard not to despair when it was his generation, the generation of Nigeria's Independence, who were failing the country.

Tayo still had not spoken with the old man, nor had he contacted his family to tell them he would be returning later than planned but he was not concerned about the latter; delays were always to be expected – 'no news is good news' Mama used to say.

Eventually, on the second day, Tayo found a way of walking alone with the old man.

"So, what shall I tell you about my old boss, Lord Lugard?" the old man smiled as he spoke. "I can inform you that I commenced employment with my boss in the year of 1912. You know that was the time when *oga* returned to Nigeria after being governor in Hong Kong? You follow?"

"Yes sir," Tayo nodded.

Occasionally the old man spoke to Tayo in Yoruba, but his preference was English in a way that reminded Tayo of his father. He spoke in a formal and somewhat stylised English with a penchant for the words: *you follow*.

"But even before the time whereby I started employment with Lord Lugard and Lady Lugard, my father was in Lord Lugard's service before me. Baba was the one who accompanied Lord Lugard to Borgu to claim it away from the French. You follow?"

"Yes sir," Tayo nodded, bemused by the man's obvious admiration for his old boss and wondering, as he continued recounting his stories, how much of his English had been learnt from Lugard.

"Even sometimes, he would ask my advice on government matters, especially if there were no other white people around, that was when he would ask us questions. *Eh-henh*."

Tayo nodded, finding this particularly interesting, as it was a side of Lugard not reflected in the diaries.

"And I'll tell you something else," the old man smiled, "my boss liked our women."

"*Eh-enh?*" Tayo smiled. "Is that so?"

"Oh yes," the man grinned. "You know it started even before his wife came to this country. He used to ask my father to find him some good woman and to this day there are some half-caste people in this Nigeria who come from him."

Tayo laughed, his mind now racing with questions as the man continued to recount details of his time with Lugard. As he talked, Tayo found himself thinking of his mother. The more he listened to people of her generation, the more he realised how little he knew of Mama's life. He thought of Vanessa too and how good she must now be at these sorts of interviews. The walk had taken them around the old man's fields and they were now retracing their steps.

"I have one more thing to show you," the man said, as they approached the house.

He disappeared into a back room and emerged minutes later with purple material draped over his arms. Tayo thought he was bringing church robes, but then as he drew closer he peered in amazement at what lay in front of him. It was Lugard's official robe – the one he apparently so detested wearing for meetings with local dignitaries but had been required to wear by His Majesty.

"Keep the robe safely," Tayo urged, "and don't let any British museum take it from you. Whatever someone offers to pay, you can be sure it won't be enough."

By the time Tayo left the village it was late-afternoon and he looked forward to returning to the Ogundeles' to rest. Three nights of sleeping rough on dirt floors and bathing in cold water had taken its toll and he dozed in the back seat. He dreamt of a proper bed, twenty-four-hour air-conditioning and the sauna that awaited him in the luxury of Uncle Kayode's home. The beautiful heart of darkness, Tayo smiled to himself. He would shower and then sit outside in the gardens, next to the pool. Or perhaps he would retire to their guest cottage and lie with Miriam.

Perhaps she would be in the mood to make love, but that was rare these days. Even when she hadn't been pregnant, their lovemaking had grown infrequent with the exception of those days of hoped-for fertility – and how he hated the precision with which she made love then. For the rest of the time, her excuse was tiredness, but even on holidays she seemed to have little desire for him. Perhaps it was biological. He knew he was not the only husband to suffer from a wife's abstinence, yet he did not go outside to feed his physical desires as others did. He had considered it, but never wanted to risk it – more for Kemi's sake than for anything else. He dozed off again and dreamt of Helene's cooking and then Helene turned into Vanessa, and the house was no longer in Lagos but in Dakar. He was lying with Vanessa in the guest cottage and kissing her when the dream stopped. The car had broken down.

Several more hours were wasted by the side of the road in the stifling heat, waiting for the vehicle to be repaired. Tayo stayed awake for the rest of the journey knowing that he would have to direct the driver to the house. At least they had managed to avoid the worst of Lagos traffic, but as they drove closer Tayo was surprised to see the gates wide open and cars parked everywhere – inside and outside. Was Uncle Kayode holding some sort of meeting or party at his home? Was someone ill? Had someone died? One of the guards ran to the car.

"*Oga sah!*"

"What is it?" Tayo asked, quickly opening his door and ignoring the driver's plea for money. Miriam was running towards him from the house with brother Remi beside her.

"Where have you been since Monday? We've been trying to contact you," she shouted. "Mama is dead," she sobbed.

"Mama?" The words reeled in his head as he gripped Miriam's arms for support.

"Where were you?" she sobbed. "Everyone was trying to find you."

*

In keeping with Muslim tradition, the family had buried Mama's body within 24 hours, not waiting for Tayo to return, but they had delayed the funeral party for him, as well as for others returning to Ibadan from overseas. When older people died, the grieving took place at the burial. After the funeral, sometimes a few days later as was the case for Mama, there was a party to celebrate the deceased's life. Now that Tayo had returned, the party would be arranged and he and each of his brothers and sisters would be expected to prepare food in Mama's house, and serve it to the guests who would arrive throughout the day.

Miriam had already chosen the special *aso ebi* for the family to wear, which bore a picture of Mama. Musicians would come and they would write a song for Mama, singing her praises and reflecting on the life she had lived as well as on her good fortune to be blessed with many children. There would be dancing, but Tayo had decided he would not dance.

Mama had died on her way to Lagos. That Sunday night she had asked her driver to take her there, and as they made their way on the darkened highway they hit a pothole, and the driver lost control. Nobody knew what had made Mama travel to Lagos at night and Tayo blamed himself, even when Uncle Kayode took him aside and urged him not to. Over and over again, he replayed the events of those days in his head. If only he had not listened to the conversation with Kemi and the artists then he would never have been tempted to leave. If only he had listened to Miriam. If only he had put family first, and it didn't help when people told him not to blame himself; the more they told him this, the more he did.

Chapter 24

Six months after Mama died, the coup that most Nigerians were expecting came to pass. All across the nation heavy glass frames were taken down from walls and pictures of the President were updated. Out came the man in white civilian robes, and back went the green military fatigues. White and green – Nigeria's colours. This routine was well-known by now, and would grow all too dismally familiar for Nigeria in the years to come, but at first people celebrated the return of a strong military that promised to stamp out corruption. At that time anything promised to be an improvement on the nation's failed experiment with democracy. However, soon the optimism vanished and university students took to the streets in protest. Months turned into a year and, with each successive wave of discontent, students demonstrated, campuses were closed, people were arrested, and some died during the protests. Many professors tried to stay out of the fray, but Tayo empathised with his students and refused to be intimidated. He vowed to himself that as long as he lived, he would work to make things better even if it meant giving clandestine assistance to student activists, which he did when students wanted explanations for controversial government policies. Armed with Tayo's notes they wrote convincing arguments against government plans, printed them on flyers and plastered them all over campus. For Tayo, it became a surreal existence, leaving no time to focus on his academic research. His days were spent either with his students or in his office preparing documents such as the one he was working on now for a British Council conference.

The theme of the conference was the future of Nigerian universities and the message Tayo wished to convey was simple – universities were collapsing and urgent help was needed from the government. The problem, however, was how to frame the message in such a way as to be taken seriously by government officials as well as by donor agencies likely to be in attendance. Tayo was tired of walking a diplomatic tightrope in front of his nation's army officers, many of whom were half his age, but what else could he do? If the army officials perceived that he was criticising them, Tayo knew they could become recalcitrant and little progress would be made, not to speak of the possible personal danger it might put him in. And so, without explicitly allocating blame, he intended to address the real and potential damage brought to a nation's economy by dysfunctional universities. He placed the lid on his fountain pen, squeezed it shut, and stood up ready to rehearse his speech, when he heard a knock.

"Are you busy?"

It was Miriam and yes, he was busy, but how could he admit this when he had already exceeded the time that he had promised her.

"Look at you," he exclaimed, admiring the results of what he knew had taken several hours in the salon. "You look beautiful, my darling." The fine black braids hung in a perfect semi-circle around the back and sides of her head. "No cooking tonight, I'm taking you out."

He thought of taking her to Hill Station for a special meal and a romantic night, but before he could say any more she was asking him if he knew who else had decided to leave the country.

"Who?" Tayo enquired cautiously, knowing that with each new departure Miriam became more convinced that they should also leave.

"The Gordons."

"Really? Is this to go and look after her parents?"

"No. She has sisters in England."

"Maybe her siblings aren't too responsible," he replied, tapping the desk impatiently with his notes.

"Even Kwame is leaving, Tayo."

"Well, I always suspected he was bogus – always running away from problems," Tayo replied, not meaning what he said but the direction of Miriam's conversation irritated him, and he didn't like her using names to try to change his mind.

"Tayo, all our friends are leaving. The Adewales, the Wisemans, the Shahs, even your beloved writers, Soyinka and Achebe, have left. Everyone is going, yet still we stay. For what?" She stepped away from the door and stood straight.

He shook his head, quietly placing his notes back on the desk. 'Why now, Miriam?' he thought. 'You know this is an important speech. Can't you just allow me to finish?' In the old days, Miriam used to listen to him and had looked up to him, trusted his judgement, but not now.

"Omotayo, look, just go and look in the kitchen. There's no rice, no bread, no eggs, no sugar," Miriam spoke quickly, rapidly ticking off the items, one-by-one, on her fingers. "There's nothing. Nothing! You can't even teach because of rioting and strikes."

"Miriam, please," he said, watching as she raised her hands above her head in a gesture of despair. "We've discussed this so many times before. Times are hard, but we can't all run away. It's not just the students. I also have responsibilities to the Union."

"And responsibilities to us? What of your responsibilities to your wife? To your child? To our relatives?"

She did not mention her nephews by name, but he knew what she was thinking. It was one of those issues that they would never resolve. He felt that he was doing all he could to support both extended families as well as so many of his students, but she didn't see it this way and wouldn't let him finish explaining.

"The hospital hasn't paid me for months," she interrupted, "and you? When did the university last pay you? When was the last time lecturers received a salary? When was the last time you were given a sabbatical, or even a little money to present work at your beloved international conferences?"

"But it's not about pay." He struggled not to raise his voice against hers.

"Isn't it? So when are you going to start driving a taxi or selling *dodo* and *garri* in the market just like your colleagues in order to support us? And what happens when Kemi's school is closed? All the time you're thinking only of your students or the past."

Tayo brought his fingers to his temples. The nagging and shouting was like a scene from television, straight out of *Village Headmaster*. Why couldn't they just have calm, reasoned discussions?

"Miriam, you know it won't come to this. You know that the money from my books provides for us."

"And that's supposed to last forever? Omotayo, why can't we move? Just for a short time at least, until Kemi is settled. You could be writing abroad, teaching abroad. You would even influence things here at home more by being out of the country, but you get so obsessed as though you're married to this cause."

"Miriam, I can't go yet, not yet. Look, I'm trying to write this speech, to show the government what has happened to the universities. Everything is crumbling and this is our last chance. We can't let our country sink into utter self-destruction. It's our last chance, don't you see? Just look at the universities – ever since 1974 the budget for higher education has fallen, yet the number of universities has been expanding. Is it any wonder that –"

"Why?" she interrupted.

"Why? Because they're following IMF guidelines and…"

"I'm not talking about that. I don't care about IMF, World Bank, whatever! All I want to know is why can't you move? Remember what you said when Buhari came to power. What did he achieve?"

Miriam always had to bring it to this – the drama and the shouting.

"It was a bloodless coup, Miriam, and a successful war against indiscipline. You remember how the neighbourhoods were clean, people queued up in an orderly fashion and arrived at work on time, and –"

"Omotayo! What are you talking about? Just listen to me. I'm not your student. I don't care about that."

"Well, you should care, and anyway you asked the question."

"What question? I didn't ask you to tell me about Buhari."

"Yes you did," Tayo sighed, thinking that she would soon start crying to make him feel guilty.

"I asked you why you couldn't leave this place."

"Miriam, how can you expect me to walk away from everything – my work, my students, our country – and establish myself abroad?"

"Why not?" she shouted, clasping her hands above the braids and squeezing her face between her elbows.

Tayo shut his eyes, and in that moment despised her.

"Look, I belong here, Miriam. These are the things I care about and must fight for. I don't have any other choice."

"And you think Babangida is suddenly going to change his mind on the adjustment program?" Miriam let go of her head and shook her hands angrily in the air.

"No, but I'm more useful here than abroad. Everyone is running away; I can't also run."

"And you believe these military men won't touch you because you're a professor, Chair of History, and big Oxford man? Look at what they did to Dele Giwa."

"Miriam, Miriam, please," he begged, walking towards her.

"No, don't touch me. Don't touch me. There's nothing here. We're wasting our time. And if we'd left earlier we wouldn't have lost the baby."

"Miriam," he pulled her gently towards him to stop her crying. "Miriam, we don't know that."

She too had heard the doctors say that the chances for such a premature baby would have been slim anywhere in the world. Still, she insisted that access to first-world equipment would have saved the child. At the very least, she had argued, had she not been living under so much daily stress she would not have gone into early labour. He stroked her arms and kissed her gently on her forehead.

"You've never been good at moving," she sighed, pulling away.

And with that, Miriam rubbed out all the goodwill and love that had been so hard for him to show in the first place. Had he not relocated to Jos because she was eager to come here? It was Miriam who argued that Jos would be better for the family – a more temperate climate than Ibadan, a good international school for Kemi, and on and on and on. Moving had not been his choice.

"But I did move – for you – didn't I?"

"You make it sound like a sacrifice."

"Damn you Miriam! I've always sacrificed for you from the very beginning. Have you forgotten who stuck with you when you fell pregnant? I didn't blame you and I didn't leave you when you lost the baby. So don't talk to me about sacrifices."

"Well if that's how you feel –"

"Miriam, look, I'm sorry, I just…" but before he had finished, she had slammed the door, and his neat stack of notes flew up and scattered. One sheet escaped and fluttered off the desk, skimming his bare foot. He reached down for it and shook off the coating of *harmattan* dust. How was he supposed to concentrate now? He scrunched the sheet of paper into a ball and tossed it angrily at the door. What was wrong with the woman! Wasn't it good enough that he had promised to stay for another year? Why did it always have to be so difficult?

Chapter 25

1990

Tayo sat at the Hill Station bar, remembering the night he and Miriam had gone there for drinks before going to the Chinese restaurant next door. He remembered sharing hot spring rolls, and each of them claiming to be better than the other with their chopsticks when neither of them could manage to bring food to their mouths without if falling off the sticks first. They had laughed a lot that night, like new lovers, and then went home to make love so passionately that it had given him hope. But that was then. Now Kemi and Miriam had left him for a life in England. Tayo sighed, pushing aside the saucer of groundnuts and shaking his head to the offer of another beer. Music pulsated from speakers half-hidden by fat bottles of Bacardi and Scotch, and the barmen sang along to a tune that Tayo recognised.

"Who's this artist?" Tayo asked.

"Michael Jackson, sir," the barman answered.

Tayo nodded. Yes, it was Kemi's music, although now that he was a frequent visitor to bars perhaps it was more accurate to say that pop songs had also become his music. He presumed Kemi still listened to Mr Jackson, but that too might have changed.

Two businessmen sat next to him sipping their lagers and debating, in hushed tones, the likely pros and cons of import-export business in the 1990s. Tayo guessed they were speaking quietly so that no one might swipe their ideas, but at times their excitement seemed to get the better of them, and he caught snatches of conversation. One believed in importing electric generators on the basis of predicted increased power shortages, which begged the question: how could Nigeria's Electrical Power Authority possibly get any worse? Already NEPA was off more than on, and hence the joke – 'Never Expect Power Always.'

"By 1994, I'm telling you," the man exclaimed excitedly, waving an index finger in front of his friend's nose, "I'm telling you that so many people… in fact I can even say ninety per cent of Nigerians will be begging for generator."

The friend seemed unconvinced, arguing instead for the importation of Mercedes Benz spare parts and the export of Nigerian curios and thorn carvings. Tayo smiled sadly to himself at what their conversation suggested about a country in which continuing chaos and greed were taken for granted. Had his father still been alive, he would have been shocked. Father had always thought that the best investments were in land, so much so that Tayo remembered it featuring in their last conversation. They had been touring the family farm, walking slowly because of Father's weakened state, past the rows of maize, yams and sweet potatoes. Tayo missed his father; now there was no one older and wiser to look to for advice. But perhaps it was better that Father had not lived to see his country fall apart while the rest of the world emerged from the tyranny and fear of the Cold War.

Of course there were always a few things Nigerians could feel proud of. Soyinka had won the Nobel Prize, Okri had claimed the Booker, and Father would certainly have enjoyed all the sporting successes. Who could forget that splendid African Cup final of 1980 when the Green Eagles creamed Algeria 3-0! But such glories could not compensate for all that was wrong with the nation. And it wasn't just Nigeria, but the whole continent that seemed to be suffering. Tayo looked wearily beyond the bar to the open doors leading to the pool. The sky had darkened to a backdrop for thunder and menacing claps of lightening. Outside, families were hurriedly gathering their towels and belongings before the first raindrops fell. Waiters dashed about, collecting abandoned deckchairs before sprinting back through the bar to the main foyer. Some of the guests would be staying at the hotel, but many, a mix of Africans and Europeans, would be locals visiting for the afternoon, the way Tayo used to come with Miriam and Kemi. He watched people running from the rain and spotted a teenage girl whose confident stride reminded him of Kemi. Tayo smiled at her, but she didn't see, or else had been taught to be wary of strangers. All day long it had been like this – one event after another, causing him to seriously doubt the wisdom of staying on while his family had left for England. It began in the morning with the broken water pump, which the mechanics insisted could not be fixed without spare parts from China. The next headache came when the houseboy announced that he would be returning home to Kafanchan for the burial of a relative and then, as if this were not enough, he had just wasted precious time with Mr Peters.

It all started when Simon wrote to Tayo at the beginning of the year. They had not been in touch since their Oxford days, but Simon had kept abreast of Tayo's news through the *Balliol Record* and, when he was appointed Chairman of a prestigious London Foundation, he immediately contacted Tayo. Tayo was thrilled to receive the letter with its mention of possible funding for his university. Foundations generally marched to the tune of the World Bank and IMF, arguing that what Africa needed was vocational and not academic education, so Simon's Foundation seemed like a breath of much-needed fresh air. Contacts were eagerly established and arrangements made for Mr Peters, Simon's Africa Director, to visit Nigeria.

In preparation for the meeting, Tayo had put together all the relevant papers and statistics. He had even cancelled plans to travel to New York where he was to have received an award for his new book. And this was all for the sake of a meeting with Mr Peters, which turned out to be a waste of time, so much so that Tayo wondered why the man had bothered to come over here when his mind was made up concerning any donations the Foundation would make. He offered second-hand books (none of which were requested by the university) as well as old software programs that were useless without the computers the university so desperately needed.

Tayo leant against the bar reflecting on the fact that he had stayed in Nigeria in order to help the university and his students, yet in reality he had provided little help. Last month he had received a suitcase full of cash, an anonymous bribe from the authorities to stop him complaining about government policies. He had refused it, but now the threats were less veiled and he could hear Miriam warning him that he would lose his job.

Tayo glanced at his watch, waiting for his students to arrive and wondering what he would tell them. He would have to admit that he had been misled into believing that the Foundation would support their graduate study. And what was he going to say to Simon? Tayo pushed his seat a little further from the bar for a better look outside and saw that the rain had stopped. Workers were busy wiping the plastic deck chairs dry and covering them again in green slipcovers. With no guests outside, the men sang loudly, clicking their fingers and rolling their shoulders to Bob Marley. *Baby don't worry, about a ting/Cos every little ting, gonna be all right...*

Tayo swivelled on his stool to look back inside. Behind the bar was a recessed lounge with leather seats and pouffes, a more comfortable area to drink and chat. Tayo noticed two Lebanese men with Nigerian women many years younger than them. The girls wore mini-skirts and strapless tops, so were probably prostitutes Tayo guessed. Why else would they be with overweight, middle-aged men? It was simply a question of economics and the amount of *naira* that could be extracted.

His gaze lingered momentarily and then returned to the woman he had noticed first who sat on her own, drinking a Fanta. She was white and wore a tie-dye dress and sandals that marked her as either someone who lived in Jos and dressed in the way of locals, or perhaps a tourist. She was reading until one of the waiters approached her and stood before her with his tray held loosely in one hand behind his back. In the background Bob Marley sang, *I don't wanna wait in vain for your love.* Tayo smiled at the irony, or perhaps the set-up as the woman looked up. She tucked her hair behind her ear, and Tayo saw that she was younger than he had initially thought. Young and beautiful, the way he remembered Vanessa.

The waiter lingered, but when the woman returned to her book, he took his cue and left. She wore a wedding band, which made Tayo wonder whether her husband was Nigerian or European. There were not many Anglo-Nigerian couples around these days; most had divorced, or left the country. Again, Tayo thought of Vanessa. He drummed his fingers on the cardboard beer mat and nodded to the new beat. It was Fela's famous *Lady*, in praise of the African woman's ability to follow her man, dance and show respect, rather than donning modern independent ways. The beat was catchy and the lyrics provocative. Vintage Fela. Tayo had never taken the words of the song seriously but, today, because he was thinking about women, he gave it more thought.

His own African woman had not always followed him and he had never demanded that Miriam do so. Or had he? Certainly when they first met, Miriam had been more eager to please him than in later years and perhaps subconsciously he had thought that Miriam would strike a perfect balance between the modern and the traditional in a way that he had never been sure of with Vanessa. But in the end, she had done her own thing anyway. He sighed wearily, wishing he could see Vanessa again, just for old times' sake. If she came to Jos he would show her all the scenic spots – the reservoir, the market places, the rocky outcrops and, of course, Jos museum. He imagined that she would enjoy explaining the significance of the art to him and he would marvel at her knowledge. They would eat at The Bight of Benin, hands touching beneath the tablecloth, and they might even stay here in Hill Station's guest rooms, which always looked charming from the outside – small cottages with wooden exterior beams. Tayo pictured the rooms with large beds, white linen and soft feather pillows. Perhaps the rooms also had plush carpeting, air-conditioning and maybe even a fireplace for the cooler harmattan months so that when she came…

Tayo shook his head as a reprimand to his flight of fantasy. He looked again at the woman and considered going to say hello, but then someone else appeared. The man looked older than her, perhaps in his fifties or sixties. He greeted the bartenders in Hausa and, from the enthusiastic replies, Tayo guessed the man to be a regular and probably wealthy. No doubt a high-ranking military officer in civilian clothes, who were the rich ones these days. He wore white shorts, a blue polo-neck shirt and loafers of a style and quality that looked imported. The couple embraced, she shyly, he less so. He grasped her buttocks and kissed her on the lips. The businessmen had stopped talking and the barman was no longer humming as the couple came to the bar and ordered two beers. Tayo was thinking of how things used to be with Miriam when he felt a tap on his shoulder and jumped.

"Professor Ajayi."

"Hawa," he replied, hoping she had not seen him observing the other couple.

He bought her a drink, apologising for Mr Peter's absence.

"What happened?" Hawa touched his hand lightly, startling Tayo with her suggestion of intimacy. It was a young hand, smooth and cool to the touch.

"Are you okay?" she asked softly.

"I'm fine." He placed his other hand on top of hers to pat it gently as best as he could, in a fatherly, professorial way.

Chapter 26

He had come to his office early that afternoon to mark papers submitted the previous year. Much of 1993 had been disrupted by strikes and campus closures, and he hoped against all odds that the New Year would be different. He asked his students to consider the Indian National Congress in the 1940s – its spokesmen Nehru, Gandhi, and Jinnah, and their respective views regarding religious tensions in India at the time. He saw many parallels between the Indian and Nigerian experience, and hoped his students would find the same, extrapolate and discuss, but the papers were disappointing. At best, students summarized text and, at worst, like the one he now read, they plagiarised.

It frustrated him to find undergraduates writing in this way, but he understood why. Students could not be expected to study when the physical conditions in which they lived were so appalling. Rooms, designed to house two, now took six or more and the library, once well stocked and up-to-date, resembled a museum with a handful of torn and dusty exhibits. And this was why he felt so compelled to write more and more against the injustices that he saw all around him. His family thought him reckless and Bisi sent him several angry letters warning that his outspokenness could endanger not only himself but also others. He felt tempted to write back and tell her to save her anger for her drunken husband, a much greater menace to family than he could ever be, but he knew Bisi wouldn't listen to him, she never did. He knew things were dangerous; she didn't need to tell him this and he was careful; a new decree gave soldiers the right to detain suspects without charge, and he had no intention of disappearing without seeing his Kemi again.

Tayo straightened the remaining stack of papers and stood up to stretch. He glanced at his watch. It was late and his head hurt; time to go home. Not that there was anyone waiting for him there. These days even his brothers and sisters had stopped asking him to take care of their children and Hawa was away visiting relatives in Abuja. Though he missed Hawa's company, he did not miss her demands. She was bright but immature and petulant at times. He had begun to wish that she would find someone else – someone she could marry, which seemed to be the thing foremost on her mind. Tayo ran his hands over the faded pictures that hung above his desk. Here was an old postcard he had brought back from Oxford with the colours of the *Aureol* now looking brown rather than the original bright white and yellow. He had read somewhere that the *Aureol* made its last voyage around West Africa in 1974, which also marked the time when Tayo saw the hopes of African nationalism begin to fizzle. Perhaps the ship's departure was a sign of times to come, which would make an interesting story for his students, and more gripping maybe than the Indian National Congress. One could start with the making of the ship and the British company that built it. For what purposes were these ships constructed and what of the slave ships that preceded them? The *Aureol* was now laid up in Eleusis Bay waiting to be broken up for scrap metal. Soon it would be gone and another marker of West Africa's history would be buried along with all the stories and desires engendered by the ship.

Tayo imagined that few would remember the way white colonial officers once looked so condescendingly at other white travellers, and how they in turn glared back in contempt at those pretending to be the African Raj. Few would remember the shock of Africans watching Europeans getting drunk at sunrise, and the even greater shock of finding some of their own providing cheap entertainment at ports, diving like dogs playing fetch-it for coins tossed into the water by the Europeans. Perhaps it was better that some of these memories be buried. Nobody knew where the ship would be taken for its final and ignoble death, but the guess was the ship-breaking shores of Alang, which brought the story back to India. Tayo sighed as he put down the postcard and looked at all the other pictures pinned to the wall – the rest were Kemi creations hanging loosely on dry bits of cellotape. "My child, my dear child," he murmured to himself. "You are grown up now. What are you doing on this Friday night? Are you with your mother or have you gone out with friends? Look after your mother, my child. See that she is happy until I come." He sighed again, wishing that he could talk with his daughter, but they hardly spoke these days – not in letters, not even on the phone. Miriam told him that Kemi felt abandoned, but he never knew whether she was projecting her own feelings, or whether this was really how Kemi felt. Sometimes he thought of writing to his daughter, to reassure her and explain that he was not abandoning her, but how could he write of these things when Kemi had not mentioned them herself? Tayo shut his door and locked it. Five years had passed since Miriam and Kemi left, and two years since he had seen them last. "Too long," he muttered, walking down the corridor and then outside where he caught the last glimmer of iridescent light. Only in Jos had he known such shimmering light after the rains, which cheered him slightly as he nodded absently to the night watchmen.

"Professor!" The guard jumped from his seat to salute.

"Goodnight," Tayo replied, shivering a little.

The temperature had suddenly dropped.

When he started the car he noticed that the petrol gauge was low – a reminder to queue for petrol tomorrow. He would wake up early, at some ungodly hour, 4.00 or 5.00 in the morning, to drive to Dogun Dutse Mobil station where he heard there was fuel. How crazy that a country exporting millions of gallons of oil each day had none for its own people!

Tayo shook his head. It throbbed now, and his arms felt like lead weights. He rested his head for a moment on the steering wheel, but it didn't help – still the same searing pain. Further down the road he saw a roadblock, one of many popping up all over the place these days. Sometimes the soldiers would just peer into the car and wave you on, but usually they wanted money and would delay a driver with questions, holding out for the biggest possible *dash*. Tayo recalled a time when this sort of thing never happened, when bribes were not the norm, and professors were treated with respect.

"Good evening," Tayo said, winding down his window.

"Good evening sah," replied the soldier, wielding a rifle. "*Where you dey go?*"

"Home."

"*Make I see driva licence,*" the soldier barked.

Tayo took it from the glove compartment and handed it to the man, who looked at it then walked off. Another soldier returned with the licence.

"*Professor. We go take you for questioning, now, now.*"

"For what?"

"*You no fit hear?* For questioning." The soldier pointed his rifle into the half-open window.

Tayo hesitated.

"Get out," the soldier barked, gesturing with his gun for Tayo to step out of the car.

"I refuse to get out of this vehicle without being told why."

"*COMOT,*" the soldier shouted, forcibly pulling Tayo from his seat.

Tayo looked quickly around to see if he knew anyone in the cars behind him, but there was no one so he surrendered his keys as ordered and got into the back seat sandwiched between two soldiers, one of whom clamped a hand around the back of his neck and forcibly thrust his head down. As they sped away Tayo prayed for the first time in years. The soldier had loosened his grip so he could breathe, but he dared not raise his face.

He tried to guess from the turns they took and the condition of the road where they were taking him, but he quickly became disorientated and began to think of how long it would be before people noticed he was missing. The houseboy would not raise the alarm and nor would his family, who were so used to him being away. Perhaps someone at the university might notice his absence, but then there was so much chaos there. He began to think that he should have thought of something earlier; his reactions had not been quick enough. Would Hawa worry if she did not hear from him? His only hope was that someone had seen him arrested. Fellow writers would notice within a day or two that he was quiet, but a day or two might be too long.

The car stopped suddenly and the soldier holding his neck let go, allowing him to sit up and get out. It was dark outside and ominously quiet. Tayo made out several rectangular buildings that looked like school buildings or dormitories. Army barracks. One had lights on and that seemed to be where they were taking him. He thought of making a dash for it, but to where? A foolish idea. They led him in, releasing his arms as they marched him to a room where another soldier sat behind a desk. The men saluted and left.

"Sit," the soldier ordered as he grinned a gap-toothed smile.

There was nowhere to sit.

"Sit!" the man bellowed.

So Tayo knelt on the ground, crossing his legs to hide his trembling.

"Yes, that's right," the soldier laughed. "I'm the professor now. Sit on the floor like we used to at nursery school. Remember those days?"

"You have no right to detain me," Tayo snapped.

"Let me remind you Professor that here you have no power

and I would advise you to watch that tongue of yours. You hear? YOU HEAR?" He banged both fists on the desk.

"Yes," Tayo muttered, squeezing his legs.

"You have been warned to stop your incendiary activities and yet you have not."

"What incendiary activities?" Tayo asked, anger making him brave.

"Are you trying to mock me?"

"No," Tayo answered quickly, watching as the soldier thumped a pistol onto the table.

"Good. Much better. I think you know very well about the articles you are publishing and those lectures you are giving. Who is giving you the right to be disrespectful?"

"It's not a question of respect, it's a question of –"

"A question of what?" the soldier shouted. He stood up and walked towards Tayo, his boots stopping just inches from Tayo's knees. "A question of what?" he sneered.

"It's a question of wanting the best for our country," Tayo replied as calmly as he could.

"You think we don't know best?"

"I think –"

"No, you don't think," the soldier interrupted, walking back to his desk to retrieve his pistol. "Anything more to say?"

Tayo shook his head.

"So I am going to call my men to remove you, but if we hear one more thing," he lifted the gun and pointed it at Tayo, "PA!" he shouted, laughing as Tayo jumped.

Then came the beating.

"Please, please! Please don't," Tayo cried, covering his head. "I beg you please," he pleaded. The soldier nearest him watched for a moment then struck him suddenly with his pistol, sending him crashing to the floor, but not before his face struck the table in front of him. He felt sharp, crushing pains in his side and back – kicks. He tried screaming, but nothing came and as he looked up something bright and strangely beautiful exploded in his head. When he opened his eyes he was cowering in a corner and there was nobody else in the room. "I won't write, I won't write any more," he whispered, cradling his knees until he heard someone coming, and then he clenched his fists, bracing himself. The footsteps stopped. "Please," Tayo pleaded.

"*Oga sah, na me, Nuhu.*"

Tayo looked up and saw it was the houseboy.

"*Oga-sah, you dey for house. Na malaria wey dey make you dream one kind.*"

It slowly dawned on Tayo that he was in his own home again.

"Where are the soldiers?" Tayo whispered, hiding his face behind his hands.

"*Dem bring you come for house when dem see say you no drive well-well and enter accident for road.*"

"Is that all?" Tayo murmured. Could Nuhu not see that they had beaten him?

III

And then ...

Chapter 27

Tayo's biography of Lord Lugard was greeted with critical acclaim. *The New York Times* named it 'biography of the year,' while the *Observer* described it as 'the most significant historical text to hail from Africa in recent times.' Vanessa knew that Tayo would be touring England to promote the book, but it still came as a surprise when her editor sent her his tour dates and she realised she would be seeing him soon. She had considered contacting him before the event, but decided against it. Better just to appear and not make a fuss, except that here she was, minutes after he had greeted her, with trembling hands and terrified to go back into the room where he was. In the early years she had dreamt constantly about this first re-encounter – they would gaze at each other, filled with longing and desire, and everyone else would disappear. Of course, she hadn't expected any of that today, after all these years, but she imagined that their meeting, nevertheless, would be nostalgic. Two old friends. Lovers. It never crossed her mind that he might not recognise her.

She had arrived a little late, just as Tayo was being introduced, and he glanced at her briefly without recognition as she slipped quietly into one of the back rows. Only at the end of his talk, when she stood up, did he see her, really see her.

"Vanessa," he exclaimed, and everyone turned to look.

"I'll be right back," she called, not knowing what else to do but run and gather some composure. Now, standing in the privacy of the ladies' toilet, Vanessa looked into the mirror. She placed both hands flat against her forehead and pulled. This way she was able to hide the grey and take away the wrinkles, but when she removed her hands everything popped back: the grey hairs and furrows that ran along her forehead and spread like fine cat's whiskers from the corner of each eye. She shook her head and sighed. Then, startled by a sharp knock on the door, she dropped the compact she was holding and watched as a powdery plume of blue and purple eye-shadow billowed across the toilet floor.

"Just a minute," she called. "Hold on," she called again, bending down to pick up the broken bits. The powder crumbled when touched, so she used her foot to kick what she could out of sight beneath the sink. Quickly, she washed her hands and opened the door, but nobody was there. Whoever had knocked had left. She returned to the seminar room where people still waited in line to meet Tayo and have their books signed.

She smiled, calmer now, watching him interact, ever gracious and charming, with only a sprinkling of white hairs. He had barely aged and was just as handsome as she remembered, though not quite as fashionable. He wore grey trousers a little flared at the ankles, and a cream coloured shirt with a wide collar. He looked up from where he sat and gestured for her not to leave. *Take your time*, she gestured back, taking a mint from her bag, as well as a notebook. Usually, the latter would have been covered with scribbles capturing what the speaker had said, his style of presentation, the questions and responses, but today she had been too distracted to write. What would they say to each other? What would she say?

She jumped in surprise when he touched her shoulder. She had not seen him coming and stood up too quickly, but he caught her before she tripped.

"Tayo."

"I'm sorry, Vanessa."

"No, it's not you. It's me." She laughed nervously.

"It's wonderful to see you," he said, as she straightened herself.

"And you."

She expected him to let go of her arms, but he didn't. Instead he held on and kept looking at her.

"I was..."

"You..."

They spoke simultaneously, then stopped, then tried again. The same thing happened.

"Dinner?" Tayo laughed, gently letting go of her arms.

Outside, day stretched luxuriously into evening, the way it always did on warm summer nights.

"So where do we start after twenty years?" Tayo began.

"Twenty," Vanessa repeated. "You left in '66 and I came..." she said, making it sound as though she were just working it out.

"Twenty-seven years. My goodness," Tayo exclaimed. "And now you're married. Any children?"

Their arms kept bumping into each other clumsily as they walked.

"Yes. A son."

He nodded and slipped his hands into his coat pockets. He still had his lovely broad shoulders. Probably always would. She was tempted to touch them, just slip a hand behind his back and rest it on his shoulder like old times.

"And?" Tayo held out his hand.

Did he want her to take his hand? She wasn't sure whether he wanted her to or whether it was simply a gesture.

"Where did you meet your husband?" he continued, slowly closing his hand. "How old is your son? I want to know everything."

"Everything?" She raised her eyebrows, feeling suddenly irritated by his words. Did he think he could simply waltz back into her life and ask whatever he wished? "Well," she paused, thinking of those first two years apart, a period that at the time had seemed like the worst years of her life. Did he know? Of course he didn't. "I found a job with *The Guardian*," she said simply.

"I didn't realise you worked with them as early as that."

"Yes, but in those days I wasn't a journalist."

"What were you doing?"

"Making tea. *Lots* of tea," she smiled. "And being paraded about at lunches by my boss. I should never have stayed, but I was young and naïve. You know how it is."

"I'd forgotten how much I missed your smile," he said.

"Oh, Tayo." She started to laugh. *I've missed you, too*, she wanted to say but couldn't.

"And the laugh," he added. "I've missed that as well."

"How is your family?" she asked. It was an awkward transition, but he obliged by telling her a few things about his daughter and her chosen field of study.

"To be honest, I really didn't want Kemi to apply for drama or music. Architecture would have been better."

"Why not something in the arts?"

"It's hypocritical of me, isn't it?" he nodded. "But it's so hard to be an artist in Africa these days. You must know. I just don't want my daughter to be discouraged when she returns home."

"If she returns," Vanessa added.

"Yes," he nodded. "I suppose one can never take these things for granted and, to be honest, I don't think she will."

Vanessa noticed his phrase, to be honest. He seemed fond of those words these days.

"But look, I'm doing all the talking. Tell me about you, Vanessa. And how are your parents?"

"Mum died in '78. From cancer."

"I'm so sorry to hear that. I'm very sorry."

"Thank you," she nodded. "But Father's fine. Getting old," she added.

Tayo nodded. "And your husband? Who's the lucky man?"

"Actually…"

"Well?" he smiled, "who's the lucky man?"

"It's Edward. Edward Barker."

"Really," he stammered, remembering back to the History don at Oxford. "Well, how is he after all these years?"

"Isabella went back to Italy," she said, knowing what he would be thinking.

But if Tayo was shocked he did a good job of disguising it, certainly better than she did of hiding her awkwardness as she told him about the divorce. She then felt compelled to make it clear that nothing had ever happened between them when they had been at Oxford. It was only by chance, she explained, that she met Edward years later in London.

"You must tell me about your time in Dakar," Tayo continued. "That was when I started reading your articles, all those fantastic pieces on Senghor, Ousmane and Ba. It must have been wonderful."

"It was," she replied, wondering what he really thought of her being married to Edward. She had not told Edward she would be coming to hear Tayo speak either.

"You know I've been following your career closely, Vanessa."

"Have you?" She turned to face him.

"Do you remember once in Oxford when you asked me what I thought of you becoming an African journalist?"

"I do."

"And now you're Africa's favourite writer. I have a file at home with all of your articles – at least, those I could get a hold of in Nigeria."

She had followed his career too. It was her job to keep track of African artists and scholars, but in Tayo's case she would have done it anyway.

"Here we are," he said, pointing to the Indian restaurant.

As they approached, Vanessa wanted to tell him how the

smell of curry always reminded her of his New Year's culinary experiment, but then she remembered that it had been in Edward's old house so she said nothing as he continued to talk about her writing.

"You know the first piece I read of yours was that article on FESTAC," he remarked as they sat down. "It was a superb article. You were critical of the organisers and used Fela's Zombie lyrics to make your point."

"Yes," she nodded, remembering her initial excitement at being in Nigeria and hoping to run into him. "So you never went to FESTAC?"

He shook his head as a waiter arrived, depositing glasses of water and a basket full of papadums. She broke one and handed half to Tayo.

"Doesn't this remind you of Oxford?"

She nodded. "What was the name of that Indian place we went to? Viceroys, or Raj, I think it was called. Something with a colonial ring." He tapped his forehead to remember.

"The Taj."

"That's right," he laughed, longer than seemed necessary.

The conversation had grown awkward again, and Vanessa wished the waiter had given them more time before returning to announce the choice of condiments.

"Mango chutney. Spicy sauce. Yogurt," the man beamed.

"You must tell me more about the books you write for children," she said, searching for a neutral topic of conversation.

"Initially inspired by you, Vanessa."

"Really?"

"You gave me a first edition copy of *Winnie the Pooh*, remember? Well, that was what started me thinking about children's literature. But I want to know more about you. Are you still in touch with friends from St. Hughs?"

"I've been to a few gaudies, but I don't really have time to stay in touch."

She didn't feel like saying much more. It bothered her that he seemed so calm.

"And Jane?" he asked.

"The last I heard, she had married a rich American and was living somewhere in California. We haven't stayed in touch. And you? What about the Balliol crowd?" she asked so that he would talk instead.

"No, I'm not in touch." He shook his head. "Except for a brief correspondence with Simon and what I've read through *The Record*, but the other day I found one of my books. I don't think I ever told you this, but I used to keep a record of all the titled people I met at Oxford. I did it for my father, but the funny thing is that most of the names I wrote down became nothing, or not famous in any case. And you, my friend Vanessa, have become the most famous of all!"

"Oh, don't be silly."

"But it's true."

"So I wasn't in your book of names?"

"You were so much in my head, Vanessa, that I didn't need to write your name down."

She ate some more, aware that he was watching her. She wished he wouldn't. It meant that she couldn't eat gracefully, papadum bits bursting inelegantly from her mouth. He hadn't touched his.

"I was so much in your head that you found someone else," she ventured.

He looked down at his plate as two waiters struggled to find room for oblong platters of rice and chicken. In the end, she removed the large vase of plastic carnations, impatient for the waiters to leave.

"I was young then," he spoke quietly, keeping his eyes fixed on the food.

Silence hung uncomfortably between them as she remembered the time in Lagos.

"To Tayo," she said finally, lifting her glass.

"And to you." He clinked his glass against hers, holding her gaze briefly.

"Will you tell me about those early days in Nigeria?" She helped herself from the plate he was offering. "Those were the good years, weren't they? I mean politically and economically." The rice clung stubbornly together so she pressed harder. Tayo's grip on the plate remained firm.

"I missed you, Vanessa."

She waited for him to say more. And just as she thought she should break the silence, someone did it for her.

"It is you! Look at you, old chap," the man exclaimed, striding across the room towards them. "You don't recognise me do you? It's Samir from Bradford. Remember?"

For several minutes, in their excitement to see each other, the men seemed to have forgotten that Vanessa was there.

"I'm sorry, Ma'am. Your wife?" Samir asked, curious now as he turned to acknowledge Vanessa.

"No, this is Vanessa Richardson. She writes for *The Guardian*."

"I see," he winked, slapping Tayo again across the shoulders. "Not another of your girlfriends then. So what's wrong with that bloody ruler of yours?" Samir bellowed, pulling a chair from a neighbouring table. "Any real chance of him returning the country to civilian rule?"

"I don't know," Tayo replied, glancing at Vanessa.

"Still waiting for your Nehru dynasty?" Samir laughed loudly, oblivious to the restaurant owner's disapproving looks. "And what a bloody mess India has herself in now. What to do? Bloody power hungry all of them. And I thought you were bound for politics old chap. What happened?"

"I teach now."

"Yes, you're wise, old chap. So look, where's your wife?"

"She's here, well not here," Tayo paused, "but in London."

"Doing the holiday shopping?"

"Actually no. She lives here now and my daughter too. My wife runs a nursing facility for the elderly."

"Then you must all come and visit us; I have three daughters now and –"

"Excuse me a moment please," Vanessa interrupted.

Tayo looked up, anxious, but Vanessa pretended not to notice. She went in search of the restaurant owner to ask for the phone and left a message for Edward letting him know she would be late. She felt angry with Samir for interrupting them, and annoyed with Tayo for letting the man stay. She contemplated a cigarette, but it had been years since she last smoked, so she went to the ladies' room instead and fiddled with her hair, straightening the side parting and removing more grey hairs. 'What am I doing here?' she thought, returning to the table. She reminded Tayo that she had a train to catch and Samir offered to drive her to the station. She would have preferred that he left them in peace, but Samir was insisting.

'Now what', she thought, staring angrily at the empty tracks as she and Tayo stood, finally alone, at Birmingham New Street. A rat scurried along one of the metal girders, and she muttered to herself.

"What was that?" Tayo asked.

"Nothing," she answered, trying not to convey her impatience.

"You're angry with me, aren't you?" He touched her arm.

"Angry?" She shook her head, knowing she was no good at pretending.

"I'm sorry about Samir."

"It's okay."

"I meant what I said when I told you I missed you," he continued. "And I'm sorry, very sorry, for the way things ended between us. Not that it means anything now, but I loved you

Vanessa. I always did and… well…" His voice trailed off.

She touched his hand, half clutching at his fingers and half stroking them. What was the point in being angry? It was too late for that now.

He stepped closer, facing her, and reached for her arms.

"Could I kiss you?" he asked, just as her train arrived.

She stalled for a brief moment then gently lifted his hands from her arms. "I'll miss my train, Tayo."

Chapter 28

Vanessa sat in the grass at the top of Brockwell Park, looking down towards Herne Hill Station. It had been two weeks since she had seen Tayo, but memories of the dinner, the waiting at the station and his offer of a kiss still lingered in her mind. She tried to picture him in his office, or at home, but found her mind always going back to his room in Oxford, or the offices at Cheik Anta Diop, which was her only model for a West African campus. She wondered what he would think of where she now lived and the life she had created for herself.

Herne Hill used to be nothing fancy, just another nondescript borough of South East London with the usual rows of Victorian terraced homes, a local pub, bank, newsagent, and post office, but things were changing. It started in 1990 with two new art shops – first the one under the station bridge and then Artemidorus on Half Moon Lane. Next came the French bistros and an ultra-pricey Indian fusion restaurant. Now, clustered around the station, were expensive shops and eating-places, marking Herne Hill as part of the new south London – trendy, but not gentrified.

There remained enough of the old Herne Hill to prevent it from becoming a second Dulwich. The bakery, for example, hadn't changed. It still sold greasy sausage rolls and stodgy buns drizzled with confectioner's sugar, topped with glace cherries. It had some new competition from the Jamaican pattie shop across the street, tastier fare, but still not upmarket. Then there was the Nigerian man with his clothes shop come tailoring business, come secretarial services. It was hard to tell which of its operations was core, especially as it was almost never open, in contrast to its neighbour, the 24-hour taxi rank. Station's Taxis was a seedy shack of a place that reeked of tobacco, even more than the pub across the street. Many of Station's Taxis' drivers were Nigerian which meant she could never pass it without thinking of Tayo.

She stretched her legs, enjoying the tickle of grass beneath her calves. Down below at the bottom of the hill, men and women were cleaning the park. They wore plastic sleeves and were using long stick devices to pick up discarded beer cans, paper plates and plastic knives and forks. Yesterday the annual Brockwell Park Fair had taken place and hundreds of Londoners had trampled across the grass, eating, drinking, and dropping their litter. She had come by herself. It wasn't the sort of the thing Edward enjoyed. *Too raucous*, he complained. Her son Suleiman had gone, but not with her. He went with friends, to flirt with the girls and no doubt smoke some hash. And so with Edward at home and Suleiman out of sight, she had wandered from stall-to-stall, sampling West African cuisine and buying things to support local artists. As usual, when the African vendors learnt that she had lived in their continent, she was greeted with added enthusiasm. Suleiman laughed at her whenever she said she felt more at home with Africans than with the English, but it was true. There was a saying that once you had tasted the waters of Africa, you would always thirst for more, and she was ready to return.

She had left Dakar in 1975, when her mother was very ill. Had it not been for this, and the subsequent need to help Father adjust to living alone, she might never have come back to live in England. Her years in Africa, most of them at least, were the happiest of her life. There where the sun always shone and where she had felt so fulfilled in her work.

In Dakar she had never worried about how to raise her son

and nor was she alone, but here, even though she had Edward to help, mothering was a lonely job. Suleiman at 18 was a very different child to Suleiman as a boy. The charming, chatty toddler was gone, replaced by a silent, troubled young man. Other mothers empathised, saying that this was simply 'the teenage years', but she knew what they really thought: *that's the problem with having a black child.*

Vanessa brought her knees to her chest and hugged them. The park cleaners had left and, down by the station, sticklike figures scurried in and out. Rush hour had begun and some of those returning from work would leave the station and walk back to Brixton, or up the hill to Herne Hill and Dulwich. She and Edward lived on Herne Hill Road, not far from St. Paul's church. "Goodness," she gasped, suddenly remembering. Today was their anniversary. She had never been good at remembering these dates, but it was strange that Edward had also forgotten. Eighteen years of marriage, she contemplated, and not to Tayo or another African as she had once envisioned, but to Edward. Edward Maximillian Barker.

After things had ended with Tayo, Vanessa had deliberately stayed away from all of Tayo's old friends, including the Barkers, but one day in the autumn of 1968 she ran into Edward in London and they had lunch together. Edward had seen how miserable she was and encouraged her to return to Dakar. The problem with returning, however, was that she had no job to go to. When she had first gone to Senegal, she had gone on impulse and stayed with one of Uncle Tony's friends in St. Louis. There was no thought of finding a job; it was just an escape from England and from her family, with the desire to be somehow closer to Tayo despite her anger. Then, when she couldn't escape her despair in Senegal, she had returned to England thinking she would throw herself back into her studies, but she hadn't been able to do that either.

Instead, she drifted for a year working silly jobs in London until the day she met Edward and he gave her names and addresses of friends at Cheik Anta Diop. Thanks to him, she left her job and returned to Senegal to start a new life. In Dakar, nobody knew about her sadness and only Salamatou knew anything about Tayo, but only a little. And then she too was gone, killed in a car accident on a treacherous stretch of road between Dakar and St. Louis.

For weeks afterwards nobody could console her, although Edward tried his best and his presence did bring some comfort. He became a father to her – a man far wiser, gentler and more self-possessed than the men of her own age. Above all, he listened. And yes, she knew that he was attracted to her in more than just a friendly way, but she chose to ignore it. He wasn't her type – too old and far too English in his way of speaking, his dress and his mannerisms.

She had said no the first time he asked her to marry him. But when he asked again several months later, she managed to persuade herself that her initial reservations were foolish. He was, after all, her closest friend and it seemed only natural that they should marry. July 15th, 1976. Eighteen years. She had grown to love him, but those things that she had not liked in the beginning never went away and what was, for a short time, the attraction of his older age soon disappeared as well. Now he was forgetful and prone to repeating stories. In his retirement he spent hours and hours in his men's clubs with his very English friends. He smoked and drank, and talked incessantly of holiday homes in the south of France. He no longer thirsted for Africa.

And then there was something else, so small and trivial that it bothered Vanessa to even notice it, yet it was worse than all her other irritations, and always there. His smell. It cloaked the house and seeped into everything they owned: clothes, curtains, the bedding – a horrible, acrid smell like old, musty books, only worse – the smell of old age and far too similar to that of her father.

"Darling Vanessa," someone called.

"Anthony," she smiled, turning around to see her friend from Sketchley's. Something about Anthony reminded her of Abubakar. Both were charming and she knew they found her attractive but only in an exotic sort of way. In Abubakar's case, she had been the young English visitor to Senegal. In those days she could be considered beautiful but, surely to him, the greatest attraction had been her naivety. She had been too stupid to realise that he was already married.

There was no naivety with Anthony, at least not on her part, but she could see that he was taken by the idea of an older English woman with an interesting past life in Africa.

"What's up, beauty?" Anthony dropped the plastic bag that he was carrying and sat next to her on the grass. "Were you here yesterday? I was looking for you, babe."

"I was here, for a while," she smiled.

"And what you thinking today? What you gonna write?"

She thought for a moment before telling him of her latest idea to write about recent immigrants to London. African immigrants.

"And what about their Jamaican brothers?" Anthony joked. "We is the original diaspora y'know. Besides, you need to use my name in one of your articles. Do me some free advertising. Anthony's Sketchley on Railton Road – the best in London!"

She laughed and tugged at his Walkman, asking him what he was listening to as he removed his headphones and placed them around her head.

"Hugh Masekela," she smiled.

"Yeah man," he nodded, lying back in the grass and closing his eyes.

His shirt had risen above his stomach, revealing a ladder of taught muscles. His hands were linked across his chest and the long dark fingers reminded her of Tayo's, but he was young, not much older than Suleiman.

Therefore, however much this man might thrill her, she had to stop imagining things. She listened to Masekela's song for Mandela, remembering the year it first came out and how she had played it continuously on the day he was released. She smiled and looked down the path to where a couple were walking slowly up the hill. The man pushed a pram and the woman hugged the man's waist, leaning gently on his side – a black and white couple. Vanessa turned away to stare at Anthony so that she would not have to nod and smile as the couple walked by. Hearing her move, Anthony opened his eyes and sat up.

"So you wanna get a drink," he suggested.

*

When she got home Edward was playing Rachmaninoff at a deafening volume.

"Oh for God's sake, you're worse than Suleiman," Vanessa shouted, switching it off.

Edward wasn't in the lounge, which meant he was upstairs having a bath. Sometimes he fell asleep there.

"One day you'll bloody drown," she muttered, stomping up the stairs.

"Hello, darling," he met her on the landing.

"Will you please not play your music so loudly, Edward."

"But I thought you rather liked Rachmaninoff, my love."

"Frankly I'd much prefer Hugh Masekela any day," she snapped.

"Who's that, my love?"

"Oh never mind." She brushed past him. He was growing deaf as well.

"Darling, let me give you a kiss, it's our anniversary."

"I know," she snapped, flinging open the windows in their bedroom.

"Is it hot?"

"It's stuffy!" She strode out of the room back to where he stood, slouched a little against the banister, and that was when she noticed the bruise on his head. "What happened?" she asked, reaching to touch.

"Just a little bump. I couldn't find my glasses and must have tripped on the carpet. But it's nothing. Come, I've got something to show you." He held out his hand, and she followed him to his study.

She slipped an arm round his waist, hating herself for being so sharp with him.

"I went to the bookshop while you were out and brought you this." He held out a book.

"Oh darling!" she exclaimed, seeing the photograph of Mandela and knowing immediately what it was.

"I thought you would like it." He smiled.

"*Long Walk to Freedom*," she read the title.

Where had he managed to find a copy so quickly? The book had only just come out. She opened it, and on the inside cover Edward had written a note. *To the woman I love, and with whom I have walked the best 18 years of my life.*

"Oh Edward!" She put the book down and wrapped her arms tightly around his waist.

Chapter 29

He still found it hard to believe that after all these years they had seen each other again. But their time had been too short. He had wanted to say more, to have talked about what happened, to have tried to explain. He tried now to say these things in a letter, but couldn't find the words, so what was he going to do? He would just have to write, write without worrying how it came out, without the emotion being burdened by explanations. The most important thing was to stay in touch, so perhaps he would start by telling her about Nigeria, about how things had gone from bad to worse. He would tell her about the schools and hospitals that were closed and the civil servants who had not been paid. But this was all too depressing. He would perhaps try to make light of the situation instead and joke about the fact that the two most lucrative businesses were theft and security; only this wasn't much of a joke. So what would he write? *Write*, he told himself, *just write.*

Since our meeting, I have given further thought to our discussion on the role of the artist, finding myself going back to some of the readings we debated at Oxford, in particular James Baldwin and Ezekiel Mphahlele. Do you remember those long nights when we used to talk about their ideas? I have found it so interesting to re-read their works and discover things I had missed on a first read. I was particularly struck this time by Baldwin's musing on what constitutes a healthy society. What is the role of the maverick or dissenter in a cohesive society? A question I ask myself. Where exactly do I fit? So often I feel out of place and, by this, I am not referring to my stance against government policies. I consider my political dissention to be a necessity rather than the actions of a misfit, given that the majority of us believe the same thing. What I mean, when I speak of not fitting in, has to do with a cultural sense of non-belonging.

Would she think him crazy to be writing this? Would she understand?

For example, I don't always comply with the demands of extended family and I'm no longer certain about the existence of a god. These are both fundamental elements in our culture that one is not supposed to question. I also find that I tire of social interaction in a way that is deemed unacceptable to most people here, and this is where one of Mphahlele's essays seemed particularly insightful to me now. I refer to <u>The Fabric of African Cultures</u>, *which is an exposé of the so-called elements that make up the 'African personality.' These characteristics are obviously generalisations, but I believe they still ring true for much of the continent, even now twenty years after the essay was written. Mphahlele speaks of the importance we attach to extended family, communal responsibility and reverence for ancestral spirits (all of which I fail miserably on), but it is his last observation that particularly struck me this time round. Mphahlele speaks of the cultural tendency to gravitate toward other <u>people</u> rather than toward <u>things</u> and <u>places</u>. This is something I was only subliminally aware of until I read the essay. In a way, 'things' (such as books filled with ideas) and 'places' (memories of places and destinations yet to be visited) are what captivate me more than people. I am not saying that people are unimportant (especially friends like you), but I notice that I do not automatically seek company in the same way as* *those around me when they have something on their mind. What then is my African personality?*

"Goodness," Tayo muttered.

I'm not sure if I'm making much sense, and to be honest I'm not sure I know what I want to say. Perhaps I simply wish to express how much I enjoyed our conversation and to share with you how it has set me thinking. If only daily life in Nigeria left more time for tranquil reflection!

What he did not say and what he was only just realising was that he had missed having someone to talk to. Sometimes he would talk with his colleagues and some of his students, but it had been years since he shared ideas about life so openly and honestly with anyone.

London,
July 1995

Dear Tayo,

It was lovely to hear from you, but I'm alarmed to hear of your detention. You do not mention it in your letter, but I have heard from others. Is it true? Promise me, Tayo, that you will be careful for your sake and your family's. The fact that you are known abroad may offer you some protection from military interference, but not much, Tayo. Look at what is happening to Ken Saro-Wiwa. You must be careful. I am so concerned by what I hear from Nigeria these days, and angry that our government won't do more to condemn the corruption and human rights violations. Please, Tayo, promise me you'll be careful.

You asked about work and, yes, I'm still with The Guardian, *but finding the job increasingly frustrating. When will serious attention ever be given to Africa? There was so much optimism when the Cold War ended, and I had such hopes that African nations might finally be treated with respect, but this hasn't happened and it continues to be a struggle here publishing articles on Africa. I'm forced to play silly games (writing at weekends or at times when certain difficult editors are away) to ensure publication.*

I'm so nostalgic for the days in Dakar and restless here in England. Perhaps I am also a misfit. I live here, yet don't feel particularly English. What then is my 'personality' – African, European, or Afropean? Is this restlessness the price we pay for having lived in other countries and tasted other cultures? And yet there are many people who have lived and travelled in various places, but who still seem most at home in their country of birth. I don't know what it is, Tayo. Do people like us just think about these things too much?

I also wrestle with the question of who can write about

Africa. Do I still have the 'right' to report on African affairs now that I no longer live on the continent? Did I earn the right when I was there? I often think back to that Oxford Union debate and what Malcolm said about foreign correspondents in Africa. I also wonder about this notion of the insider and outsider that we once discussed in France. Do you remember? To what extent does being an outsider allow a person unique insights into a culture? To what extent might the outside status blind rather than illuminate? And then at what point does one cease to be an outsider? So now you have set me thinking too!

I would like to hear more about your views on faith and the church. I find it ironic that we seem to have moved in opposite directions on this topic. I now attend church regularly. It gives me a sense of belonging and a feeling of peace. You say that Nigerian society expects one to believe, whereas British society almost presumes the opposite. Could it be that our societies have driven us to our respective points of belief and unbelief?

My son recently joined the Muslim faith, which has grown increasingly popular here among young black men. They say that Islam brings a sense of purpose and discipline, but I have yet to see it in Suleiman. It has been a difficult year. Suleiman left University in April, just before finals. We don't know why and he won't talk to us about it. He was doing so well, but now he's unemployed and living with friends in North London. Edward thinks we should let him do as he wishes, but I find it hard. We used to be so close and now it's as though we are strangers. I feel guilty for not being a good enough mother. Perhaps I've focused too much on my career and not spent enough time with Suleiman.

It's at times like this that I miss my own mother. I miss her all of the time of course, but especially now. I would have gone to her for advice or perhaps simply sympathy or empathy... I don't know, Tayo. Perhaps it's always hard for mothers and fathers. Please be careful Tayo and stay in touch.

Love,
Vanessa

November 1995

My dear Vanessa,

You are a wonderful mother, and Suleiman knows this. It is just a stage that he is going through and it will pass, you will see. You must not feel guilty. I know that finding the balance is hard, but I am very proud of you, Vanessa – proud of you for being so good a mother as well as a writer dedicated to this continent. I am also touched that you are concerned for my well being, but I'm fine so you mustn't worry. I was detained for the so-called offence of showing my students Perry Henzel's, The Harder They Come. *It was deemed subversive but I was released shortly thereafter. It was no big thing, and I do promise you that I am taking care of myself.*

Since I last wrote, Miriam has been back but things have sadly not gone well. We both tried in our own way to see each other's point-of-view, but it wasn't enough. Last month I decided that I must move to England for the sake of the family, but by then it was too late. Miriam is asking for a divorce. The very word 'divorce' makes me feel so ashamed. How could I have failed my wife and daughter like this? If anyone should feel guilty about placing profession before family, it is me. I am like one of your Forster characters that never seize life.

He wanted to tell her more, to tell her about Hawa and how she had been the last straw for Miriam. He wanted to tell Vanessa, as he would any close friend, how he had struggled with the affair, not wanting to start it from the very beginning. But what was he thinking? He couldn't possibly share this with Vanessa.

I only wish I had faith, Vanessa, I really do. I still pray sometimes, but I lack the conviction that anyone hears, let alone answers, my prayers. Kemi blames me for what happened, and no doubt rightly so. When she was a child, we discussed all sorts of things together and I would tell her stories, but now we hardly speak. Things have certainly been difficult for her even without the added strain of what has happened between Miriam and me. She did her degree in African Studies and Art History, which I'm afraid, has made it hard for her to find a good job. For the time being, she is working as a secretary in London. She says she wants to return to Africa to teach English as a second language, but this is not the time to do such things. Nowhere, with the exception perhaps of Zimbabwe and Botswana (and neither of these countries need ESL), are conditions in this continent stable enough.

She has also mentioned going to America, but I am afraid I'm not keen on that either. America is so far from Nigeria. She speaks of doing something in the arts – setting up an African art gallery or some such thing. Do you think there are prospects for this in the UK? She complains of racism in England, but surely America is worse? I tried to bring Kemi up to be her own person, to be an independent young woman. I didn't want to raise her the way I was raised, but maybe in the process I failed to give her enough direction. I'm sorry Vanessa. I don't mean to complain. I think of you so often and wonder how you are. I miss you.

Yours lovingly,
Tayo

Chapter 30

Vanessa stared at her computer thinking of Tayo's most recent letters. She had remembered something that her mother once told her about love, and she tried to remember when the conversation had taken place, deciding that it must have been late in the summer of 1967. They had been sitting in the garden, she with a book on her lap and Mother doing cross-stitch. It was one of those rare warm English summers that had lifted Vanessa's spirits. Mother could have been telling any story, the mere cadence of her voice was enough to soothe, but it wasn't just any old story. In retrospect, Vanessa wished she had asked more questions, but at the time she could only think of how things related to her and Tayo. Now she wondered what the story might have meant to Mother, and who might have told her the story.

Her mother had told her that there was a saying among the Hausa that a person never married their first love. A person always married someone else, but later in life that person would be reunited with their first love. The Hausa apparently even had a phrase for it: they called it the *pick-up-your-stick-and-sandals* marriage, which referred to the way that an old man would go and visit his childhood sweetheart later in life. The woman cooked, the man brought presents, and then they shared companionship. *Pick-up-your-stick-and-sandals*, Vanessa repeated to herself, hitting the space key to banish the silly animated fish that floated across her screen every time she stopped working. In large letters at the top of the page popped the title: ***Shona Art – Stunning Sculpture from Zimbabwe Takes Art World by Storm.***

Her fingers lingered on the keys. If Father was indeed Mother's first love, what did the Hausa say for those who married first loves only to be disappointed later in life? And what did other African cultures have to say about romantic love? She hit the space key again. The article was due tomorrow and she had been wasting time. She would begin with a brief history of Frank McEwan at the National Gallery of Rhodesia and his role in encouraging art in the 1950s. Then she would describe Tom Blomefield and the establishment of the Tengenenge Community in the 1960s, paying special attention to Agnes Nyanhongo and Colleen Madamombe. *More on women sculptors*, she made a mental note. She shook her hair out of its loose ponytail, rolled her chair closer to the desk and placed her fingers back on the keys.

At a time when reports from Africa are dominated by famine, starvation, and AIDS, Shona art holds the promise of...

She did not want to start like this, but it seemed the only way to move the reader from the pervasive images of naked, skeletal Africans with flies buzzing round their faces. Or was it? This dilemma always presented itself. Was she in fact perpetuating stereotypes by mentioning them, or was she helping readers to see past the clichés? And who was her audience these days? Was it British lefties? Immigrants? African students, or all three? She stared absently at the screen and wondered if she should abandon the whole thing.

Eventually she stood up and went to the kitchen. There she poured herself some wine and, as she drank, she peered into the cupboards thinking she should eat, not just drink. She found tins of baked beans, high fibre soups, packets of pasta and dried mushrooms that Edward always kept on hand. On another shelf were his box of bran flakes and her Swiss muesli. Nothing caught her fancy, so she wandered into the lounge, leaving her glass behind.

The balloons from Saturday's party were still stuck to the ceiling. One popped as she opened the outside doors to catch some fresh air. The room smelt stuffy from old wine and cigarettes, and outside it was still drizzling. She took another drink, holding the bottle with one hand and tapping its skinny neck with her wedding band. This was the real English summer, grey and rainy. What a dismal country! She turned back to the room and saw that the wind had blown off most of the cards from the bookshelves and mantelpiece.

Saturday had been another of Edward's surprises. He was good at this, but she didn't like the unexpected anymore, especially not when it involved lots of people. She had secretly hoped that he might surprise her differently. He might have cooked, or taken her for a ride in the country, just the two of them. Of course she had smiled all evening, suffering and smiling. She played the required role, saying how blessed she felt, how wonderful it was to turn fifty (what nonsense!), but all the time she was wishing she could disappear.

Edward had bought her several CDs, picking the music he thought she liked: *The Best of Sarah Vaughan, The Best of Miles Davis*. She hated 'best ofs'. Suleiman had asked her what she wanted for her birthday and had taken her at her word when she said nothing, presenting her with a token bunch of wilting flowers, still wrapped in crinkly Tesco paper marked 'Summer Special £4.99.' He might as well just have picked something from the garden. At least that would have shown originality. And then they had parted so badly when she had driven him to the airport.

"Well you drive then!" she had finally shouted after Suleiman kept complaining about her driving.

"I should have never let you take me anyway," Suleiman

grumbled. "I was perfectly happy catching the tube."

And it was true, he had not wanted her to drive him to Heathrow, but she felt that as a mother she ought to. He was going off to Senegal for an indefinite period of time. Of course she should take him.

"You've never wanted me to do this trip anyway."

"I'm happy you're going, Suleiman, but it's just the timing. You haven't finished university and what happens when you return?"

"Who said I'm coming back?"

"Don't be so ridiculous."

"Ahh, fuck you, Mum!"

"What!" She slammed her foot against the brakes, skidding onto the hard shoulder. "How dare you speak to your mother like that?"

"Mother? What *mother*? Did you think you were doing some nice charity work for Africa when you decided to adopt me?"

She drove off again, speeding this time. If that was how he felt, then fuck him too. She would drop him and leave.

"You just thought you'd take me out of Africa, didn't you, and turn me into some middle-class bourgeois project? You thought you could send me to Oxford or Cambridge, and I'd come out looking like you or dad, collecting nice art from Africa, writing nice stories about Africa. Well that's fucked up. I'm going back to learn about where I came from and to mix with my Muslim brothers and sisters. A place where Islam is respected and revered, and not mocked like it is in this fucking place."

"Go then," she shouted, "but remember I adopted you because I love you, because your mum was my best friend and I promised Salamatou to take care of you. Call us your bourgeois parents, if that makes you feel better, but I've never, *ever*, tried to mould you into anything."

And then it was silence all the way until just before he went through security. With tears in her eyes she had watched him disappear, her tall, handsome son, and all the phases of his life flashed by. The day that Salamatou died and the years that followed in Dakar. Of them making toys together out of cardboard boxes and empty Fairy Liquid bottles; swimming in the sea; nursing him back to health after his fevers; leaving for England to see Grandma before she died when Suleiman had been ecstatic to travel for the first time on an airplane. He had loved England then, the changing seasons, fish and chips, Cádbury's chocolates and his new school. Even the teenage years had not been difficult, but then came university.

She worried constantly about him, especially now that he was so far away. What were Tayo's words? *It is a stage he is going through, and it will pass, you will see.* She longed for Tayo now. She stood up, closed the back doors, and stared for a moment at the bottle. She left it where it sat, empty between the fallen cards. She had received two letters from Tayo yesterday. In one, he had asked about her faith. "Tell you about my faith?" she mumbled to herself. *How can I speak of it when I'm like this?* She covered her face with her hands. *Look at me now – just look at me.* But in his letter he had also mentioned the possibility of a visit and at that thought she lifted her hands from her face, flicked away the tears and began to write.

My dear Tayo,

If only you knew what happens when your letters arrive. If only you knew. There was the letter you wrote to me in 1967, the letter we both avoided talking about when we saw each other last. Have you ever imagined the pain it caused me? Had it not been for Mother... but I will tell you one day. And now you have written again and I am filled with despair, depression perhaps, although I hate the word 'depression' – so gloomy and self-indulgent. I'm sure I never once heard the word used in Africa – there was no time to be depressed. Of course people had their anxieties, but it wasn't spoken of as it is here in Europe. Perhaps when depression is discussed, so scrutinised, it leads to more of it.

But today your letter has lifted my spirits and as I think of you I try to imagine what life would be like with you. Do you sometimes think the same? I tell myself that you do, but then I fear that this is just what married people use as an escape. Perhaps we all cling to fantasies of some other person that allow us to keep going with our day-to-day lives. I wonder if this is what my parents did. Father always working; Mother drinking. There must have been something else in their lives, some hope. And now, when I look at myself... it's not that anything is terribly wrong, but I long to be in love again. I want passion. To be with you.

I wonder if you have ever come across the saying: 'a pick-up-your-stick-and-sandals marriage'. This was what Mother called it. I don't know where she heard it, or whether it even exists, but she said it was a Hausa belief that in later age one is reunited with one's first love. Perhaps it was just a story to console the lovelorn. I know that everything would not be pure bliss between us, no marriage ever is, but I like to dream, and when have I not? I was born with a restlessness in my soul, the restlessness of an artist who is never fully satisfied. One moment I long to be surrounded by friends, and in another I am wishing to be alone, far away from anyone I know. Is this me being selfish or is it simply a function of growing old? I certainly don't recall feeling this way in my 20s or 30s. So you see, when you ask me about faith, I'm hardly the person to talk. My faith is weak. I strive to be closer to God, to release myself from self-centeredness, but with little success. The issue of suffering that you raised in your last letter has always bothered me, always.

Vanessa stopped and blocked the text. She paused, then pressed delete.

Chapter 31

Rain fell lightly from all directions like fine sifted flour being shaken from the heavens. This was England, Sussex to be precise, in the middle of summer. Joy, the Zimbabwean care worker, opened the front door and nodded without speaking as she let Vanessa in. Not for the first time did Vanessa wonder how a person so dour-looking could be so named. The lack of communication with joyless Joy bothered Vanessa. Usually others warmed to her, and especially Africans who were always delighted by the mere fact that she knew so much about their continent. But then perhaps it was not fair to blame Joy. Working in such a place was bound to squeeze out every last bit of joy from a person.

The Carrington home for the elderly had a steamed up feel – warm and stuffy, like a second-hand clothing shop with the added lingering smells of Sunday roast, disinfectant and urine. When Vanessa arrived, three people sat in the lounge: her Father, Mrs Halliday slouched in her chair, fast asleep, and dear old Mrs Murdoch, staring absently at the Zimmer frame around her knees, who had moved to the home at the same time as Father and followed him everywhere even though most of the time she didn't remember who he was. Father had long since stopped paying any attention to her, but she never noticed, mumbling away to herself regardless. Father was the only one active at that moment, bent over his armchair and rummaging through his briefcase. The case would be empty, but he would still be searching for something – a handkerchief, pencil, fountain pen, or some other item that he would soon ask Vanessa to find.

"Hello, Daddy," she announced her arrival.

"Fancy that," Nancy muttered.

"Is that you darling?" Father looked up briefly to squint in her direction. "I can't find my pen, darling. Have you brought me some more?"

"No, Daddy, but I'm sure we'll find you one in your bedroom."

It still shocked Vanessa to see her father like this, with his collar uneven and bits of breakfast lodged between his teeth. She sat down at the edge of a chair that stank of urine and used her fingertips to remove a wad of pink toilet paper from Father's hand. There was something horrible stuck to the paper that she dared not inspect. This was an expensive residential home yet sometimes one had to wonder where all the money went.

"Daddy, have you got your hearing aid in?"

"No, he doesn't," Nancy replied.

"Thank you, Nancy," Vanessa nodded, as she would to a child who had given the right answer. 'Perhaps not as demented as we all think,' she thought to herself as she went to her father's room and found his hearing aid under the bed.

On most days, Vanessa said little to her father. She cut his nails and listened patiently to his latest complaints but today, when he suggested that Mary and all the other black carers be sent back to where they came from, she had had enough.

"Will you come back tomorrow to shave my whiskers?" Father asked, when she stood up to leave.

"No, Daddy. I'm going to the airport tomorrow."

"Not off to interview more coloured people, are you? They ought to ship them all back to where they came from. Pack them on the Windrush," he muttered, cradling his raised knee with both hands.

"Oh dearie, dearie –"

"Yes, we all know what you both think," Vanessa cut Nancy

off. "I'm going to meet Tayo. He's coming to stay with us for a few days."

"Oh dearie, dearie me." Nancy shook her head.

"Who?" Father asked. "Oh God, not him! All he wants is your body, haven't you worked that one out yet? That's all the coloured men ever want."

"Well, I'd be jolly happy if he wanted my body now," Vanessa snapped back.

"I say," Nancy exclaimed. "Betty, did you hear that!"

"All these years your mother and I tried protecting you, but still you want this wretched man," Father shouted. "That black man used black magic to put a curse on you – I've always known it."

"Oh shut up, Daddy!"

"I say, Mrs Halliday, did you hear that?" Nancy continued to prod her neighbour. "That'll be the father of 'Nessa's black child."

"The child is adopted, you old cow," Father shouted.

"Ssh!" Joy pleaded, running in to see what the commotion was about. "They do get into a state, don't they?" she said, looking to Vanessa for moral support.

Vanessa nodded.

"Pork chop, cauliflower and raspberry jelly," announced Khalid the cook, who had also come to the door. Lunch was being served.

"Did the Arab leave the fat on my pork chop?"

"I'm sure he did, Mr Richardson. I'm sure he did," Joy repeated, taking Father's arm, almost kindly, while Vanessa waved goodbye.

There were meetings Vanessa was expected to attend in London but she had decided not to go. She called in sick and walked to the High Street where she had every intention of pampering herself – treatment for the stress of life. The Lewes shops were at least one consolation for coming all the way to Sussex to visit Father. As she thought of what to buy, she remembered last night's dream. She was at Heathrow standing in line waiting for Tayo. Many people waited like her: his old friends from Oxford, various human rights personnel and some United Nations officials.

He was looking for her, she could tell. He kept peering down the line, but when he got to where she stood, he looked straight past her as though she were invisible, and then he turned around. Suddenly, she realised that he was searching for her with the long hair and the short Oxford skirts. "Tayo, I'm here!" she called, but he didn't hear. He kept on walking back through Customs and away, and only she knew why. It was just a dream, probably caused by the fact that he hadn't at first recognised her the last time they'd met, but it was enough to make her want to leave her hair loose and buy something that would remind him of the way she used to look, just in case.

As she peered into the shop windows, she thought of how he had held her the last time they met. Four years ago, she sighed, touching the spot on her neck where he might have kissed her. She was finding nothing in the Lewes shops. She looked in Monsoon but the colours were too gaudy and the fabrics too delicate. In Caprice, the styles were all wrong – a bizarre mix of skimpy and maternity – but just as she was leaving, something caught her eye. It was a dark brown linen skirt, long and hip hugging – the sort of thing that would go well with one of her cotton shirts worn open at the neck, so she bought it and now felt ready. She planned to arrive at Heathrow early in the morning, collect Tayo and bring him home. She felt certain it was going to be a wonderful first evening. She had pictured it all in her mind's eye, except for Edward and Tayo together, which was a consideration she kept pushing aside until this moment. Edward knew nothing of her correspondence with Tayo, nothing at least of the intimate details and her rekindled feelings for Tayo. What in the world was she thinking?

Heathrow seemed to grow more unbearable each time Vanessa visited – the sticky heat, the sweat and the crowds, but she stood patiently waiting for the British Airways flight from Lagos. The last time she had come here was to see Suleiman off on his travels. She sighed, recalling how they had fought. At least they had both apologised, but it was one of those fights that were not easily forgotten; it would take time to heal. She watched as the line of Nigerians snaked its way out with trolleys piled high with suitcases, baskets and cardboard boxes of all shapes and sizes. She expected Tayo to be delayed. Customs would be asking questions about his length of stay and the purpose of his visit, but he would get through. They had double-checked. Soon the line of passengers disappeared and a new set of travellers arrived. Where was Tayo? She looked again at his telex.

Passport returned! Arriving Heathrow 16:30. BA 263.
Kind regards
Tayo

The time was right. Where was he? She walked to the desk to enquire. At first they would not tell her whether he was on the passenger list. *Policy*, they said. She asked for a supervisor and then the supervisor's boss, and eventually they checked for her. Tayo was not on the list.

Chapter 32

Abdou was driving him to the airport and Tayo was sitting in the back seat wondering if he had forgotten anything. He had informed all the necessary people at the university and told his neighbours and editors of his departure. He had also remembered to lock the phone as well as the windows. There was really nothing of value in the house – just the house itself – but these days thieves took anything, so everything had to be locked, double locked, even triple locked.

He had met with the gardener and night watchman, and given them their instructions. They were to guard the property until he got back. This time, however, he did not tell them when he would return. He suspected that the last time he went away they had used the garage to house relatives from Gindiri and Kafanchan, and sold produce from his garden – maize, oranges, tomatoes and bananas, even though he had specifically instructed them not to. So this time he gave no indication of when he might be back and asked Yusuf to check on the house from time to time. Yes, things in Nigeria were tough, but this did not give workers the right to take liberties with his property.

Usually he travelled for two to three weeks – enough time to attend several academic conferences and present a paper or two. But this trip would be different. He was going to Europe for the first time in four years and it would keep him out of Nigeria for at least six months, which was the length of the visiting professorship in London. After that, he was not sure what he would do. A lot depended on what happened in Nigeria and to the university, but for now the University of Jos remained closed and no one knew when it would reopen.

"*You dey craze*!" Abdou shouted suddenly, pressing his palm forcefully against the horn.

"Foolish man!" Tayo added, seeing the petrol tanker overtake within yards of oncoming traffic, and with it the memory of his mother's accident flashed through his mind. Tayo shook his head angrily. It was pure chance whether or not you were in an accident caused by these lawless drivers. "Professor, if you can find me a job in England I will be so happy," Abdou broke into Tayo's thoughts.

"I will see what I can do. But you know in England if you don't have working papers they won't employ you these days. When I was a student we didn't need visas and that sort of thing, but everything has changed now. It's not like the old days."

"Yes, sir." Abdou paused for a moment. "But by God's grace I must go. Maybe I can find an English wife, so as not to be troubled by the authorities."

"Maybe," Tayo contemplated, "but make sure you love her and not just the papers. Marriage is *a very serious thing*, young man," he said, wincing as the words came out.

A very serious thing was just the sort of utterance that a man his age was supposed to make, especially given that his marriage had not survived. *Listen to me, because I've failed, I should know.* It was so easy to declare marriage 'a serious thing' and yet such a cliché, and what use had it served him? He had ended the relationship with Vanessa because he had lost his nerve, and then sensibly married Miriam because, from all indications, it was the right thing to do. If he had followed his heart, and not his head, he would have chosen differently. Perhaps it had nothing to do with head versus heart and everything to do with him and his inability to understand women and relate meaningfully to them.

In a few hours time he would be seeing his old love, a married woman whom he still loved. A woman married to his old benefactor. *Marriage is a very serious thing*, so what was he doing thinking constantly of the age difference between Edward and Vanessa? Edward would soon die and then Vanessa would be free – free to be with him. He wasn't proud of this train of thought, but could not stop the thoughts nor prevent himself from expressing affection in his letters. Of course he did it in such a way that could be interpreted by a third person as simply an expression of deep friendship. Her letters were the same. It seemed to him that they both understood what the other was doing – each discreetly expressing their love. But what if he were mistaken? Perhaps this was simply what he wanted to think. Vanessa had never said she was unhappy with Edward and, even if she had, what were they to do? How wrong it would be to come between two people in a marriage. No, he would never do that. Life must go on. He had brought Vanessa's diary with him and would return it. Whatever he might feel, he must behave responsibly and keep his desire in check. And so he tried to think of other things. He pictured their home with Edward's history books stacked high on the shelves as they were in Oxford, and his art. There would be plenty of African art now, the combined collection of two art *lovers*. Lovers, the word echoed uncomfortably in Tayo's head as he recalled Edward's advice on marriage.

Tayo looked at himself in the rear-view mirror and realised that he had not imagined how he might appear to Vanessa. In four years, he had aged. Gaunt and balding now, not young and muscular like his younger self. He looked away. Outside, storm clouds had gathered and within minutes the sky had turned from pale blue to a threatening charcoal grey. Birds took flight and a lone monkey dashed across the road running for cover. Tayo thought that the lorry behind them must also be trying to out-run the storm. Abdou must have presumed the same as he pulled to one side to let it pass, but it did not overtake.

"What's wrong with these people?" Tayo shouted, gesturing

at the driver to keep his distance.

Abdou pulled over further to give the driver more room, but still the driver did not overtake; it was then that Tayo saw the military uniforms, and knew.

"Abdou!" he screamed.

IV

...

Chapter 33

Kemi lived in a one-bedroom apartment on Franklin Street – one of the few streets in San Francisco that never went to sleep. At all hours of night, just like the day, cars accelerated down the hill, filling the air with exhaust fumes that rose to the level of her second floor apartment. The noise of engines, brakes and the occasional blaring of horns meant that the night was never silent and nor was it dark. There was always a steady stream of headlights and sometimes the whirling lights of emergency vehicles, their sirens piercing the night with their high-pitched wails. Sleep was hard, but then it always was these days. If Tayo did fall asleep, he dreamt of Nigeria and woke sweating. He had two recurring nightmares: one where he was drowning in a prison cell and the other where Abdou floated away in the form of a sheet of paper that Tayo could never catch.

People said that after the accident Abdou appeared fine. When they pulled him from the wreck he was able to walk and insisted on helping carry Tayo. The nurses had bandaged Abdou's facial lacerations, but it was the bleeding inside, the bleeding nobody saw, that later caused Abdou to collapse and die. They said that little could have been done, even had they caught the internal bleeding, but Tayo was not convinced. He knew that more medical attention had been given to him that day than to Abdou. Now Abdou was dead and there was nothing Tayo could do to bring him back. Here Tayo was in America, far from Nigeria, unable to comfort Abdou's family, and not even able to support his own family.

The plan was for Tayo to stay with Kemi in San Francisco for a month, enough time to be seen by the medical specialists and wait for his leg to recover. While abroad, he would contact universities to find out what jobs might be open to him. Kemi had organised his trip to the US, flying him via France. He regretted not being able to fly through London to see Vanessa, even though he knew that not only was it a miracle that he had survived the accident, but also that he had got out of the country. Now he was safe and living in Kemi's apartment that she had rearranged to accommodate him.

She had insisted that he use her bedroom while she slept in a room created out of a storage cupboard. He tried to take the makeshift room, but she wouldn't let him, and, even though she never said anything to suggest that he was being a burden, he felt that he was a great encumbrance. What father, he repeatedly asked himself, should be relying on a daughter in such a way? And then, when he found out that Kemi was working as a nanny to fund her artistic endeavours, it felt even worse. How could his daughter be doing such a menial job while he lived with her, in her flat, doing nothing?

His days dragged by, and the television became his companion. He watched the news on CNN and CNBC – morning, afternoon and evening. He watched in hope of international news, but almost always the coverage was domestic, of child abuse, murders and serial killings, with just one lone 'global minute' to cover the rest of the world. Sometimes he thought he should listen to music rather than watch television, but he could not muster much interest in music these days. And yet there was plenty of music in the apartment. Kemi owned CDs of African musicians with names like Les Nubians, and Positive Black Soul. He guessed that this was the music she used to teach her students African dance and found it curious that his daughter, living abroad, probably knew more about African music than Africans in Africa.

Kemi also owned some of Miriam's favourites, such as Sunny Ade and Miriam Makeba, and whenever she played these it brought back memories for Tayo, some happy, but mostly sad. He wondered what Kemi told Miriam about him these days. Sometimes, when mother and daughter spoke on the phone, he would say a few words to Miriam. He would ask her how she was, and she did the same – short and perfunctory, speaking more for Kemi's sake than for theirs.

Kemi left early every morning for work and returned around 6.00 in the evening. The routine was then to go out for cheap food on Polk or Union Street, or to have food delivered to the apartment in paper boxes and Styrofoam cups, and Tayo worried that his daughter wasted money on such food. He also feared that she would not find the right husband without culinary skills. It wasn't that Kemi didn't know how to cook, she just didn't like it, and the fridge was always bare on the inside. Outside, it was crowded with magnetic letters, photographs of Kemi's friends, and an assortment of poems and sayings. Her boyfriend, Laurent, could cook, but that was his job. Tayo presumed Kemi saw him during her lunch breaks and perhaps on the occasional evening when she came home late. He never asked. Laurent was a nice enough man but not, in his view, suitable for his daughter. The fact that he was a chef was bad enough, but he didn't have a degree either. Tayo wondered if this was the price he now paid for encouraging Kemi as she grew up to have a mind of her own. He was pleased that at least Laurent did not visit the apartment or stay overnight.

"You should get out, Daddy," Kemi insisted as the days passed.

He told her that he did, even though it was obvious that he rarely left the apartment. He wanted to return to Nigeria. Here, in Kemi's San Francisco, he did not belong. He remembered one day going to buy his daughter some tea. He had been walking along Polk Street when he passed a shop selling international papers and spotted a story about Nigeria on the front page of *Le Monde*.

He did not buy the paper – he was careful with the dollars Kemi gave him – but he sat down on the bench outside and read what he could from the front cover on display. The news was not good – falling oil prices and continued government corruption. "No hope for Nigeria," he muttered, covering his head with both hands. The next thing he knew, someone was tapping his shoulder and, when he looked up, a middle-aged woman was handing him a bagel. At first he was puzzled, then shocked. It was not even a whole bagel, but part of one, half-eaten.

"You need to see a therapist," Kemi insisted. "You're suffering from depression."

"I'm perfectly fine," he snapped.

What right did she have to say such things? Besides, he did not believe in therapists and nor should she. Therapy was a Western thing, a fad, and a waste of money. If he did not want to go out, why should he? His leg had not healed, his country was in chaos and he was trapped in America.

Still, Kemi persisted. "You're depressed and you need to do something about it. You should contact the universities, plan for your future –"

"Don't tell me what to do, Kemi. I'm not going to stay here any longer than I have to if that's what you're concerned about."

"I'm not concerned about that. I'm worried about you."

"It's not your responsibility to worry about me. You've already taken care of the medical expenses."

"You could see my therapist."

"I should do what?"

"You could see my therapist," Kemi repeated.

"*You* have a therapist? For what?"

"Oh, for goodness sake!"

"What do you need one for?"

"Do you think it was easy to live without a father for so many years and then to watch you and Mum divorce?"

"But…"

"It doesn't matter why I see a therapist, Daddy. The fact is I do and it helps me."

"Well, I really don't understand." He shook his head.

"And you wouldn't!" she shouted, thrusting her hands into the air in a gesture that shocked him in its resemblance to something her mother would do.

"You hardly know me. You sent us off to England, never caring what happened to your wife or daughter. All that mattered was your work."

"So is that what your mother tells you?" Tayo asked, struggling to contain his anger.

"She didn't have to. I could see for myself."

"And this is how you speak to your father now. With no respect."

"Respect! Respect! Is that all that matters? What about love? I've always wanted to be close to you, but all the time you just talk about respect, bloody respect. Well no, if you must know, I don't respect you. I don't respect what you did to us; I don't respect how you left us, how you always thought about work first. Now you come here and I try to help, I try to make suggestions, even Laurent tries and –"

"Listen, don't talk to me about Laurent."

"Why? Because he's white?"

"No, because in our culture –"

"In our culture? Whose culture? The one you made up?"

"In *our* culture Kemi; you listen to your father!" he shouted.

"Don't you dare shout at me!"

He stared at her, too shocked to speak. Never before had he seen his daughter behave so disrespectfully.

"You always wanted me to marry an African, didn't you?" she persisted. "Nothing is good enough for you, is it? I teach African dance, I search for my roots, I try to help you by making suggestions, but nothing is good enough. Nothing!"

He kept quiet as she stormed out of the room but he couldn't let her go and cry on her own. He tapped gently on the bathroom door.

"Kemi, please, let's not talk this way."

There was no reply, so he tapped again. No answer. He left for a while, pacing up and down, listening to her sobs and wondering what to do next. Then she left the apartment, slamming the door behind her. Not knowing what else to do, he went to the bathroom where she had just been. The smells of Kemi reminded him of Miriam – the soaps, shampoos, and perfumes of these two women, the women he had wronged. Why was he so incapable? So inept? What was wrong with him? Why couldn't he love another person the way one was supposed to? Mama, Miriam, Christine, Vanessa, Kemi, and even Hawa had despised him. It would be better that he went away and left everyone in peace.

Later that evening when Kemi finally returned and he saw that she was fine, he told her that he was taking a walk. The fog had rolled in and the air hung damp and cold, but he could not be bothered with a coat. He walked as fast as he could, ignoring the pain in his leg, past Fort Mason, past the Marina, and up to the Golden Gate Bridge. How easy it would be to jump. *Just jump!* While he calculated the odds of certain death – the height, the fact that he had never learnt to swim – a car whizzed past playing Michael Jackson's music. Tayo turned and saw a little girl waving from the open window. He thought of Kemi again and turned from the water.

She was on the phone when he got back. "I have no idea where the hell he is," she was saying.

He pushed quietly on the door handle to let himself out again, but then he paused with his hand still there, listening.

"I don't want to call the police, Laurent. I know he's just off somewhere sulking. He doesn't care."

Pause.

"He won't even speak to his friends and he doesn't know that Mum's the person sending all this money to pay for his medical bills. He doesn't give a shit."

Miriam sending money?

Tayo stepped back into the apartment, shutting the door noisily.

Kemi refused to talk after she hung up the phone but, later that night, Tayo found a way to start a conversation.

"You know, Kemi, when I was young, we didn't talk about our girlfriends or boyfriends to our parents," he began, "and I forget sometimes that you were not always raised in Nigeria as I was, but you must believe that I have nothing against white people, nothing at all. Thinking about race is the American way, not ours."

"So you wouldn't mind if I married someone white?"

"To be honest, I'd be more concerned if you married a Nigerian. There are so many crooks about these days. And besides, well," he paused for a second, "you're not the first person to fall in love with a white person, you know."

"You did?" Kemi looked up and smiled.

"Oh, a long time ago." Tayo shrugged, feeling silly now for having brought it up. "Vanessa was someone I met at Oxford."

"Did you think of marrying her?"

"I suppose we did, but then I met your Mum and…"

"And what Daddy?"

"And then, well that's all."

"You don't have to worry about what I'll think, Daddy," Kemi smiled. "This is Vanessa Richardson, isn't it?"

"Yes, as a matter of fact it was," Tayo replied, trying not to sound too surprised.

"It wasn't hard to guess, Daddy," Kemi laughed. "You've

mentioned her several times since you've been here."

"Have I? I really didn't think… well, in any case she's married now and…"

She looked at him, perhaps expecting him to say more, but there was nothing more to say. He met her gaze and she nodded with grown-up understanding that made him uncomfortable.

"Sometimes I wonder how Laurent's parents really feel."

"You've met them already?"

He was not used to this grown-up child of his. Nobody had ever prepared him for this.

"They lived in Africa, you know. Laurent's father worked with *Medicins Sans Frontiers*. His father is very nice, but it's his mother… well, maybe all mothers are protective of their sons. Do you think so Daddy?"

He shrugged as if he didn't know, but he did because Mama had been that way.

"I'd like his mother to accept me."

"And she should, my love. She should." He squeezed Kemi's hand. "Which parent wouldn't be delighted to have you as a daughter-in-law?" he said softly, resting his head on her shoulder and shutting his eyes.

"I hope you know that I didn't mean any of those nasty things I said this afternoon," Kemi whispered, placing a hand on his knee. "I love you Daddy, very much, and even respect you."

He squeezed her young hand, fighting back the tears – his first tears since his arrest, which his daughter knew nothing about and hopefully never would.

Chapter 34

The kitchen table had become Vanessa's favourite place to write. The clock said 3am and the house was silent except for the ticking of the old, familiar clock. *Tick tock, tick tock*; she rocked her head from side to side in time. After a while she got up to make some tea. 'Yes,' she thought, this was what happened to mothers later in life; they became nocturnal creatures. She would always go to bed early with Edward, but then get up at these quietest moments of the night – the perfect time to think. Edward would sometimes join her for a minute or two, frequently getting up at night too, but only to use the toilet. He would tell her that she worked too hard, and she would promise to stop. He knew she wouldn't, and she knew he knew, but this was their script and there was a certain comfort in sticking to it. Now, as she waited for the water to boil, she thought of Tayo. It would still be daytime in California. What would he be doing? At least he was safe now. She sighed and returned to the table with her mug of rosehip tea.

Everything was laid out: the manuscript, the photographs and Saratu's letter. Shortly after Father's death, Edward had suggested that she read Father's book and try publishing it. She had been reluctant to do so at first, given that her relationship with Father had grown worse over the years. For a long period, between Mother's death and Father going into care, she had hardly spoken to him because of his refusal to accept Suleiman as his grandson. She had thought many times of cutting him out of her life, but could never bring herself to do so. Instead, she hid

Father's nastiness from Suleiman and visited him in the home as little as possible.

When he died, she had wanted to burn all his papers, but it was Edward who coaxed her out of this, forcing her to confront Father's writings which, after much procrastination, she did. She found, as feared, a manuscript full of racist and patronising comments about Africans, but it also contained many interesting details of the colonial period, and this presented something of a dilemma for Vanessa. While the blatant racism was deplorable, she couldn't deny that the writings were of some historical significance. There were detailed notes on what was accomplished in the course of a District Officer's day and descriptions of journeys made on the *Aureol*, similar to those she remembered hearing about from Tayo. All that was missing, and of course it was an important part of the picture, was the perspective of the Nigerians who worked with her Father. In the end she had written to friends in Nigeria, hoping that some of his old workers might still be around to give their stories. At first nobody replied, but then she had received the letter from Saratu.

Dear Mrs Barker,

Praise God that I obtained your letter dated 7th March, 1997. I am now living in Gindiri and so the letter took some time to reach. I am happy to hear you are writing about Africa. God bless you. Mama would be very happy to know this. I am sorry to inform you that Mama passed away on 5th August, 1986. Until her death, she was talking of your mother, who was her favourite Madame. She was still angry with the gardener for causing irresponsibility for your mother to leave our country when you were a child. I am hoping that you return to Nigeria again very soon. I would like to see you. God has blessed me with six children. Four boys. Two girls. Praise God. The eldest is named Elizabeth, the same as your mother. I am sending you a picture of your mother that Mama used to keep.

Also, I am giving you one picture of myself. I am in the maternity ward at St. Teresa hospital, where you can dispatch future correspondence.
MRS SARATU JANU c/o Mother Theresa Hospital
P.O. Box 16, Gindiri, Nigeria
I wait to hear from you sooner rather than later.
God bless you and your family.

Vanessa smiled as she placed the letter back in a pile. She would have loved to see Saratu again. She fingered the picture, remembering times when they had played like sisters, climbing trees, running, jumping or playing at being mothers. The photograph was a Polaroid and the colours were faded, but the resemblance was clearly there. Saratu was looking like her mother now – round and short with the same beautiful smile, dressed in the pale blue nurses' uniform with a wide, navy blue belt and silver buckle. How different their lives had become. Saratu was a competent mother of six and, she, the somewhat dubious mother of one. She put the photograph down and touched the second photograph of Mother. Then she picked up the picture of Danjuma and held them side-by-side. Danjuma's photograph was one that Mother had kept in a drawer along with other pictures from Nigeria. Danjuma was posing in a smart shirt and formal trousers. He stood at an angle, looking across his shoulder at the camera. "Where did you take this picture?" Vanessa murmured. "Did you send it to Mum? And what is this 'irresponsibility' that Saratu speaks of?"

As a child, Vanessa had always believed that the reason she and Mother returned to England before Father was for her education but, last year when she had broached the topic with Uncle Tony, he had told another story. Something had happened to upset Mother in her second year in Nigeria, but nobody knew quite what. All Uncle Tony knew was that Father travelled a lot, leaving Mother behind, and he speculated that

Father had had an affair. Now another story began to form in Vanessa's mind. 'What if,' she thought and began to scribble on her notepad.

June '46 –Elizabeth and John marry
March '47– Vanessa born
June '47 –Set sail for Nigeria.
Elizabeth excited to go to Nigeria – first time. Parents alarmed that she's leaving with young child, but can't dissuade. Elizabeth has always been strong-willed (married man they disapproved of).
1948 – difficult year
Elizabeth gets malaria and Vanessa too. Jonathan thinks bad idea to bring wife and daughter to Africa. Elizabeth insists they stay. She loves the sunshine, the outdoors and the friendly nature of the locals. She makes friends at the market, at the clinic, with the house servants. Not as Jonathan expected. Embarrassed that wife befriends locals, esp. house servants.
1949/1950? – Jonathan tours Mambilla plateau without Elizabeth and Vanessa. Elizabeth's closest friends: maid (Rose) and gardener (Danjuma)

And then it struck Vanessa. What if Danjuma was the man who had told Mother the sticks-and-sandals story? If so, might there have been some personal significance in him being the one to tell her? Vanessa looked again at the two pictures. She wished she had asked her mother more about life in Nigeria, but she had always felt scared to; fearful that dredging up memories would trigger Mother's depression. But now she wondered if talking about Nigeria might have helped her mother.

Danjuma is a young man, nineteen or twenty-years-old. Only a few years younger than Elizabeth. Danjuma is strong and muscular and easy-going by nature. He laughs a lot and teaches Elizabeth all that she wants to know about gardening. He offers to take her around the Jos Plateau, to show her the waterfalls and lush forests that she has not seen, and it is on these trips perhaps... that something starts between them. His youthful spirit and good looks attract her. He finds her beautiful and he likes the way she makes an effort to speak Hausa and understand his culture and religion. Soon they are doing things in secret. For months they enjoy each other's company, until Jonathan returns and their secret is discovered. Jonathan refuses to believe that his wife loves a local servant. He wants Danjuma punished, flogged and imprisoned, but Elizabeth tells Jonathan that she will reveal the truth if such a thing is done. And so they compromise. Elizabeth returns to England with young Vanessa, and Jonathan remains in Nigeria. Danjuma is sacked.

Then what? Would Danjuma and Mother have corresponded in secret? She simply put together pieces of a story and guessed at the rest. She had replied to Saratu's letter and now she would find Danjuma to ask him his side of the story. She looked at the pictures again and thought of Tayo.

"Mum." Someone shook her shoulders.

"Mum, why are you crying, Mum?"

"I'm sorry," Vanessa sobbed.

"Mum, you're shaking. What's wrong? It's Granddad's writing, isn't it?" Suleiman rested one hand on the table and the other on her shoulder.

"Yes," Vanessa nodded, thankful for this excuse. "Can't you sleep, darling?" she asked, sliding her hand over his. She looked up at him and smiled.

"I was reading but then I heard you crying." He squeezed her shoulder gently. "Look Mum, don't let Granddad's stuff get to you. You know what I've been thinking," he let go and walked to the fridge, "one day I'll run a sort of literary agency for African writers."

Vanessa watched as he poured himself a drink – her grown up son who was so kind these days. It made her happy to see him excited about ideas and particularly about Africa, which was a passion they now shared. All they had talked about since his return was his business ideas and desire to promote African art by setting up an arts shop. She and Edward still wanted him to finish university, but Suleiman had inherited some of Salamatou's stubbornness and his mind was set. Vanessa looked at the way her son was standing, drumming his fingers, just like Tayo, against the fridge.

"Well, if you're interested in books, you should speak to my friend Tayo."

"You talk a lot about him." Suleiman returned with a glass of water.

"Do I?"

"I always wondered what it might be like to have a black father."

"And was that a –"

"No, it wasn't a problem, Mum, it was just one of those things I used to think about. I got so tired of everyone always being surprised that my parents were white. So tell me, were you ever in love with Tayo? Was he in love with you?"

"You'll have to ask him."

"You're blushing, Mum."

"No, I'm not."

"You are now."

"Oh Suleiman, you're distracting me!" She reached across the table and tapped him playfully across the head.

"I'm just teasing, Mum. I know you love Dad and all that, but you've always been so passionate about Africa that I reckon you've still got some feelings for your African ex.

Yeah?" He winked as he left the room. "Oh, did you remember to wash my sweater?" he asked, popping back.

"Suleiman!"

"Just checking Mum, just checking."

Chapter 35

A few days after her father arrived, Kemi introduced Tayo to John Harris, Professor of Ethnic Studies at San Francisco State University and grandfather to the children she babysat. Professor Harris was delighted to meet Tayo and later offered him a part-time job in the department. The offer came as a surprise and not a particularly welcome one to Tayo. He had little desire to interact with people and a teaching job, he felt, would force him to do just that. Moreover, what would he teach? He would have politely declined the offer had it not been for the fact that he knew Kemi needed the money. So Tayo started teaching and, to his surprise, he enjoyed it – the students, the easy access to materials from the library and the opportunity to work on his own writings. He taught two classes: one on the political history of West Africa and a second on oral histories in Northern Nigeria. A few weeks into the semester, as he was walking from the department to the library, someone tapped him on his shoulder.

"Professor Ajayi, I do believe!"

"Yes?" Tayo turned, expecting to see a student. "Ah ah!" Tayo exclaimed. "What are you doing here?"

"What are you doing here?" Kwame laughed as they embraced.

Kwame had been at the university teaching theatre arts for the past seven years and had only just heard of Tayo's arrival. The meeting felt like a homecoming to Tayo and from that day on he had a friend with whom he talked about Nigeria as well as his experiences in America. It was with Kwame that he would soon rediscover his love for jazz, occasionally going to Rasselas in the city or to Yoshi's across the bay. Tayo's leg soon began to show signs of improvement and then came the news that General Abacha had died, which filled Tayo with hope.

Tayo stopped minding when Kemi stayed out late at her boyfriend's and even looked forward to Laurent coming to the apartment, as he did more often these days, to cook them a decent meal. Tayo bought himself a radio, listened to the BBC and NPR, and stopped watching television. He began to take buses to Grace Cathedral and listened to the boys' choir on Sundays. He bought music now, feeling better that he was earning some money. And as his leg steadily healed he became more adventurous with his walks. He went to the water every day, sometimes more than once for the exercise. His route was down Franklin Street to the Wharf, across to Fort Mason and onto the Marina.

As he walked, he liked to look at the houses and imagine who lived in them and where they came from. Most of those on the stretch of Franklin Street between Lombard and Bay were split into apartments where young people lived. He would see them sometimes jogging or carrying their washing to a laudromat. Sometimes he would smell their food from open windows – mostly eggs, bacon and cinnamon. He presumed that most of them worked in the computer industry because of the hours they worked and they were often in coffee shops with their cell phones, beepers and laptops.

There were not many children in this part of town, but a few elderly people would venture out from time-to-time, accompanying or accompanied by their funny-looking dogs. He sometimes walked back along Bay through Fort Mason, where the houses looked to him quintessentially American – pretty little box-shaped homes with white picket fences. Military personnel owned these, or so he thought, but he was never quite sure. Then there was the Safeway supermarket and the long stretch of stunning houses that stood behind the Marina. Occasionally he would see fancy cars parked in the driveways and bright lights glowing in some of the rooms, where curtains were never closed. But many of these mansions looked uninhabited – holiday homes for the rich.

By the water's edge, Tayo watched the boats and the fishermen. It was where the ordinary, even the poor, mingled with locals and tourists, and Tayo always paused to watch the fishermen. Some would be squatting and fixing bait to their lines, others would be standing about casting their rods, while others would be sitting, waiting patiently for a bite. Sometimes they caught little fish and occasionally big ones, but mostly nothing. Tayo chatted to the fishermen and surprised them with a smattering of Cantonese that he still remembered from a visit to Shanghai. He practised the language with them and gradually added to his vocabulary.

Back in Kemi's apartment, he also began to cook rice and a rudimentary tomato and onion stew. He discovered, to his surprise, and with Laurent's encouragement, that he was not a bad cook. Time went by more quickly now that he was due to return to Nigeria. Obasanjo was back in power and Tayo looked forward to participating in a new Nigeria. He was in touch again with Vanessa and had even taken the time to track down other old friends. Bolaji had been appointed Professor of International Law at Nottingham; Francis had acquired an American accent and citizenship, and was working for the State Department in Washington; and cousin Tunde was the pastor of the fastest growing Nigerian church in London. Yusuf was still in Jos and had started, of all things, several Christian television stations. Tayo supposed that Yusuf had converted to Christianity, but it might simply have been one more opportunistic 'Yusufian' move.

When Tayo went on his walks he held imaginary conversations

with these friends. He usually walked for an hour, or longer if his musings needed more time, as was always the case when talking to Vanessa. There were many tourists who walked the path behind the fishermen: young, old, black and white, and the question of race was something that he had discussed on many occasions with Kwame.

"Why do you think I left this country to go to Nigeria in the first place?" Kwame had laughed when Tayo first broached the topic. "Look Tayo, if you live in America long enough, you'll see there is no way of avoiding race. Race is a part of the fabric of this nation. You're either black or you're white, and this affects every aspect of your life. That's why so many of us left in the 70s."

"But it strikes me that it's not as simple as black and white," Tayo mused. "I see race playing out in my classroom between blacks, whites *and* Latinos."

"True."

"And some of the worst tension I find is between Africans and African-Americans."

Kwame laughed. "That's because most West African brothers and sisters don't understand or appreciate our history."

"And the same could be said for African-Americans."

"Yes, you're right, of course," Kwame nodded. "The misunderstanding is mutual and easily exploited by whites. How many times have you and your daughter been told by white people how wonderful you are, and how different you are to African-Americans?"

Tayo nodded.

"So why don't you talk about it in your classroom? See what the students have to say. Hold a debate."

So he did. Tayo chose a topic that he hoped would make his students think more carefully about Africa's history, as well as America's history. In the style of debate that he had grown to love at Oxford, he chose a quotation and asked his students to use it as the basis for the debate. The quote, which he considered suitably provocative and sure to solicit some good debate, came from Trevor-Roper:

'Perhaps in the future there will be some African history to teach. But at present there is none, or very little: there is only the history of Europe in Africa. The rest is largely darkness, like the history of pre-Columbian America, and darkness is not a subject for history.'

As expected, the statement provoked reaction from the students, but not quite what Tayo had expected. Firstly, none of his white students wanted to take a position in favour of the motion, so that was the first hurdle – to make it clear to his students that arguing a position was not the same as agreeing with it. Easier said than done. White students for the motion kept apologising and the one African student in the class became offended when an African-American spoke convincingly in favour. At the end there was almost a fistfight between Kenyan Thomas and African-American Damion. Tayo would not repeat the exercise.

A ship's foghorn broke Tayo's thoughts as he made his way back to Kemi's apartment. It cried its long lonesome call, warning others of poor visibility in the Bay and reminded Tayo of the *Aureol* and crossing the Irish Sea. A bird hopped close to where Tayo walked. He paused to watch. Were there many one-legged pigeons by San Francisco's bay, or did he just keep seeing the same one over and over again? It was injured, but still able to fly. 'Like me,' Tayo thought. Injured, yet pulling things together, and metaphorically, if not literally, flying again. When he returned to the apartment, he found a Federal Express package waiting by the door. He put it to one side, thinking it was for Kemi, but when she returned home she gave it to him.

"From the Nigerian Embassy," Tayo noted, cautiously turning the package this way and that. He thought of Dele Giwa and had the package been any heavier, he would not have opened it. Still, as a precaution, he went to a different room from his daughter and opened it at arm's length. A diplomatic pouch fell out onto the floor. Tayo picked it up and found a letter inside.

"A letter from the President," he murmured, reading the note. "What's this?"

Kemi had now joined him. "It says you've been awarded an honorary degree from Oxford," she read over his shoulder.

"If it's true then I'm shocked, but how can this be when I've heard nothing from Oxford?"

"Probably because they sent the letter to Nigeria. Daddy, this is fantastic! Look, it's congratulating you on a lifetime achievement!"

"Well, if it's true, I can hardly believe it. Do you think this is really true? They give these sorts of things to famous people with Nobel Laureates, or OBEs and MBEs, not ordinary people like me."

"Well now it's you Daddy! We'll call Oxford later tonight – first thing UK time."

Tayo smiled to himself. If this was really true there was someone else he would call first.

"I must call my friend, Vanessa," he said, thinking aloud before he had time to check himself.

Kemi was smiling mischievously and Tayo tried to recall how much he had told her about Vanessa. With all the excitement, he couldn't remember, but perhaps it didn't matter.

Chapter 36

Tayo received an honourary degree along with five other honourees: two were awarded doctorates of Civil Law, one, a doctorate of Music, another in Science, and two (one being Tayo), were given the honorary doctorate of Literature.

Encaenia took place in the Sheldonian – a long and rambling ceremony conducted in Latin for six distinguished persons but, in Vanessa's mind, this was a celebration mainly for Tayo. At last, he was receiving the recognition he deserved, and after the ceremony she stood and watched him with pride as he mingled with his guests. She had met Tayo briefly before the ceremony and they had hugged, but hardly spoken; too many people and not enough time. She thought at first that it was perhaps the way it should be, no time for sentimentalism, but no, she decided, that was not the way it should be. They needed more time.

"Do you know all these people?" Suleiman whispered.

"No." Vanessa shook her head, even though she did. The only one that mattered was Tayo.

"Come!" a young woman called as she ran towards them. "You must be my father's friend, Vanessa."

"Yes," Vanessa smiled, "and you must be Kemi."

"I am." Kemi gripped her hand tightly before turning to Suleiman.

Suleiman took Kemi's hand and Vanessa breathed a sigh of relief. Suleiman could be funny about things like this sometimes.

"Come," Kemi urged, "let me introduce you to everyone."

Again, Vanessa hugged Tayo and congratulated him.

"When will I see you?" he asked, releasing her from the hug, but not letting go of her hand.

"I'll see you soon." Vanessa squeezed his fingers, which were being taken by others as more well-wishers surrounded them, jostling and making it hard to stand still.

She moved away, following Kemi to be introduced to Bisi and Bolaji, and re-introduced to Uncle Kayode. Vanessa did not recognise Uncle Kayode at first and, despite his enthusiastic greeting, he seemed unable to remember her either, which saddened her until she realised that he had had too much to drink and others were busy trying to find a place for him to sit down. Then Kemi introduced Vanessa to Miriam and Vanessa was stunned at how youthful Miriam looked. She had always imagined Tayo's wife as being someone of her age, and perhaps she was, but she looked younger. She was friendly too, and instead of feeling jealous she felt strangely sorry for Miriam – sorry for Miriam and for Tayo. They spoke for a while about what each other did and then about their children, who stood not far away engaged in a conversation of their own.

"So what's America like then?" Suleiman asked Kemi.

"Great! The weather's good, the music's great. It's totally happening. You should come."

"But I hear they don't care much for Muslims over there, especially after 9/11."

"Not in the Bay Area. You can be any religion you want in San Francisco, it doesn't matter. You should come. Come and stay with me."

"Serious?"

"Of course."

Vanessa smiled, wishing she could hear more, but Bolaji, whom she only vaguely remembered, was keen to talk as their group started walking towards Balliol, where a reception was being held in Tayo's honour. Miriam announced that she was leaving early and Vanessa felt she must do the same.

"Oh, but you can't go!" Tayo insisted.

"No, you can't!" Kemi insisted. "Dad's been dying to see you."

Vanessa's heart leapt as she heard these words, and she was touched by Kemi's kindness.

"I'd love to stay, but I must get back to London for Edward."

"Don't worry about Dad," Suleiman interrupted. "I'm going back. Dad will be fine."

And so she went with Tayo and talked to more of his friends, still wishing there had been time for just the two of them. Perhaps they would meet up in London before he returned to America. And then, as she was lost in her own thoughts, he walked towards her and took her arm.

"Come," he said, "if we don't escape now, we never will."

"So now it's Professor Ajayi, *Doctoris in Litteris,*" she said, smiling as they walked together, past Christ Church, towards the river.

"*Ego auctoritate mea et totius Universitatis admitto te ad gradum Doctoris in Litteris honoris causa*," he replied.

"So you haven't forgotten your Latin?"

"Oh yes, I have," he laughed. "Truthfully, that's the only line I can remember, and I'm not sure I could give you a good translation."

She listened to the familiar tenor of his voice and thought that it hardly mattered what he said. Of course they would both make conversation because that was what one did, but just to be with him and alone with him was wonderful. She was due back in London before dark, and Tayo, she knew, could not abandon his own reception for long; but for a short while they were alone together.

She watched him, as he looked across Christ Church meadows where cows basked lazily in the late-afternoon sun. Just before they left the reception, Tayo had retrieved a small parcel from the porter's lodge, which he now carried in one hand. He had stopped for a moment, turning back to gaze at the college, and she thought he looked more casual and relaxed than the last time they had met. He had changed out of *sub fusc,* and was now wearing pale khaki trousers and a light blue shirt. After all these years, he was still handsome, unnervingly so. She wore the blue cotton dress that Suleiman had chosen, a pair of cream suede shoes (a last minute extravagance) and a straw hat.

"What are you thinking?" she asked quietly.

"Sorry?"

"You seem deep in thought, what are you thinking?" she said, louder this time so he could hear.

"It's the history of this place, Vanessa. There is so much history here. Did I mention that I'm staying at the Master's Lodge?"

She nodded.

"In the Master's Lodge, there's a guestbook that starts in 1909. In America, something like that would be treated as ancient, wouldn't it? But here it's just an ordinary guestbook, and one that I'm supposed to sign alongside all these very famous people. There are Prime Ministers, world leaders, and all sorts. I saw the names of Harold Wilson, Isaiah Berlin, Gandhi, and even Seretse and Ruth Khama."

"The Khamas, now that's interesting," Vanessa remarked, remembering their story.

"Sorry?"

"I was just saying how interesting – the Khamas, Wilson, Gandhi, and now you."

He laughed, and then they walked for some moments in silence, each with their own thoughts. She wanted to ask him about Kemi, and about his plans for the future. They had not yet spoken about his accident, or the months of depression in San Francisco (something his daughter had mentioned to her in confidence). She wanted to tell him about Father's book and her plans to return to Nigeria.

"Oxford really hasn't changed, has it? Look at Christ Church, and this." Tayo pointed to the meadows. "If I close my eyes it could still be 1964. The sounds are the same: the bells, the coaches shouting to their rowers on the river, light aircraft in the sky and the sounds of trains in the distance. There is even the same smell of grass and river." He paused with his eyes still shut. "And then, when I look again – here you are! It's like a beautiful dream come true."

"Well, I've certainly changed in the space of thirty or so years."

"Ahh, but you are still the gracious, generous soul that I knew, and the beautiful woman I fell in love with," he said, walking more slowly.

She smiled sadly. They had reached the river and walked along the path that ran in front of the college boathouses.

"Do you remember Summer Eights?"

She laughed, knowing what he would say next.

"When you and Gita got completely drunk and wanted to get into the boat with the rowers from St. Johns."

"Are you sure it wasn't the Balliol rowers?" She laughed.

"Shall we?" Tayo pointed to a bench by the riverbank.

"But shouldn't you be getting back?"

"I'm sure they won't miss me. This is where I want to be and I must also thank you because I know you had a hand in my receiving this award."

"Not at all," she said, even though it was true that she had written something to support his nomination, but her voice alone would not have been enough to have him selected. She sat down, pleased for the rest from her new shoes.

"Kemi's a delightful young woman, Tayo. I wish that Suleiman had been able to stay a little longer."

"So that we could match-make our children?" Tayo smiled.

"Oh Tayo! But it sounds like Kemi is already spoken for."

"Not until I say so," he laughed. "And how is Suleiman?"

"He's well, very well," she smiled, remembering the way her son had teased her as she struggled that morning over what to wear. She had gone into his room to model her clothes, and at first he said nothing, too busy listening to his ragga. "Chill, Mum, chill," he said, when finally he had noticed her. "You look terrific. You'll look beautiful for him."

"So you haven't told me much about your stay in America," she remarked. "What is this book you're thinking of writing?"

She listened as he told her about his writings on American racial politics. His perspective as an African in America sounded interesting, but as hard as she listened it was only him that she thought of as he talked – who he had been and who he still was.

"Perhaps you should have written about your time in England as a student and the racism here, and I suppose my father…" She let the words trail off.

"It wasn't just your father 'Nessa. I was proud, too proud in those days and so stupid too." He paused. "Oh, Vanessa –"

"Tayo," she said, speaking before he had time to say any more and then, not wanting to dwell on regrets, she asked him to tell her more about San Francisco. "What's the other project you had mentioned and what about retirement?"

He paused for a long while before answering, perhaps like her sifting through thoughts, trying to determine when and what to say. What was worth saying?

"So I take it you won't be retiring when you return to Nigeria?" she added.

"I ought to retire because the age of retirement in Nigerian universities is sixty. But I'll continue to teach, if not officially, then unofficially."

"Oh, but surely now you have this honorary degree they will dispense with all official rules and make you Vice-Chancellor for life."

"I hope not," he exclaimed, turning to face her. "I just want to go back quietly. I don't want to be involved in university politics anymore. I've done my time. I'm too old now." He placed one hand along the back of the bench and the other in the space between them. "Will you come and visit me one day?"

"I'd love to. And in fact —"

"And of course, you must bring Edward," he said, before she could finish.

She smiled. It was thoughtful of him, but Edward found it hard to travel these days. Even the short journey from London to Oxford, which he had wanted to make today, proved at the last minute to be too much for him.

"I know." Tayo nodded. "You've told me that it's difficult for him to travel. But I pray that he regains his strength. I shall pray for a miracle."

"Thank you," she replied. "Does this then mean you believe in prayer now?"

"In my own way," he mused.

She nodded and gazed at the river, watching the rowers. *And how I prayed that you would return, that we would find a way to make things work.* She looked back at Tayo. He was watching her, so she turned away.

"Oh, look at that!" she exclaimed, spotting a squirrel close to their feet. Its tail was arched and nose lifted, sniffing the air. "Do you remember what you used to call them?" The squirrel scuttled a few feet away, rising now on his hind legs with paws up, waiting.

"What?" Tayo asked, looking bemused.

"I remember you calling them rats with bushy tails."

He laughed. "They were good times together, weren't they?" He removed his hand from the back of the bench and rested it with the other on his lap.

"Yes and …"

"I miss those days," he said softly, filling in for her silence. "Sometimes I wish I could just go back in time and re-live them. I would make different choices now."

"And what would you change?"

"I would have married you."

"Oh Tayo," she exclaimed.

"No, it's true. As an old man, I realise what I've missed." He sighed, giving her knee a friendly tap.

She took his hand and squeezed it as if there was nothing more to say; yet every nerve in her body itched to speak.

"I have some things for you." He picked up the parcel from the bench and gave it to her.

A letter lay on top of a book. She read the letter first.

I am writing to inform you that I have serious intentions with Vanessa.

"I wrote it a long time ago," Tayo said, interrupting her reading. "It's a letter to my uncle and… well, I just wanted you to know that I was serious and that I had wanted to marry you."

Tears came to her eyes as she read more.

"And this?" she asked, brushing away the tears. "My goodness! How did you get this?" She flipped quickly through the pages of her old diary and saw the places where she had scribbled *Oluwakayode,* the name she had dreamed about one day naming their child.

"My God, my God," she mumbled and then, as she struggled to hold back more tears, a middle-aged couple approached them and asked if they would mind taking a photograph for them.

"Certainly," Tayo offered, standing up to take the camera from the strangers who now stood in front of them.

The man held his lady by the waist, sucked in his stomach and smiled as his wife leant her braided head against his chest. Vanessa watched them as they posed and, as she watched, she felt a wave of *déjà vu*. Her mind raced across time to find the answer. Was it a memory of her photographer friend, Seydou

Keita? Was it the way he asked his subjects to pose? Or was it Salamatou in 1970, with her hair braided like this woman's? Or perhaps she was seeing an image of her parents before she was born, in a time that she had only imagined? Sticks-and-sandals, she thought. Mum and Danjuma. Tayo and Vanessa.

"Now let's get one of you two," the man offered.

"Okay," Tayo agreed, cheerfully handing back the camera.

He sat down and moved closer to Vanessa, until their hips touched and she prayed for the tears to stay put.

"Aw come on, my brother," the man urged, lowering his camera. "Let's see a little more loving."

Vanessa clenched her jaw in an even greater effort to hold back her tears and smile for the camera. Tayo laughed and slid his arm around her shoulders. Instinctively, she turned her head to his and, without thinking, tired of thinking, she kissed him gently on the lips, and then it was fervently, not caring what the other couple thought or said as the tears ran down her cheeks.

*

Night had fallen and three students who had passed them on their way out to the river now passed them again, still sitting on the bench, hand-in-hand, with her head on his shoulder, staring across the river.

"They must be mad," said one. "It's freezing."

"Probably tourists," whispered another, "or parents p'haps."

And then the ringing of Christ Church's bells drowned their voices out. The cows in the meadows paid no attention to these hourly chimes. The moon, however, took notice of the bells and rose from behind its clouds to light up the sky and send silver ripples across the Isis.

Legend Press

Independent Book Publisher

This book has been published by vibrant publishing company Legend Press. If you enjoyed reading it then you can help make it a major hit. Just follow these three easy steps:

1. Recommend it
Pass it onto a friend to spread word-of-mouth or, if now you've got your hands on this copy you don't want to let it go, just tell your friend to buy their own or maybe get it for them as a gift. Copies are available with special deals and discounts from our own website and from all good bookshops and online outlets.

2. Review it
It's never been easier to write an online review of a book you love and can be done on Amazon, Waterstones.com, WHSmith.co.uk and many more. You could also talk about it or link to it on your own blog or social networking site.

3. Read another of our great titles
We've got a wide range of diverse modern fiction and it's all waiting to be read by fresh-thinking readers like you! Come to us direct at www.legendpress.co.uk to take advantage of our superb discounts. (Plus, if you email info@legendpress.co.uk just after placing your order and quote 'WORD OF MOUTH', we will send another book with your order absolutely free!)

Thank you for being part of our word-of-mouth campaign.

info@legendpress.co.uk
www.legendpress.co.uk